TRIPLE CROSS

A LUCIUS WHITE LEGAL THRILLER

ALAN P. WOODRUFF

THANK YOU READERS

Thank you for buying and reading my book and I sincerely hope that you enjoy it. As an independently published author, I rely on my readers to spread the word, so, if you like my book, please tell your family and friend. And if it's not too much trouble, mention me on your social media pages and **post a review on Amazon**. If you would like to tell me your opinion directly, please visit my website – **www.alanpwoodruff.com** – and send me a message. If you have a question, I will respond as soon as possible.

PRESENT DAY

1.

The sad fact is that I lie some. That is, I lie in the interest of self-preservation and noble causes and, to be perfectly honest, whenever else it suits my purposes.

My name is Harris Masters, but most people just call me Masters. It doesn't make any difference to me—it isn't my real name. Like I said, I lie some. However, in the case of my name, the need to lie was forced on me by the Department of Justice. They want people in the Witness Protection Program to have new names and identities. I can understand their thinking. Besides, I believe that lying to stay alive is an exception to the commandment—I forget which one—that says lying is a bad thing. In any event, I've grown accustomed to my new name. It's too bad I may need to change it again, but I'm getting ahead of myself.

Autumn, and its burst of colors, had come suddenly to the Smoky Mountains. At least it felt sudden to me. It was my first autumn away from New Orleans, so I didn't have anything to compare it to. Mountains covered with trees, green or any other color, never held much interest for me. They still don't.

I'm not sure how long it took for the trees to change color. All I know is that when I stumbled into bed at some ungodly hour one night, the trees were green, and when I woke up, the leaves were all various shades of red, orange, and gold. It probably wasn't an overnight occurrence, but that's how it seemed. I could have been asleep for more than one day. That happens occasionally. It may have something to do with the fact that I also drink a lot. That's one of the reasons I got disbarred, though I'm sure it's not the only reason the Louisiana Bar Association yanked my law license. If the excessive consumption of alcohol were a disqualifying personal flaw, there wouldn't be many attorneys in Louisiana. I think my disbarment was the result of more than just my drinking. Punching out a judge might have also had something to do with it.

Being disbarred wasn't the worst thing that could have happened to me. I never particularly wanted to be a lawyer, but some things are inevitable. Three generations of doctors, lawyers, and honest politicians—I know the last is an oxymoron, but it's true—defined my future long before I had a choice in the matter. I couldn't imagine spending half my life sucking up to people and hustling campaign contributions, and I knew I'd never make it through medical school. All that left me was door number three.

I always thought JFK Jr. had the right idea: Go to law school, graduate, and take five tries to pass the bar exam. By that time, his family had gotten the message, and he was free to do something else. I don't know what he did, but that's not the point.

I knew I wasn't cut out to work in a big firm that expected new associates to work seventy-hour weeks, so I started with a cubby-hole of an office in a building where a lot of other sole practitioners shared a library, a couple of small conference rooms and a lunch-room. The other attorneys in my building all had established practices that kept them busy, and they sent me enough small cases that I managed to survive.

I had been practicing law for a couple of years when my

aunt and uncle, both very successful surgeons, were killed in an automobile accident. I had not had any great successes as a lawyer, but I was family, so the family decided I should handle the case. It didn't hurt that the driver of the truck that killed them was high on crack and was driving with a suspended license when he ran a red light in front of thirty witnesses. Even I, as inexperienced as I was in handling such cases, couldn't lose that one. My fee from the settlement set me up for life, but I came to learn that I wasn't cut out for the life of the idle rich. I needed to have something to do, and the law, despite my ambivalence to it, was the only thing I knew. I suppose I could have learned a new trade, but I couldn't come up with an alternative that appealed to me.

I don't know what caused me to drift into criminal law. I never represented clients charged with violent crimes—only people accused of victimless crimes like gambling, drugs, and prostitution. I suppose there is something that drew me to those who only violated stupid laws. If you look at my record, you'd conclude that either I wasn't very proficient or I specialized in representing clients who were guilty. But I digress. Maybe I have attention deficit disorder.

An annual invasion of the tourists followed the changing of the colors in the early fall. The attraction that colored leaves held for the thousands of people who clogged the narrow country roads of eastern Tennessee for a month each year was lost on me. I could do without them — the tourists, not the leaves — but they're good for the local economy, and they don't really bother me. Not personally.

The leaves were now turning brown, the waves of gawking tourists had diminished to a ripple, and a light rain was beginning to fall as I pulled my classic '63 Porsche into the gravel parking lot outside The Red Rose. As usual, a few pickup trucks shared the lot. More would arrive shortly as the afternoon crowd of construction workers and other laborers stopped by for a libation before heading home to face the bitching wife and screaming kids. By six, they would have moved on, and the place would have quieted down until the bikers started arriving at seven. It had been that way as long as I had been coming to the Rose. It's not an important fact, but I notice such things.

A draft beer showed up at my usual place at the bar before I was across the room.

Out of habit, I checked the booth in the far corner of the room. It was empty. I drank at the bar, but the booth in the corner was my office. Not officially, of course. It didn't have a sign or anything. It's just that people came to me for advice from time to time, and it was useful to have a place where we could talk undisturbed.

Unable to practice law, I had turned to detecting. After a year, the people who patronized the Rose generally knew that I was a private investigator. The fact that I was hardly ever investigating anything never occurred to anyone.

When I do work, I mostly find lost people. Some of them, generally runaway ex-husbands with alimony or child support obligations, are lost by choice and don't want to be found. Others, such as lost heirs, are glad to be found. Occasionally I locate birth parents for children or reunite parents with children they'd given up. I do it mostly to keep busy. The work is easy and generally risk-free, but the things that have occupied my time since becoming an ex-lawyer have nothing to do with my present situation. The reason I am where I am goes back to when I was still a lawyer and had the misfortune to become associated with Salvador "Sonny" Falco, but that's another story, and we'll get there soon enough.

When I entered the Rose, Delores (I never knew her last name) was behind the bar polishing glasses. Delores was the primary reason the proletariat found the Rose so pleasant. There was little doubt that she had the finest pair of hooters in three counties. I know that may not be the politically or socially correct way to describe Delores's most outstanding (no pun intended) qualities. But let's face it, when they're as big, round and firm as a grapefruit, it would be an injustice to merely call them breasts. Besides, she did little to conceal her considerable attributes, so I don't think she'd mind my reference.

As was her custom, tonight she wore a low-cut blouse knotted in the front with her hooters just tantalizingly out of full view. Delores knew her clientele.

"How ya doing, Delores," I said as I slid onto my customary stool.

"Can't complain," she said as she leaned just far enough over the bar to be sure I could get a peek at her erect nipples. Delores didn't wear a bra and was a bit of a tease.

"But you will anyway," I chuckled as we completed our ritual greeting. We were long overdue for some new material.

The national news was on the television. No one else much cared what happened more than thirty miles away, but I tried to stay informed.

A face I knew appeared on the screen. Sonny Falco. He was all smiles as he strolled down the steps of the federal courthouse in New Orleans. A phalanx of lawyers, all of them with smiles of their own, surrounded him. A dozen microphones and cameras were thrust in front of him. The banner at the bottom of the screen said in big red letters "MOBSTER MISTRIAL."

I started to ask Delores to turn up the volume when my cell phone chirped. Usually, I leave my phone turned off when I'm not using it. After all, the phone is for my convenience; not for the convenience of someone trying to reach me. However, after seeing the news headline, I expected an unavoidable call. I was sure I knew who it was, but I checked the caller ID to confirm my suspicions. Sometimes I hate it when I'm right.

A voice I had come to detest asked, "Have you heard the news?"

The voice belonged to Barbara Blain, assistant U.S. attorney for the Eastern District of Louisiana.

"I'm watching it now." I wondered if she could tell how pissed I was about the implications of the news. "What happened?"

"Don't know. We figure he probably got to a juror."

"Uh-huh," I said. I wasn't going to give her the satisfaction of asking anything else.

"We'll get him next time."

Where had I heard that before? I braced myself for what I knew was coming.

"You're going to have to stay lost for a while longer."

"That wasn't the deal," I said. A few colorful expletives came to mind, but little would be accomplished by suggesting that she perform a physiologically impossible sex act. "'One year,' you said."

"Things change. We've been through this before."

"I haven't seen Becky in almost a year," I said. *Not that you give a damn.* Becky is my… I suppose 'girlfriend' is as good a word as any. She's a struggling artist who pays the bills by working in an upscale gallery on Charles Street. After five years together, the last two sharing a small bungalow in the French Quarter, we had started to talk about making the relationship something more official when my life as I knew it came to an end.

It wasn't as if I had many choices, but the people from

the Department of Justice had at least made it look like I was doing the right thing. All I had to do was tell them what I knew and name names. I wouldn't have to testify, and my name wouldn't appear anywhere in their files. But just in case, a new identity and a new location were strongly recommended.

I couldn't have agreed more. But the people the feds were investigating were much smarter than the government gave them credit for being. They also had sources inside more agencies than anyone was willing to consider—plenty enough to find me if they wanted to. Even if the feds had gotten a conviction, I would have been in danger. I knew too much, and the people in Falco's organization weren't likely to ignore me. 'Forgive and forget' is not in their lexicon.

I briefly wondered if Becky would recognize me when she saw me again. There isn't much to do in the mountains of eastern Tennessee, and I had taken up running. I was up to ten miles a day on mountain roads. My weight was down from two-fifty to one-seventy-five. And I'd quit smoking. No more two packs-a-day, so I suppose there were some benefits to my temporary exile, but I'd had enough. A year of playing Grizzly Adams was all I could take. I'd given the feds everything they'd asked for. I fulfilled my part of the bargain. The fact that they couldn't get a conviction wasn't my fault.

"We have to locate the documents," Blain said.

Tell me something I don't know.

"You're the only one who can find them."

I hated to admit it, but she was probably right.

"Falco knows that you know about them…"

Your grasp of the obvious is amazing!

"…and I'm certain he believes you know where to look for them."

She was right about that, too. I'd hoped it wouldn't come to this. I'd thought about it for a year, but that was in the abstract. Now it was real. The documents were my only hope, but not because they would convict Falco. I was no longer confident that Blain could convict him—and even less confident that I would be safe if she did. With the documents, I had a chip for bargaining with Falco. Without them, I didn't have a chance.

"Harris?"

It took a moment to respond. It was still strange to be addressed by the name they'd given me. "Yeah. I know. It's him or me."

"That's not what I was going to say."

I knew the air conditioner hadn't suddenly kicked on, so the chill I was feeling must have been my response to her statement.

"I'm not going to like this, am I?"

"I don't see any other way of getting Sonny. You may have to testify at the next trial."

Damn. Cold sweats *and* a burst of acid in my guts. "That wasn't part of my deal." I would have screamed at her, but that would have drawn too much attention. Besides, I'm sure the tone of my voice, as low as it was, conveyed at least some of what I was feeling. The rest of it—the in-my-marrow dread and greasy uncertainty of ever getting to leave *château backwoods*—seemed to be a weight that I was damned to carrying alone.

"Things change."

"*Bullshit.*"

"Your plea agreement says you'll provide, and I quote, 'all necessary co-operation.'"

I was in no mood to be reasonable. "I suppose you know where you can shove your agreement."

"Harris, if you violate the terms of your agreement, we'll have no choice but to prosecute you."

I was about to suggest what part of my anatomy she could kiss but thought better of it and didn't say anything. After all, she'd only said I "*may*" have to testify at the next trial, and no good could come from pissing her off unnecessarily.

"Harris?"

I realized that, in my moment of pique, my mind had drifted off. "Yeah. I'm still here."

"I'll send some Marshals to pick you up and bring you in when we're ready for you. And don't worry. You'll be safe."

No. By the time you take Sonny Falco to trial again, I'll be dead.

2.

I don't know how long it took me to drive back to my cabin. I'd made the drive so often that I could do it with my eyes closed, which, given the condition in which I frequently left the Rose, I had probably done.

This time I was cold sober, but my mind wasn't on the road. All the contingency plans I had worked out over the last year churned through my mind. One by one, I reconsidered them, saving the portions that continued to make sense and discarding the parts that no longer looked feasible.

Things had begun falling into place when I realized that I'd reached the end of the gravel road leading to my cabin. The rain, which had just started when I left the Rose, was now coming down in torrents. Through the veil of falling water, I could barely make out my cabin thirty yards from the road. I sat in my car, debating whether to wait out the storm or make a run for the porch. The steady trickle of water from the hole in the convertible top of my Porsche–unnoticeable when I was underway and the wind blew the rain off the roof—helped me make up my mind. I crawled out of my car–there is no other way for a six-foot-two male to get out of a Porsche–and sprinted down the hillside trail and around the end of the cabin toward the porch. By the time I reached the front steps, I was soaked.

At the top of the steps, I felt an involuntary shiver that

had nothing to do with the rain. The door to my cabin was half-open.

I rarely locked my door—only when I was going to be gone for a day or more. There wasn't anything inside worth stealing, and leaving the door unlocked was my way of saying I wasn't going to be held captive to the fears that permeated society. I did, however, always close the door, and the wind had never blown it open before. Granted, I hadn't experienced a storm as bad as the one that was blowing tonight, but I wasn't taking any chances.

I reached under my jacket to the small of my back and removed the 9-mm Glock that I'd grown accustomed to carrying. The sound of the rain on the tin roof of the porch drowned out any sound that might have been coming from inside the cabin. It also covered any noise I might be making, or so I hoped.

I crouched by the steps and scanned the darkness. Without conscious thought, I retraced the drive, or what little I could remember of it. I couldn't recall passing any other cars, and there hadn't been any other vehicles parked along the road. But I guess that was irrelevant. Whoever had paid me a surprise visit, or was waiting for me, wouldn't have been *following* me.

I was hyperventilating and told myself to relax. It didn't do much good, but at least it was something. I had no clue what to do next. Locating missing persons—most of which involved chasing information through public records that were accessible on the Internet—wasn't training for covert activities.

After a few seconds, I concluded that I was being paranoid. I started up the steps with my gun at the ready. Being paranoid didn't mean I was also stupid. I approached the door and pressed myself against the wall. I took a deep breath and kicked the door the rest of the way open like they do on television.

Whoever had been there didn't seem to have found whatever they were looking for. They also didn't seem to care whether their intrusion was discovered. Every book I had was on the floor. Every drawer had been opened and searched. The cushions on the sofa and matching chair had been torn and searched.

I don't know how long I stood at the door, gazing at the surreal destruction. At some point, I closed the door and started picking my way through the wreckage before returning to the door and turning the knob on the bolt lock. Better late than never.

The circumstances demanded a cold beer and I headed for the kitchen. I was pleased to see that at least the refrigerator door was closed. Either the intruder didn't expect to find anything of importance inside or he understood the importance of a cold drink at times like this. The thought that the intruder was not a complete savage was somehow comforting.

Three beers later, I began to form rational thoughts. Someone knew who I was and where I was. There wasn't much doubt who that was. The only question was why anyone had waited until now to come looking for whatever they hoped to find. The only explanation I could come up with was that he, or she, was waiting until after the Falco trial was over. I didn't have any idea why that would be important, but this kind of detecting was new to me. I was sure I'd get better at it, though. Either that or, I concluded, I'd better make sure that my life insurance policy was still in force.

I pushed myself away from the kitchen table and headed for the living room where I stopped at the threshold and once again absorbed the reality of the invasion. Inevitably, my focus went to the desk. Its top, and the floor around it, were littered with the contents of old client files, but the desk itself hadn't been damaged. I held my breath as I reached for the latch that, when released, allowed the top to be raised. Inside, my laptop remained tucked where I'd left it.

An hour later, I had stowed my computer and my meager belongings into the absurdly small trunk of my Porsche and was heading west on I-40. I didn't know where I was going or what I was going to do when I got there. I only knew that I couldn't stay where I was.

3.

Driving on a crowded interstate at night in the pouring rain is probably a good time to stay focused on what you're doing, but doing the wisest thing was never my strong suit. If it were, I wouldn't have gotten into my current predicament in the first place.

As I've said, representing criminals has a certain allure. Yeah, yeah, I know what the public thinks of criminal defense lawyers, but defendants aren't always guilty of the crimes they've been charged with. They may be guilty of *other* crimes—they almost certainly are, and they're probably going to do something else that's criminal if they get off—but I can't worry about such things. Besides, I represented them before I represented the estate of my aunt and uncle—may they rest in peace—and I needed the money. But I digress.

Suffice it to say that while representing Sonny Falco, I learned some things about him and his business activities that he wouldn't want anyone else, especially any federal agents, to know. And maybe, just maybe, I did some things that might have been a little bit illegal. (Did I mention that in addition to my drinking I have been known to partake of some agricultural substances whose possession and sale is frowned upon by the government?)

The point is, my clients trusted me with information, and I couldn't disclose anything I learned from them.

Attorney-client privilege and all that. What I could do with that information when I stopped being a lawyer was another matter. If I'd stopped practicing law voluntarily I might have been more compliant with my lawyerly responsibilities. However, as far as I was concerned, having my law license revoked liberated me from the rules. At least that's what I told myself when the U.S. attorney made me an offer that, as they say, I couldn't refuse. That was a little over a year ago, and now I had my posterior in the proverbial sling. So, there I was, running away from God knows what and heading to God knows where. (God also probably knew *who* I was running away from, but even I could figure that one out.)

Two thoughts were uppermost in my mind: How the hell did anyone find out where I was? What did anyone expect to find in my cabin, and how could I placate Sonny Falco? (Yes, I understand that those are three things, but they're all part of the same problem, so let's not quibble about how many thoughts I was having.)

My first question had only one answer. No one, not even Becky, was supposed to know where I was. Only the Marshals and the U.S. attorney knew that. So the only answer to my question had to be that they, or someone in their offices, had spilled the beans—or ratted me out if you prefer. Whoever the culprit was, it meant that I couldn't let Blain know where I was going.

My first conclusion posed yet another problem. Who was I supposed to be? Could I still be "Harris Masters," or had my new identity also been disclosed? I still had all my identification from before I became a protected witness, but I was sure Sonny Falco had people looking for me under that name too. Fortunately, I knew people who could provide me with identification under a new name, but that would take time—and such people couldn't always be trusted. I had to give the matter of my identity some thought.

The next question on my list had a simple answer. Whoever had ransacked my cabin must have been looking for the documents. The fact that the government hadn't used them in Falco's first trial couldn't have escaped his attention. But the fact that I had disappeared would have led him to conclude that I had been co-operating with the government. Falco may be a criminal, but he wasn't a stupid criminal. The question was, is he a forgiving criminal?

I needed help, and my options were limited. As I paged through my mental Rolodex, I repeatedly found myself drawn to one name, Horse McGee, but I'm not exactly sure why. His boss, a guy named Lucius White, had a cabin on Douglas Lake and they, along with White's girlfriend, Leslie Halloran, spend time in Tennessee when they're not at his office in Fort Myers, Florida.

McGee is what you might call a drinking buddy. When he's not involved in some investigation for White, he hangs out at The Red Rose. We got to know each other by swapping stories about our investigations and sharing professional insights. I didn't know much about White or his girlfriend. I only knew that White was some hot-shot lawyer, and Leslie was just plain hot.

About ten miles south of Knoxville, I-40 intersects with I-75. I-40 heads west, and I-75 goes south. West and I head for New Orleans. South and I head for Florida. As I approached the split, I made a decision.

TWO YEARS AGO

4.

Mardi Gras in New Orleans is one of those events that should be on everyone's bucket list. There's nothing like it. Yes, I know, other cities have Mardi Gras celebrations that they're proud of. But, with all due respect to those cities, nothing can compare with the madness and uninhibited, occasionally raunchy, insanity the consumes New Orleans. Except for the hotels, bars, and restaurants, businesses might just as well shut down for the week, and a fair number of them do close on Fat Tuesday. But some businesses must go on, and mine was one of them.

As I've told you, I practice criminal law—at least I did until I got disbarred—and crime doesn't take holidays. Fortunately, most of the crime that comes with Mardi Gras is minor stuff. Prostitution, public indecency, public intoxication and public urination (that's pissing, for those of you who didn't finish high school) lead the list. Oh, sure, there may be an upsurge in muggings and assaults—maybe even an extra killing or two. It's just what happens when you crowd a bunch of committed partiers together and promote drinking in public.

Most of the people who fill the jails and the arraignment court docket during Mardi Gras have been arrested for petty crimes. But regardless of what they've been arrested for, they have one thing in common—they all need lawyers. The problem is that no half-way competent attorney wants to work nights—especially not on Fat Tuesday. The result is that the public defenders are overwhelmed, and I had offered to help if they got too busy. I didn't remember that I had volunteered—I must have been drunk at the time—until I got an urgent call from Jack Crowley, manager of the local legal aid program, asking me where the hell I was.

As it happened, I had been indulging in an afternoon of carnal activities with my beloved Becky and was preparing to have another go at it when I got the call. I wanted to tell Jack I couldn't help him, but a promise is a promise. Besides, I liked Jack. We drank together with some regularity, and my first commandment is that you never screw a drinking buddy. But what the hell, another few minutes wouldn't make that much difference, and Becky, dear sweet naked Becky, would never let me hear the end of it if I put work ahead of satisfying her desires.

Driving to the courthouse was out of the question. All the major thoroughfares in downtown New Orleans—or, as we say, N'Orlins—were blocked for the parades, and every surrounding street, to say nothing of those in the French Quarter, was so crowded with tourists and local celebrants that a car didn't stand a chance of getting through. It was an unusually cool afternoon, and I didn't break a sweat as I hoofed it out of the Quarter to a hotel where there were a few taxies.

Half an hour after leaving home, I headed up the steps of the courthouse. Once past the metal detectors, I stopped by the vending room for a coffee. It wasn't the kind of chicory coffee that is the mainstay of N'Orlins coffee drinkers, but I needed something to keep my head in the game.

Jack Crowley was waiting in the corridor outside the courtrooms on the second floor. He looked harried as he

shouted instructions and dispensed advice to his subordi-
nates who were meeting with their clients for the first time.
Crowley breathed what could only have been a short sigh
of relief when he saw me approach.

"What do you have, Jack," I said without going through
the ritual of the handshake and greeting thing.

"It's a madhouse. Half of my staff is so new that they
don't even know where the men's rooms are."

As if to prove his point, two of his attorneys, both
apparently fresh out of law school and making their first
solo appearances in court, interrupted our conversation
with questions about the arguments they should make on
their new cases. Crowley didn't even return his attention to
me as he handed me a small stack of files. I glanced through
them as I wandered over to the benches where most of the
miscreants who were charged with misdemeanors waited.
In a normal week, they would have been waiting in the
courtroom or the pre-appearance holding facility. (Don't
you love political correctness? "Pre-appearance holding
facility." It's a fucking *cell*, for God's sake.)

Anyway, as I was saying, I was heading for a row of
partying perpetrators when I was approached by a woman
who made me think of my grandmother. She was eighty
if she was a day, but she was spry, and she navigated her
walker through the crowd like Mario Andretti on the back-
stretch at Indianapolis. (If the simile is too obscure for you,
think of a Pakistani cab-driver in New York City.) Anyway,
she grabbed me by the coat sleeve and asked how long she
was going to have to wait. I thumbed through my files to
see if she was one of my cases. She wasn't, but I couldn't
avoid the urge to help granny—and satisfy my curiosity.
"What were you arrested for?"

She looked at me as if I was daft, and I suppose I
deserved it. Let's face it; there were a limited number of

ordinances that she could have violated. "They busted me for public indecency." Her words suggested that she's watched a few too many episodes of *Law & Order,* but her accent was pure Channel Irish. For some reason, I found the combination of words and accent hilarious, but I managed to suppress the urge to laugh.

"What did you do?" I shouldn't have asked the question when I was about to take a sip of my coffee.

She beamed at me. "I flashed my boobs at a mounted cop."

I choked, spewed a mouthful of coffee, and dropped my files. I knelt to pick up my papers and lowered my head to hide my face. I tried to avoid laughing, but I think the convulsing of my body gave me away. I should have known better, but when I regained control of myself, I looked at her and asked, "Why did you do that?"

She responded with a wide-eyed look and the kind of a throaty laugh that made me think she smoked too much. "It's *Mardi Gras!*"

I chuckled, shook my head, and wandered away. I remember thinking that she had given me a plausible defense for my other clients, but I don't think I ever used it. (This was all before I had become wealthy enough to not worry about pissing off an overworked judge whose tolerance for humor was inversely proportional to the magnitude of his docket.)

I found several of my assigned clients and had a perfunctory chat with each of them. Most of them weren't facing anything more than a fine. I would plead them out, and the bored judge would announce their penalty. My clients would hustle to the clerk's office to pay the declared amount and scurry off to rejoin the festivities outside. *Yes,* I thought. *It's Mardi Gras.*

I was halfway through my assigned files when I came

to a name that rang a bell. I couldn't immediately place it, but I knew it was familiar. I glanced at a copy of the arrest report and charge—possession of cocaine with intent to distribute. I'd handled a few possession cases—mostly misdemeanor pot-related cases for the wayward offspring of friends—but nothing like this. These charges were serious felonies, and I had to remind myself that I was only going to represent him for this one bail hearing. I knew he would be in the pre-appearance holding facility and headed for the stairs while still trying to remember why I knew the name. Then it occurred to me. He was an "associate" of Sonny Falco. I didn't realize it at the time, but that was the start on my path to the trouble I'm in now.

5.

I told the guard outside the area where those who were charged with "real" crimes were held who I was and who I was there to represent. He directed me to a small, non-descript room with a metal table and two chairs where attorneys were able to meet with their clients in privacy. I assumed that the case had been assigned to the office of the public defender by mistake and that the meeting with my client would be brief. Sonny Falco's associates generally had at least one attorney on speed-dial, and I assumed that he would be handling the man's case when it went to trial. But I was there, and I had to go through the motions.

Louis LeBlanc strolled into the interview room looking no more concerned than if he was entering a room at some social event. His demeanor and body language suggested that he was not a first-timer. He was also not what I expected. For some reason, the charge—possession with intent—made me think that he would be a low-level street dealer—correction, an *accused* street dealer—and would be dressed accordingly, whatever that meant. Instead, he was wearing a pirate costume. It wasn't the kind of outfit that was just thrown together by a typical Mardi Gras reveler. It was more like the custom-tailored costume worn by members of one of the Krews that sponsored floats in the many parades held during the week of celebration.

He slid easily onto the chair opposite me. I introduced

myself and extended my hand. He smiled, and we shook. His grip was firm and business-like. His hands were those of someone who was not averse to labor but probably didn't use his hands in his job.

We studied each other for a few seconds before getting down to business. I explained that I was not a public defender and was there as a volunteer. This interested him, and for the next few minutes we chatted like people who had met at a cocktail party. Mostly, he asked me about my practice and background, and I answered his questions. I may have embellished a few facts here and there. As I have said, I lie some. Besides, I didn't expect to see him again after tonight, so where was the harm. I don't know why he cared about anything he was asking, but I wasn't in a hurry to get back to the rest of my assigned cases.

Eventually, my temporary client learned whatever it was that he wanted to know, or just tired of the small-talk, and was ready to move on to the business at hand. I was about to embark on my usual spiel about what would happen next when I realized how meaningless it was. I knew, or at least I suspected, that my client had more experience with the criminal side of the justice system than I did.

I said, "I assume you have already called your attorney."

"Couldn't," he said. "My regular attorney ain't available."

"Oh," I said. I intended the statement as a mere acknowledgment that I had heard him, but he took it as a question.

"He got his self… He died—suddenly."

I couldn't help wondering what he had started to say. There weren't many ways he could have completed the sentence that wouldn't have made my heart rate rise. The more I thought about it, the happier I was that he hadn't finished the sentence. There are some things I didn't want or need to know. Besides, I reminded myself, I was only going to represent him for one hearing. What did I care about the

demise of his former attorney? I was about to say something else when the guard knocked on the door and said,
"You're up soon. I have to take Mr. LeBlanc to the courtroom. You can meet him there."

I was startled that the guard referred to my client as *Mr.*
LeBlanc. Respect. My back stiffened reflexively. Who was
LeBlanc? What was I missing here?

As we stood, my client said something that I was not
prepared for. "Are you available?"

I didn't immediately say anything. But my look, which
was probably somewhere between surprise and lack of
comprehension, spoke for me.

"I want to hire you. Are you available?"

It would have been easy to say I had a full plate and
couldn't take any new clients. But the fact is that my calendar was virtually empty, and I was intrigued. A little
intimidated maybe, but interested, nonetheless. Even as I
was about to speak, I knew I was doing the wrong thing.
I quoted him a ridiculously high fee as my retainer and
secretly hoped that he would reject it.

"Done!" he said. "I'll see you upstairs."

6.

My heart was still pounding as I hurried up the stairs, taking them two at a time, to tell Jack Crowley about my encounter with Louis LeBlanc and beg off any more cases for the rest of what was by then evening. When I told him that I had agreed to represent LeBlanc, he responded with a long, low whistle and said, "Are you sure you know what you're doing?"

I admitted that I didn't.

He shook his head. "How the hell did he even get on the list to be represented by my office?"

I said I didn't have any idea how that had happened but guessed that he had thrown out some gibberish about a non-existent Constitutional right and a flustered clerk had put him on the list. Or possibly everyone in the courthouse knew more about my new client than I did, and someone wanted to get him processed as quickly as possible.

Junior attorneys from the public defender's office were urgently throwing questions at Crowley when he said, "Meet me tomorrow. I want to hear all about this."

"Okay," I said over my shoulder as I headed the court-room. "How about Café Du Monde? Twelve o'clock."

"Make it one," Crowley shouted.

As I plowed through the crowd, I raised a hand with my index finger touching my thumb and gave him an 'okay' sign.

§

The courtroom was packed when I entered. I recognized a few attorneys who, like myself, were still in need of business and hung around the courthouse hoping to pick up a client who didn't qualify for Jack Crowley's services. I made my way past the swinging wooden gate into the well of the courtroom—the part where the real business of the court takes place. (In olden times, the spectators were separated from the action by a simple bar past which only attorneys were allowed. Hence the term "passing the bar" meant that you were a lawyer. This fact isn't relevant to the story, but I think it's an interesting piece of trivia that I like to share whenever I get the chance.)

I took one of the empty chairs at the defense table and settled in for what I was sure would be an interminable wait.

The judge was in the middle of hearing arguments for and against the amount of the fine to be levied in a solicitation case when a police officer led my client into the room. The judge glanced toward them and I think—although I can't be sure—he raised his eyebrows. The officer led LeBlanc to a seat in the empty jury box and stationed himself beside my client.

Half an hour later, LeBlanc was led to my side while the clerk read the charges: possession of cocaine and possession with the intent to distribute cocaine.

The judge took off his glasses and began to polish the lenses. Without looking up, he said, "Appearances."

I stood, stated my name for the record, and identified myself as counsel for the defendant. The prosecutor, David Hillis, who I'd spoken with at several bar functions but didn't know well, did the same.

The judge inspected his glasses and put them on before

giving us his full attention. "What's the State's position on bail?"

"Your Honor," Hillis began. "The defendant is charged with a major felony. Cocaine is becoming—"

The judge rolled his eyes. "Save it, counselor. We all know that cocaine is a scourge on society. But as you can see, we have a lot of cases to hear tonight, so just tell me how much you want."

"Fifty-thousand dollars."

I looked toward LeBlanc. He nodded.

"That's acceptable," I said.

"Then fifty-thousand it is. Cash or bond."

I remained standing at the defense table. "Just one more thing, your honor."

The judge slid his glasses down until they rested on the tip of his nose and he glowered at me. "What is it?' He didn't attempt to conceal the impatience in his voice.

"My client would like an immediate probable cause hearing."

The judge released an exasperated sigh and turned in the direction of his courtroom deputy, who was rummaging through what I can only assume was the court calendar. The judge leaned back, seemingly studying something on the ceiling as he waited. Finally, the clerk wrote something on a piece of paper and handed it to him.

The judge glanced at the paper and announced, "Friday at two-thirty with Judge Henderson, if that's convenient for you."

"That will be fine, your honor."

"I'm so glad." Sarcasm was not his best quality.

I glanced toward my client, who appeared to be having a difficult time keeping a straight face. He did, however, manage to give me an approving nod before the police officer came to escort him to the clerk's office.

As they left the room, I felt a tap on my shoulder and turned to see a tall, slender man with dark hair and a goatee.

"I'm Pete Whitacre. I'm here to post bail for Mr. LeBlanc. I'll walk you down to the clerk's office."

I couldn't decide whether I was comforted or concerned by the realization that LeBlanc had a bail bondsman on speed-dial.

§

Whitaker and I worked our way through the crowd outside the courtroom and went to the clerk's office where LeBlanc, who had already collected his personal property, was waiting for us. LeBlanc was reclining against the back of the wooden bench. His legs were stretched in front of him, and he was absently examining his manicured fingernails. When Whitacre and I entered, he stood and smiled and, while ignoring me, hugged Whitacre. "Thanks for hustling over here. I know you have big doings scheduled for tonight."

"That's not until later. Are you still planning to drop by?"

"We'll see. Me and my attorney are going to have a drink and discuss some business."

This was news to me, but I guessed LeBlanc was accustomed to having his every wish be someone else's command. That should have told me something, and it did. I just wasn't sure what.

"What's the pain, Pete?" LeBlanc asked Whitacre, although even then I was sure he knew that the price of a bond was ten percent of the bail.

"For you, I have a special deal. Ten percent."

They both laughed. I surmised that they had been

through their routine before, but I didn't know which one was Abbott and which one was Costello.

LeBlanc pulled out a roll of bills, hundreds, that was bigger than my fist—and I have a big fist. He peeled off the requisite number, gave them to Whitacre and signed a few forms before turning his attention to me. "Come on. Let's go get a drink, and we'll talk about my case." My availability, or lack thereof, didn't seem to be of any concern to LeBlanc. "I assume you don't mind if I pay my retainer in cash."

I'm not sure, but I may have stuttered when I responded. "Yes. I mean, no. Cash isn't a problem. But we can't talk about business over drinks somewhere. To preserve the attorney-client privilege, we have to talk where no one can overhear us."

LeBlanc chuckled. "Don't worry about it. I've got a private club, and it has rooms where we can talk."

My mind suddenly flashed to scenes from gangster movies with social clubs with someone big and ugly guarding the door and a crime boss holding court in the backroom and getting his hand kissed by one or another supplicant. I couldn't avoid thinking, *What the hell have I gotten myself into?*

7.

LeBlanc's Lincoln Town Car was waiting when we headed down the long flight of steps in front of the courthouse. A man who I assumed was the driver was sitting on one fender with his foot on the bumper and smoking a cigar. No uniform, just a black suit, unbuttoned, and a maroon shirt open at the neck. It struck me that his choice of attire was odd. Oh, it was a nice-looking suit, but in New Orleans almost no one wears a suit unless they have to.

As we approached the car, LeBlanc—it wasn't until later that I started calling him Louis—had his arm draped over my shoulder like we were old buddies. We hadn't spoken since leaving the clerk's office, and I found his act of familiarity a little off-putting.

I was still thinking about the driver's suit as we reached the sidewalk. As the driver slid off the fender he crushed his cigar under his heel. The movement made his coat open, and I saw the reason he was wearing it. At the sight of the gun, the *big* gun, in his shoulder holster, I wondered again what I'd gotten myself into. My heart skipped a beat. I know that's a cliché, but my memory is clear on the point.

The driver opened the rear door, and LeBlanc guided me in. It wasn't until the door closed that I realized how late it was—or it might have been that the dark tint on the windows made it seem later than it was.

As the car pulled away from the curb, LeBlanc finally

spoke. "You like oysters?" (He pronounced the word for the bivalve as "yersters." It was the first time I'd paid attention to the sound of his voice. He was obviously a native.)

"This is New Orleans. Who doesn't like oysters?" At least one of us pronounced all the words in a way that could be understood beyond the bayou. Although I was born in New Orleans, I'm a military brat (my father was a flight surgeon), and most of my formative years were spent overseas or among Yankees so I never picked up the local accent.

"That's good. We always have the freshest oysters in town, and we have a chef who does wonders with them if you're into cooked ones. Me, I'm a fresh oyster kind of guy." If it hadn't been so dark in the car, I'm sure I could have seen him licking his lips.

I didn't pay much attention to where we were headed. Even though we were well away from the Quarter and the area of downtown where the revelry was taking place, the streets were so constricted that we had to make quite a few turns as we wended our way through the throng. I soon realized we were on St. Charles heading in the direction of the area now listed on the National Registry of Historic Places as the Uptown New Orleans Historic District. To the locals, it's just Uptown.

In the daytime, I always enjoyed this part of the city. The tourists may think that the French Quarter epitomizes New Orleans, but the streets lined with nineteenth-century mansions and big old live oaks covered with Spanish moss are my version of the essence of New Orleans. Many Sundays, Becky and I took the old trolley to the Camellia Grill, at the end of St. Charles, for breakfast.

We'd only traveled a couple of blocks on St. Charles when I asked LeBlanc where we were going.

"I told you. We're going to a private club." As I came

to learn, there were times when you couldn't shut LeBlanc up and others when you couldn't get him to talk. This was one of the latter.

We drove for another ten or so minutes, made a couple of turns that took me from being generally oriented to woefully lost. Eventually we pulled up in front a modest (by Uptown standards) mansion.

LeBlanc opened the door without waiting for the driver to do it. What a guy. Man of the people and all that.

We got out, and I made a quick survey of the surroundings. It was a fairly typical neighborhood as Uptown neighborhoods go. Big houses with spacious porches set well back from the cobblestone street. Lots of trees and Spanish moss. I could hear the sound of parties emanating from a few houses. It would probably get louder as the evening wore on and the raucousness that is Mardi Gras reached its zenith. On any other night, I would have realized that an exceptional number of expensive cars were near the house where we were parked. The only significant thought that occurred to me was that we hadn't had to hunt for a parking place and that two other spots in front of the building were still available. Perhaps they would be taken by late-arriving party goers, but I didn't think that was the case. Even in the absence of any signs, it seemed to be understood that these were reserved spots.

We joined a couple of costumed men on the sidewalk. In retrospect, I think I was a little grateful that they were in costumes. That way I wouldn't be able to identify them. Even then my detecting skills were starting to emerge.

LeBlanc hugged each of them but didn't introduce me. They chatted for a while, but I tried not to listen to anything they said. Instead, I surveyed the neighborhood and watched as a police cruiser inched up the street at well below the speed limit.

As we headed toward the house, it occurred to me that there weren't any women around. Not on the veranda in front of the house and not, as far as I could see through the windows, inside.

Once inside, LeBlanc told me to wait by the door while he took care of a little business. I was happy to oblige. As he disappeared into the modest but growing crowd, I took the opportunity to do a little more detecting. I couldn't get the image of a mob "social club" out of my mind.

A tuxedoed waiter offered me a Hurricane. I could have used a drink, but I declined. The later offer of a few oysters was another matter. I took two or three and a small china plate from the offering waiter. LeBlanc was right; they were fresh and delicious and just what I needed to satisfy my palate until he returned. When LaBlanc reappeared he was holding a Hurricane and, with a tilt of his head, beckoned me toward a winding staircase.

LeBlanc led me up the stairs and down a long hallway. We passed several rooms furnished as dens and sitting rooms. As we passed, their occupants glanced at me and quickly closed the doors. At the end of the hallway, LeBlanc led me into a large room that had probably once been the master bedroom but was now furnished as a sitting room. It had an understated opulence that reminded me of the lounge of the Harvard Club in New York, which I'd once visited with an uncle who'd attended that institution. The room even had the same smell: the scent of rich leather mixed with the lingering scent of tobacco—expensive cigars, if my nostrils weren't deceiving me.

LeBlanc touched my arm and indicated that I should wait by the door. From there I could see that the glass in the expanse of windows was covered with a layer of tinted material that had a metallic feature. LeBlanc crossed the room, lowered the mini-blinds, and closed the heavy drapes before signaling me inside.

LeBlanc lowered himself onto a leather sofa and stretched out. I took a seat on the love seat opposite him. LeBlanc extracted an envelope from the pocket of his pirate pantaloons and casually tossed it onto the antique coffee table between us. It slid across the table and came to a stop at the edge in front of me. I wondered if that was merely chance or if he was accustomed to performing the action. I assumed the envelope contained my retainer. I picked it up and fought the urge to open it. I'd never seen the amount of my fee in cash, but counting the money in front of him would probably be deemed an insult.

He took a sip from his Hurricane and placed the glass on the coffee table. "You really should try one," he said, pointing at his drink. "They're delicious."

"I'm sure they are." I hoped that my voice was more controlled and professional than I was feeling. —"Just what kind of a place is this?"

"I told you. It's a private club—men only."

"That's all?"

"That's all."

In retrospect, I admit that I may have been a little naïve in accepting his explanation at face value.

LeBlanc took off his pirate's hat, wig, and beard and tossed them on the sofa. Now that I had my first good look at him, I realized that he was nothing like the stereotypical image I'd conjured up.

I already knew that he was about my height, a little under six feet, and just a few pounds overweight. I also knew that he carried himself with confidence—not the ramrod stiffness of a Marine, but erect and relaxed. What surprised me was his head and face. He was bald—whether by choice or the process of nature I couldn't tell—and had bushy brown eyebrows over his dark brown eyes and a neatly trimmed mustache over thin lips. And he had an old scar on his left cheek.

My examination of my client was interrupted when he said, "I suppose you want to talk about my case."

It sounded more like a statement than a question, and I assumed that he wanted to get business out of the way quickly so that he could rejoin his friends. That suited me just fine. We had to do it eventually, but I had hoped we could do it later at my office. I was sure there weren't any bugs planted there, but I wasn't so sure about here. Besides, I was anxious to get back to Becky and enjoy the last of the Mardi Gras festivities.

LeBlanc must have read my mind. "Don't worry. We sweep this place for bugs regularly."

I responded with a slight nod. "Then why don't you tell me what happened?"

He raised his arms and smiled. "I'm guilty. Now, what's *your* plan?"

I admitted that I didn't have one.

8.

At eleven the next morning I rolled out of bed and headed for the bathroom. My head was throbbing, and I desperately needed an aspirin or two—or three. I sat on the edge of the sink, taking time to be sure I could maintain my equilibrium, before turning on the shower. God did that feel good.

I was halfway through what I had intended would be a therapeutic cleansing when I suddenly remembered that I had promised to meet Jack Crowley for lunch. When I walked into the bedroom, a towel wrapped around my waist, Becky rolled over and muttered something unintelligible that I took to be "good morning." I kissed her lightly and told her that I had to go to a meeting. She moaned softly and snuggled under the covers.

At twelve forty-five I was dressed in my usual Ash Wednesday attire—jeans, a polo shirt, and running shoes—and seated at an outside table at the Café Du Monde. I was on my second cup of chicory coffee and third beignet. My headache was beginning to subside, and I was able to think coherently about the events of the previous evening. I didn't have any idea about how I was going to defend LeBlanc and was anxious to get to work researching his case. I'd thought about canceling my meeting with Jack, but decided against it in the hope that he could give me some ideas about how to handle my new case.

Jack rolled in at a few minutes before one and slid into a chair opposite me. His eyes were bloodshot, and he was wearing the same suit he'd had on the night before.

"You look like the guest of honor at a funeral," I said.

He slumped, closed his eyes, and rolled his shoulders. "Death would be an improvement."

"Long night?" I said as I signaled the waitress to bring another coffee and an order of beignets for Jack.

Jack rubbed his eyes and yawned. "And it's still not over."

I figured Jack could use a little downtime, so I just nibbled at one of my beignets and waited.

I was beginning to think Jack had dozed off when, a few minutes later, his coffee and beignets arrived. He slowly opened his eyes enough to form slits and glance at the table. When he was satisfied that there was a reason to rejoin the living, he sat up, stretched and muttered a "thank you" to the waitress before taking a swallow of coffee drink. As he replaced his cup on the table he yawned and rubbed his eyes with the palms of both hands. "We handled more than two hundred cases."

I didn't know whether or not that was an exceptional number of cases for a Fat Tuesday, so I didn't say anything.

He shook his head. "What a night!"

Jack took another long drink of coffee and reached for a beignet as he asked, "How did your evening with Mr. LeBlanc go?"

Another *Mr.* LeBlanc. Did everybody but me know who my client was? "What's to tell? I have a new client."

"You *do* know who he is, don't you?" The sound of a horn from a barge on the Mississippi belched out before I had a chance to respond. Jack's hand returned to his forehead, and his eyes pulled tight until the rumbling noise subsided.

"I know he's connected to Sonny Falco."

"That's putting it mildly!"

"You obviously know more than I do. Why don't you fill me in?"

Jack shook his head. "For a smart guy, your ignorance sometimes amazes me. Sonny Falco is the godfather of the Mafia in New Orleans."

I must have opened my eyes pretty wide because Jack started to laugh. "You didn't know that, did you?"

I suddenly felt defensive and maybe a little stupid. Sure, I'd heard stories and seen occasional references to "organized crime" in *The Times-Picayune*. But this is Louisiana. Around here, you're still a nobody if you haven't been indicted for something. "Okay, smart guy," I said. "If you know so much, tell me how LeBlanc is connected to Sonny Falco. The Mafia is a purely Sicilian and Italian organization, and LeBlanc sure isn't either of them."

Jack shook his head again. The action was starting to irritate me. I liked him better when he was bleary-eyed. "You watch too many old movies. We're talking about the modern Mafia—or what's left of it."

"So where does LeBlanc fit in?"

"He's Falco's political guy. He makes sure that things get done right in city hall and Baton Rouge."

"He pays bribes?"

Jack shrugged. "Maybe, but I doubt it. That's too blatantly illegal. I'm sure money changes hands somewhere along the line, but LeBlanc is more of a deal-maker. He puts people together and arranges for the exchange of favors." Jack took another gulp of coffee before adding, "But I suspect there are times when he makes people offers that they can't refuse."

I still wasn't sure what Jack was trying to tell me, but I could guess. I found myself taking solace in the knowledge that my representation of Louis LeBlanc was a one-time thing.

We chatted for a few more minutes until it became apparent that Jack was too exhausted to concentrate. It was just as well. I was anxious to get to work on my new client's case—especially now that I knew more about who he was.

§

I spent the rest of the afternoon holed up in my office in front of my computer researching the latest rulings in drug cases. I hoped to find some opinions by Judge Henderson, but I didn't come up with anything. That was hardly a surprise. Trial judges don't generally issue written rulings, and the few that are written are rarely published in any of the electronic databases used by lawyers. On the chance that some of his drug cases had been appealed, I also researched the appellate court database but again came up with bupkis. That could mean one of two things: either he didn't hear many drug cases, or he didn't make errors of the type that would justify an appeal.

You don't need to be a rocket scientist to know that the first alternative was unlikely. I didn't doubt that Henderson had heard at least his share of drug cases—probably a lot more than I'd even handled—which left only the possibility that he rarely made reversible errors. That scared the crap out of me.

I spent a few more hours educating myself on all defenses I might assert, but things weren't looking great for my client. My mind began to drift. If things weren't looking so great for Louis, where exactly would that leave me?

Shortly before five, my telephone rang. The caller ID

showed the call was from the police lab. I swallowed hard and picked up the receiver.

As expected, the caller informed me that the lab had completed its analysis of the substance taken from LeBlanc and that it was, indeed, cocaine. Of course, I wasn't surprised, but hope springs eternal, so I hustled over to get a copy of the report before the lab closed.

§

An hour later I was back in my office studying the lab report. Nothing was obviously out of line, and I was about to close up shop for the day when I had an idea. I returned to my computer and began my search for information on crime lab procedures and tests used to identify cocaine. To my surprise, I found a site where I could determine the procedures used by the crime lab of the New Orleans Police Department. According to what I read, the testing protocols were pretty straightforward. But as everyone who watches crime shows on television knows, there's more than one procedure for testing for just about everything.

I made a couple of calls to criminal-attorney friends in hopes of getting some more information on testing for cocaine, but most of them were either gone for the day or had taken the day off to recover from the previous night's festivities. I was about to call it a day when I got lucky and connected with a lawyer who I knew could at least point me in the right direction, assuming there was such a place. I explained my dilemma and silently prayed that he knew something that would help me. All he could tell me was that there were other judicially recognized tests, but he didn't know enough about them to put an end to my ignorance. I thanked him for his help and leaned back while running my fingers through my hair and thinking about what I could do. Whatever it was, I knew I wouldn't be able to sleep until I had some answers. Instead of going home I headed for the Tulane med school library.

9.

The next morning, I met LeBlanc outside Judge Henderson's courtroom and led him to an attorney conference room down the hall. He was dressed in a dark blue silk suit and a white dress shirt, both obviously custom-made, and a striped tie in the colors of LSU. I had told him to wear a suit, but I, who still bought off the rack at discount stores, hadn't expected that it would be quite so unmistakably elegant. My first thought when I saw him was that he looked like a pimp, and I was glad he wasn't charged with promoting prostitution.

We settled into uncomfortable chairs on opposite sides of a small, scarred conference table, and he asked me to explain what I would be trying to accomplish. I was surprised that he wasn't familiar with probable cause hearings and needed me to tell him what I was doing, but I was glad to oblige. Giving a little lecture on the law gave me an opportunity to take my mind off the upcoming hearing and relax. It was almost enough to make me believe that all would be well.

"In a trial, we'll be focusing on evidence and legal issues regarding the admissibility of evidence. In a probable cause hearing, the prosecution has to prove it has enough evidence to justify a trial. There's an opportunity to make the prosecutor disclose his theory of the case and how he intends to prove the charges against you. That will help me prepare for a trial if there is one. The prosecutor isn't likely to have prepared for the probable cause hearing as carefully as he will for a trial. He's only had two days to work with his witnesses, so they aren't likely to be as well-rehearsed for the probable cause as they will be for the trial. I'm hoping his witnesses will let something slip or say something we can use to impeach their testimony if the case goes to trial."

LeBlanc must have been satisfied with my explanation because he nodded thoughtfully but didn't say anything.

"Just one more thing," I said as we stood to go to the courtroom. "No matter what a witness says, don't react. This isn't the time or place for us to challenge any testimony. Understood?"

"You're the boss."

As LeBlanc and I entered the courtroom, I spotted Paul Baker, the District Attorney.

Interesting, I thought. *The DA himself is handling this case. LeBlanc must be more important than I thought.*

After the bailiff called the court to order, Henderson took his place behind the bench and said, "Be seated," as he slid into his black, high-back chair.

Baker and I both entered our appearance, stating our names and the names of the parties we represented.

"All right, what do we have here?" the judge said impatiently.

Baker and I both stood, ready to state our views of the proceedings.

"One at a time, gentlemen," Henderson said as he turned toward me. "You called for this hearing. What do you have to say?"

"Your honor," I said before I coughed. "Your honor, it is my client's position that the state has insufficient evidence to allow this case to proceed to trial."

Baker jumped to his feet, but the judge held up a hand with his palm facing outward and Baker returned to his seat. "Go on, counselor."

"Thank you, Your Honor. It is my client's contention that the state cannot establish beyond a reasonable doubt that the substance in my client's possession was cocaine. It is also my client's contention that his arrest was procedurally flawed."

I admit that I was winging it. LeBlanc and I had spoken at length the previous evening, but he could only tell about the circumstances surrounding his arrest. He was leaving his social club and about to get in his car when a patrol car pulled up and stopped him. He was told to empty his pockets, which he did, and the officer found the plastic bag containing cocaine. He was immediately placed under arrest and taken to the police station and booked. I didn't have much to work with, but I had some ideas.

The judge turned to Baker. "Call your first witness."

Baker stood. "The state calls Margret Nelson."

A slightly built woman of about forty wearing a forest green pants-suit entered the courtroom, took the witness stand, and was sworn in.

From behind the prosecution's table, Baker said, "Please state your name and position."

"Margret Nelson. I'm a technician with the crime laboratory of the New Orleans Police Department." Her words were delivered without so much as a quiver, and she looked right at home on the stand.

"On March fifth, were you provided with a sample for your analysis?"

"Yes."

Baker approached the witness and handed her a small plastic bag. "Can you identify this item?"

"It's a plastic bag containing a white powder that I was

asked to analyze for the presence of cocaine." She pointed to a tag on the bag. "Those are my initials on the evidence tag."

She had clearly testified before. She knew everything the prosecutor was going to ask and offered her answers in her statement. Baker asked for the bag to be entered into evidence. The judge asked if I had any objection. I didn't, and the packet was marked as evidence.

"In analyzing this sample, did you strictly follow all procedures in the laboratory manual?"

"I did."

"And what were the results of your analysis?"

"The substance tested positive for the presence of cocaine."

It was all very straightforward. The state's justice machine was practically humming.

"I have no further questions for this witness," Baker said and returned to his seat.

I stood and walked to the center of the well of the courtroom, where I stood silently and looked at my legal pad as if I were studying my list of prepared questions. I was merely hoping that a period of silence would make the witness a little nervous. There was no indication that my ploy was having any effect on her so I proceeded.

"Exactly how did you determine that the substance you tested was, in fact, cocaine?"

"We did a standard test by mixing a small sample with a chemical reagent that turns blue when it comes in contact with anything containing cocaine."

"It that the only test you used to make your determination?"

"Yes."

"How many different chemicals can be used to test for the presence of cocaine?"

"I don't know. There are probably many. We use chemicals that have been accepted by the courts as reliable."

She was calm and professional, and her responses didn't sound rehearsed.

"Does a sample have to be pure cocaine for it to react with the chemicals you use?"

The witness's expression turned proudly smug. "Our test will identify even trace amounts of cocaine."

"How much cocaine has to be present for your test to be positive?"

"Let's put it this way. We can establish the presence of cocaine on a dollar bill if it is even touched by someone who had any cocaine on their hands."

I hung my head as if thinking about how to follow up on her answer. In reality, I was only giving her time to wonder what my next question might be and worry that she might not be able to answer it. But she was cool and sat virtually motionless. I concluded that my gambit wasn't working and moved on.

"How many times did you conduct your test?"

"Two."

I knew that that was the requirement of the laboratory manual, but I wanted to make a record of her actions before I switched gears.

"What is a false positive?"

"That's when a test says a drug is present when it isn't."

"How can you be certain that your test didn't result in a false positive?"

"We tested it twice."

"Is it possible that you got two false positives?"

The witness shifted her position in the witness chair. "I suppose it's possible."

"Uh-huh." *No points, but a short gain.*

"Does the chemical you used to test for cocaine also react to any other substance?"

"Not that I know of."

Moving the ball. "So, you don't *know* the answer to my question?"

Baker stood. "Objection. Asked and answered, and it's not a proper question."

Before the judge could rule on the objection, I said, "I'll rephrase. Do you *know* that the chemical you used to test for cocaine does *not* react with any other substance?"

"No. I don't know that."

"Is it possible that your test determined the presence of something other than cocaine?"

The witness squirmed slightly before responding. "I… I suppose."

I glanced toward Baker. He must have also noticed the witness's reaction to my question and was feverishly writing on his legal pad. A glance at the judge told me he was also aware of Baker's action. I wasn't sure if I'd scored any points, but I knew I was making progress. I seizing whatever momentum I had gathered and I forged ahead.

"Was the sample you tested pure cocaine?

Nelson chuckled.

"What's so funny?"

"Counselor, you must know that cocaine is only pure when it is first made. It's always cut before it reaches the street."

"How much cocaine was present in the sample you tested?"

"I can't answer that question. We only test to determine if cocaine is present. We don't test for the purity of a sample."

I gave her a skeptical look. "Why not?"

Baker stood and objected. "The purity of the sample isn't relevant to the charge."

"But the quantity of cocaine in my client's possession *is* relevant to whether my client can be charged with intent to distribute. If he was only in possession of enough for personal use, he can't be charged with intent to distribute."

Judge Henderson sighed. "The objection is overruled. The witness may answer the question—if she can."

Nelson acknowledged that she hadn't made any effort to determine the amount of cocaine present in the sample.

"Does your laboratory have a gas chromatograph?"

"Objection," Baker said without standing. "The question is irrelevant."

Before Baker had finished making his objection, I said, "The relevance of the question will be made clear in a moment."

The judge stifled a yawn. "Overruled."

"Yes. We have a gas chromatograph."

"And isn't it true that with that instrument you can determine the actual quantity of a drug present in a sample?"

The witness didn't seem prepared for the question and hesitated before responding. "Ah… Yes."

"Then why didn't you determine the quantity of what you claim was cocaine that was in the sample you tested?"

The witness hesitated again. "We… I mean, I… wasn't asked to make such a determination."

I was ready to ask more questions about the lab's testing procedures when the judge glanced at his watch. I wasn't about to let time dictate my examination, but keeping the judge's attention was another matter. I sensed that he was growing bored and chose to move on to another topic.

"Is your test sensitive enough to identify cocaine if it represented only one-millionth of a sample?"

"Probably not."

"Exactly how much cocaine would have to be present for your test to detect it?"

"I can't say."

"Did you test my client's blood or urine to determine if *he* had consumed any cocaine?"

"Objection. The defendant is charged with possession, not use, of cocaine."

The judge didn't wait to hear any argument I might have had before saying, "Sustained."

"I have no further questions."

The judge tilted his head in Baker's direction. "Call your next witness."

Baker called Officer Pete Bower. Bower eyed me nervously as he took the stand and was sworn in. Baker went through the usual ritual of establishing Bower's full name and position and the fact that he was the arresting officer. As he answered Baker's questions, Bower kept stealing furtive glances in my direction. I couldn't tell if he was looking at my client or me, but I did sense that he was nervous. Considering his age—which I guessed to be no more than the mid-twenties—I assumed this was the first time he'd been a witness. I figured I could use that to fluster him during cross-examination.

Baker must have read my mind and understood the need to make his witness comfortable.

"How long have you been on the police force?"

"Two… two years." He was looking in my direction as he spoke. I pretended to write something on my legal pad. Nothing makes witnesses more nervous than seeing an opposing attorney making notes of their testimony.

Baker moved to a position between Bower and me. "Please describe the circumstances under which you arrested the defendant."

"Ah… well… I was on patrol in Uptown, near the university, and I saw Mr. LeBlanc, I mean the defendant, in an area where we were supposed to be on the lookout for drugs. He was on the sidewalk, and he looked kinda suspicious, so I stopped to question him."

Baker walked to the side of the witness box away from me, and Bower shifted positions to face him. "What happened then?"

For a moment, Bower hesitated. The vacant look in his eyes suggested that he was uncertain about what to say. He was probably trying to remember what he had been told in the meeting I was sure Baker had held with him before the hearing. When he finally spoke, he sounded as if he was trying to determine what Baker wanted him to say. "I asked to see some identification."

"What did he do?"

"He showed me his driver's license."

Baker waited silently. I'm sure he was expecting Bower to give a more expansive response. Any police officer with experience as a witness would have told the whole story of LeBlanc's arrest without additional prompting by Baker.

"And then?"

"I told him to empty his pockets."

Baker was too experienced to show the frustration I knew he was feeling. "And that's when you found the bag containing the cocaine?"

I could have objected on any number of grounds: improper form of the question, leading question and a few others. But there wasn't any real reason for interrupting the proceedings. Baker would merely rephrase the question, and I would have risked irritating the judge unnecessarily.

"That's right. Then I arrested him and put him in my squad car and took him to the station."

"Did you read him his rights?"

"Oh… yeah. I told him about his rights before I put him in the car."

Baker paused and glanced through his notes before saying, "No further questions."

I was surprised by the brevity of Baker's examination, but I suspected that he was concerned about what his witness might say in response to any further questions. Or maybe he knew he had problems with how the arrest had been made and didn't want to expose them. I'm also sure Baker knew I wasn't an experienced criminal attorney, and he may have hoped I wouldn't pick up on the clues.

I stood and reclaimed my place in front of the judge. I thought about trying my silence gambit but concluded that Bower was already nervous enough.

"You testified that you thought my client looked…" I paused and consulted my notes. "…'Kinda suspicious.' Exactly what was he doing that you thought was suspicious?"

"Ah… He was… It wasn't anything in particular. He just looked suspicious."

"Is that the only reason you detained him?"

"Uh-huh. I mean, yes."

"Was he wearing a pirate costume when you stopped him?

"Yes."

"Hat, beard, eye patch?" I looked toward the judge to see if he was showing any interest. If he was, he didn't give any indication of it.

"That's right."

"Is that how you concluded that he looked suspicious?"

"Objection," Baker said without standing. "Asked and answered."

The judge overruled the objection.

Bower squirmed. "He just did."

"And you base this conclusion on your two whole years of experience."

The judge glowered at me. "We don't need any sarcasm, counselor."

I apologized to the judge and returned my attention to the witness. "You also testified that you were supposed to be on the lookout for drugs in the area you were patrolling." It wasn't actually a question, but that's how the witness took it.

He leaned closer to the microphone. "That's right."

"Is that area known for drug dealing?"

"I don't know. That's just what we were all told before we went out on patrol."

"Are you saying that the instructions to be on the lookout for drugs were general instructions given to *all* the patrol officers?"

"That's right."

"Were *you* specifically told to be on the lookout for drugs in the Uptown area you were patrolling?"

Bower nervously shifted his position. "No."

I concluded that I had exhausted my line of questions and changed the subject.

"Where did you find the substance that you thought was cocaine?"

"It was in a plastic bag in your client's coat pocket."

"How do you know it was *his* coat?"

"He was wearing it."

"How do you know he wasn't wearing someone else's coat? Did you ask him if it was his?"

Baker rose and said, "Objection. It's a compound question,"

"I'll rephrase," I said before the judge could rule on the objection. "Did you do *anything* to determine whether the coat where you found the substance was *his* coat?"

"It didn't make any difference. It was in his possession."

He was right, and I kicked myself for asking the question.

"You charged my client with possession with intent to distribute—"

"That's right," the officer said before I completed my question.

"What made you think he had any intent to distribute whatever he had?"

Bower squirmed and looked toward Baker who avoided his gaze by looking at his notes. The officer waited, apparently hoping Baker would rescue him with an objection.

I waited for several more seconds before asking, "Would you like me to repeat the question?"

"No. I heard you."

"Then what is your answer?"

He lowered his head and studied the floor. "I don't know."

"Did you do anything to determine whether or not my client had touched any cocaine?"

Bower looked at me. "Like what?"

"Did you do a wipe test of his hands?"

"No."

"Did you do a wipe test of *any* part of his body?

"No."

"Exactly what did you do when you brought my client in?"

"Like I said before, I arrested him and put him in my squad car. Then I drove to the station, took him inside, and booked him."

"Was he wearing his coat the whole time?"

"I had already confiscated the package containing the coke."

It wasn't an answer to the question, but it covered what

I was getting at. "Where was the package when you took my client into the station?"

"It was in my squad car."

"So, for a while, it was not in your *personal* possession?"

The witness's face flushed. I sensed that he knew he had not followed proper procedures and it took him a few seconds to admit he hadn't maintained possession of the evidence.

I had more questions, but his answer to my last one was a killer. I decided to end my examination on a high note.

"I have no more questions for this witness."

The judge turned toward Baker. "Any redirect questions, Mr. Baker?"

Baker's taut jaw and deep breathing suggested that he was struggling with thoughts about how he could save his case. I didn't think there was anything he could do about Bower's admission. Baker must have concluded the same thing. He shook his head. "No, your honor."

I rose, ready to make my argument for suppressing the evidence and finding that the laboratory tests were not sufficient to prove that the recovered substance was cocaine. I thought I had done a reasonably good job, and I was anxious the give my prepared closing statement, but the judge gave me a flip of his hand indicating that I should return to my seat.

"I've heard enough," he said. "I'm ready to make my ruling."

I felt confident that he would rule in my favor. I glanced toward Baker. He didn't look happy.

"For the record, I'll say that I'm a little troubled by the testimony regarding the laboratory's tests. But that's not the basis for my ruling. When the police officer left the evidence unattended in his car while he took the defendant in for booking, the chain of custody was broken. Therefore, I rule that the bag and the substance contained in it are inadmissible. Without that evidence, the state cannot make a *prima facie* case, so I am going to dismiss this case."

I stood. "Your Honor, any case the state may try to make would require the evidence you have suppressed. Therefore, I request that you dismiss this case *with prejudice*."

The judge looked toward Baker. I think he was hoping Baker would give him a reason to deny my request.

Baker shook his head. The judge sighed and said. "Granted. The case is dismissed *with prejudice,* and this hearing is adjourned."

I allowed myself to smile, though I worked hard not to let it bleed into smugness.

Baker came to my table and congratulated me. I know losing attorneys hate to congratulate their opponent, but it's a ritual we all follow.

After Baker was out of earshot, LeBlanc leaned toward me. "What does the ruling mean?"

"Dismissal 'with prejudice' means the charges can't be refiled. You can't be tried on the drug charges."

LeBlanc beamed and wrapped his arm over my shoulder. "You did well, counselor. It was fun watching you in action."

I was glad someone thought it was fun.

"Yes, sir. This was fun." He continued to beam. "We have to do it again sometime."

I examined his face, trying to determine if he was serious. I sincerely hoped he wasn't. "Maybe sometime when you didn't do what you've been charged with."

10.

As LeBlanc and I walked to the front of the courthouse, I was feeling pretty good about myself. He patted me on the back again and congratulated me for the third time. "We need to celebrate," he said.

As good as I felt, I was exhausted and just wanted to go home. Besides, I didn't see a point in spending any more time with LeBlanc. I'd done what he paid me for and, despite the trepidations that had manifested after learning about his connection to Falco, we had gotten off essentially unscathed. As far as I was concerned, that was the end of our relationship and I was glad for it.

"I'm not taking 'no' for an answer. I need lunch, and there are some things I need to talk to you about."

Having missed breakfast, I also felt the need for something to eat. But the second part of what LeBlanc said had me feeling a little queasy. I knew LeBlanc was a criminal, and I didn't have any desire to become a criminal lawyer, or at least *that* kind of criminal lawyer. I'd promised myself, and Becky, that my representation of him was a one-time thing. But I was hungry and a little curious as to what he wanted to talk about so I agreed.

"Where do you want to go?" he said.

"There's a good café on the corner up the block."

"I know where you're talking about."

His statement only confirmed my suspicion that ours was not his first experience with the criminal justice system.

"Wait here," he said. "I have to make a call."

He wandered to the corner of what passed for a terrace outside the courthouse and pressed the speed-dial on his cell phone. The call only lasted a few seconds, and it didn't look like he said more than a sentence or two. I assumed he'd gotten someone's answering machine.

With a sweep of his arm, LeBlanc indicated he was ready to proceed and we headed down the steps.

§

Up the block from the courthouse was a small restaurant that served breakfast and lunch. I don't remember its name, but it doesn't matter. Everyone in the courthouse and the legal community referred to it as the Coffee Shop. It wasn't the only nearby eating establishment, but it was comfortable, the food on the limited menu was unusually good, and the prices were relatively low. But most importantly, the service was fast, and it was large enough to accommodate the crush of lawyers who descended on it every day for a quick meal between hearings. The Coffee Shop also had one other feature that made it popular with lawyers. It had two small rooms in the back where attorneys and their clients could meet in private.

It was shortly after eleven when LeBlanc and I entered the Coffee Shop. It was only about half-full when we arrived. Nonetheless, I thought it was advisable to use one of the attorney-client conference rooms. I still didn't know LeBlanc well and wasn't sure what he might want to talk about. We didn't have anything particularly confidential to discuss, but I couldn't be certain that he wouldn't inadvertently blurt out something that could come back to haunt him, or us. The last thing I needed was for him to say something to which a handful of lawyers would be potential witnesses.

Lunch was, happily, uneventful. We both had oyster Po'Boys and agreed that they were delicious. Mostly, we talked about growing up in New Orleans—at least that's what LeBlanc talked about. For some reason, he wanted me to know about his youth and about how we happened to come together. I didn't understand why he thought I would want to know about his past, but it seemed significant to him.

There wasn't anything noteworthy about LeBlanc's formative years. He'd been raised by a single mother—his father having been killed in a shooting when LeBlanc was nine. I didn't ask about the incident, and he didn't volunteer any details. He hadn't been in any trouble to speak of, just one arrest, for smoking weed, that earned him an overnight stay in the county lockup. I guess the judge thought that was enough to put a little scare into him.

We didn't get into his later life, and I was happy to leave it that way. But I have to admit that I was beginning to like the guy and felt a little disappointed that our relationship was at an end.

When we left the coffee shop, a white stretch limo was parked outside. I didn't give it any thought until LeBlanc sauntered over and opened the door. "Come here," he said. "There's someone I want you to meet."

I can't say that I was thrilled by this surprise. Instead, I was a little pissed that LeBlanc had arranged a meeting for me without telling me about it first. Besides, I had a pleading brief that was due the following day for one of my few clients, and I wanted to get back to my office. But I was curious.

"Come on. This won't take long."

Against my better judgment, I followed his gestured instructions and slid into the car.

The man who was waiting was somewhere in his 60s and nearly bald. From the look of him, I'd say that he had an extraordinary fondness for New Orleans' famous dining and an aversion to exercise. He held a cigar between his index and forefinger. I would have bet anything that it was Cuban.

As I entered the car, he blew a puff of smoke out the window, turned toward me, and held out his hand. "I'm Sonny Falco."

11.

My representation of other "associates" of Sonny Falco started slowly. As I came to learn, the usual mainstays of organized crime—prostitution, loan sharking and the like—were not among Falco's businesses, but some of his associates did freelance in such activities. It wasn't long before I was on the receiving end of a steady stream of referrals. Becky wasn't pleased by the direction of my practice, but I assured her it was only business. I even tried to make myself believe what I told her.

A few months, five or six, after getting LeBlanc out from under his drug charges, I received a telephone call from LeBlanc. I hadn't seen or talked to him since the day of the probable cause hearing, so I was surprised to hear his voice when I picked up the phone.

His first words were, "I hear you're doing good." No, "Hello." No, "This is Louis."

After I got over the initial surprise at hearing from him, my first thought was that his grammar needed improvement. Then it dawned on me that his use of the word "good" was a reference to the quality of my work and not to me personally. I thanked him for the acknowledgment of my successes and waited, with some trepidation, for him to get to the reason for his call.

"Sonny has some work he needs done in a hurry. Are you interested?"

I hesitated. To satisfy my curiosity, I'd done some research on Falco. What I'd discovered was mixed. Most of what I found confirmed what Jack Crowley told me when I first represented LeBlanc. My few friends in the police department were, surprisingly, a little less damning. Yes, there was a time when the Mafia was well-entrenched and active as a criminal enterprise in New Orleans. The fact is, the organization that became "the Mafia" started in New Orleans in the late 1800s. According to my friends, drug dealing, gambling, and various forms of racketeering had replaced violent crimes as the *sine qua non* of organized crime.

I realized I was ruminating and hadn't responded to LeBlanc's question.

"It depends on what he needs."

"Just some basic legal work. The attorneys Sonny has don't have time to do it right away."

"I have some time, but I need to know more. I may not be qualified to do it." I wasn't enthusiastic about doing work for Falco. What little I knew about him made me think that representing him was a bad idea, but I was willing to keep an open mind and, to be perfectly honest, I was curious about why he would want to retain me.

LeBlanc didn't immediately respond. I don't think he was accustomed to having anyone not jump when a representative of Sonny Falco made a request.

"You need to talk to Sonny," he finally said. "I'll send my driver to pick you up. You can have lunch with Sonny at our club."

His reference to "*our* club" got my attention. It confirmed my belief that the people I'd seen on the night of my first visit weren't members of the general public. "Okay. Pick me up at twelve-thirty."

"My car will be in front of your office."

§

I confess that I felt some degree of uneasiness when I got out of LeBlanc's limo at his club.

Of course, I'd met Falco after LeBlanc's probable cause hearing, but that wasn't the same as meeting him to discuss business. That had been a preliminary getting-acquainted meeting—more about him learning about me than the other way around. He'd asked most of the same questions LeBlanc asked during our first meeting—general questions about my background, my education, and my law practice. He'd come across as being genuinely interested, and I guess I was a little flattered. It wasn't until later that I concluded the call LeBlanc had made after the probable cause hearing had been to report the results and LeBlanc's opinion of my performance.

Now, as I stood outside his club, it occurred to me that my first meeting with Falco had been something of a job interview and the uptick in clients after the probable cause hearing had been a probationary test.

LeBlanc met me at the door and greeted me like an old friend—even though we hadn't spoken since my representation of him had concluded. But that was okay. As I've said, at our post-hearing lunch I found myself liking the guy.

Inside the club I saw a couple of men playing cards and a table full of men having lunch. They looked in my direction and exchanged puzzled looks before returning to their various activities. LeBlanc headed up the stairs and signaled for me to follow. At the end of the hallway, he stopped in front of a closed door opposite the room where we'd had our first meeting. Without knocking, he opened the door and gestured for me to enter. The room was, to my surprise, relatively small and sparsely, albeit elegantly, furnished. A large mahogany desk faced two matching leather chairs. I was struck by the fact that I didn't see a telephone.

Behind the desk, Sonny Falco leaned back with a cell phone in one hand and a cigar in the other. He pointed toward the chairs with his cigar, abruptly ended his call, and extended his hand.

"Louis said you don't want to do a project for me." It sounded more like an accusation that a statement or question.

"It's not that. It's just that I don't know what it is or whether I'm qualified to do it."

"I see."

"And I wouldn't want to disappoint you."

Falco seemed to be pleased by my addendum, though as soon as I said it I felt a quick flash of regret.

"Exactly what is it that you want me to do?"

"It's nothing special, but I need it done in a hurry."

He nodded at LeBlanc and then turned back to me. "There's a bill pending in the legislature that we have an interest in. We want to see some changes in the bill. One of our friends is willing to sponsor an amendment, but he wants something he can use to justify what we want. We need you to research our proposed changes, see how other states have handled our problem and write up an amendment and something that supports our position."

"That doesn't sound too difficult. But I'm sure you have other attorneys who could handle it. Why not use them?"

"The vote is scheduled for the end of next week, but we have to get something to our friend by next Monday. My attorney didn't think he could do what we need in time."

This sounded logical enough, but I didn't believe Falco's attorney couldn't make time for him. Still, I had the time, and the project would be a welcome change from what had become my routine practice. I thought about it for a few seconds before saying, "It's not what I usually do, but I think I can handle it."

Falco bobbed his head and threw me what I think was his version of a smile. "Good." He slapped his hands on the desk. "Now let's have some lunch, and we can talk specifics. I've asked our chef to make us some oyster Po' Boys. I hope that's okay."

I said it was fine. Falco stood and walked around the desk to what I had assumed was the door to a closet. It turned out to be another room, about the same size as his office, with a conference table and eight chairs and what must have been a combined linen and china cabinet. The table was set, and our oyster Po'Boys were waiting.

For the next hour, we discussed the bill Falco was concerned with and the changes he wanted. LeBlanc gave me a copy of the bill, which proposed some changes in Louisiana's gambling laws. I can't say that the subject of the proposed legislation surprised me. Gambling had been legalized in Louisiana in the 1990s, and casino and riverboat gambling had become an important part of its tourist economy, but it was strictly regulated. The bill in question would have changed some of the regulatory provisions and the requirements for licensing gambling establishments. As we ate, I read it and made a few notes about what Falco wanted to see changed.

At the time, I didn't know enough about the business to understand why the changes were important to Falco, but I would learn that soon enough.

12.

Collecting copies of the relevant legislation for other states was simple enough. With electronic databases provided by the big legal-research companies, all you have to do is type in a few keywords and push a button. In a matter of seconds, the computer identifies every statute containing your search words for every state. My first couple of searches produced a list of more laws than I could review in a month. But after a few tries with different search words, I started getting what I wanted. Fortunately, there aren't that many states where gambling has been legalized. (I'm not counting states that have lotteries. That's not gambling—it's throwing your money away. Besides, I wasn't interested in the regulation of lotteries.)

I printed out all the plausibly relevant laws for the states that authorized the kind of gambling Falco was interested in. I knew it would take me a couple of long days to read everything, but Falco was paying me by the hour and I figured he wouldn't mind.

By the time I finished reading all the statutes, I knew more about gambling laws and gambling regulation than I had any desire to know. Then I started working on the second part of my assignment: finding justification for what Falco wanted the Louisiana legislation to provide. That's when I started racking up the billable hours. I began by researching and analyzing the legislative records for statutes that were relevant to Falco's interest. Then I spent half a day doing Internet searches for articles and blog discussions relating to the pros and cons of what Falco wanted. There wasn't much, but I wanted to make a good impression on my new client. Besides, as I said, I was being paid by the hour, so I figured I might as well be thorough.

By Saturday, I decided that I knew enough to write up the analysis Falco had requested. But putting everything I had learned on paper was going to be an arduous task, and as you may have concluded, I'm not the best writer. I prepared myself for an all-nighter.

I called Becky and told her we were going to have to cancel our plans for the evening. She wasn't happy. She didn't even try to console me. But a promise that I would take her to Commander's Palace for dinner when the project was complete made her a little more accepting. A *little*.

My shoulders were aching after six days bent over the computer. I thought about taking an hour off to get a massage but decided that I had to get to work on my analysis.

To make a long story short, I finished my report at about two o'clock on Monday morning. I can't say I was totally satisfied with it, but it was the best I could do under the circumstances, and I hoped it was enough to meet Falco's needs. I'm not sure what the consequences would be if he weren't satisfied with something, but I didn't think he was the kind of man who didn't do anything when he was displeased.

§

LeBlanc called me at home at nine the next morning. I don't know how he got my unlisted number. It didn't surprise me, but it wasn't exactly welcome either.

I mumbled something that was intended to be a 'hello,"

but even I didn't recognize it as such. I think it came out sounding more like 'mellow' or 'yellow."

He said something that didn't quite register. I hoped it wasn't anything important because I didn't want to ask him to repeat it. All I remember was that he said, "Sonny wants to know when you'll be delivering your report."

By then, the fog that engulfed my mind was beginning to clear and I told him it was ready and could be picked up later that morning. There was a long pause. I don't think he was accustomed to having to schlep to an attorney's office to collect a work product, but I was too tired to care. I guess he decided to give me a break—what a guy—because he agreed to meet me at my office at eleven.

§

LeBlanc arrived at my office at precisely eleven. He was wearing a custom-tailored dark-blue power suit. I don't remember what I was wearing.

I gave him a copy of my report and leaned back, fighting to keep from dozing off.

For ten or fifteen minutes, he reviewed my report. Every once in a while he looked up to ask me a question about something and made a notation on the report. He nodded a few times, and I heard a few closed-mouth "uh-huhs." When he finished reading my analysis, he spent a few seconds thumbing through the appendix—a compilation of the statutes of other states that I thought were relevant and an article discussing the merits of what Falco wanted to have included in the proposed amendment.

Finally, he laid the report on my desk, leaned back, and gave me a whimsical smile. "This is good work. I think it's just what our friend in the legislature needs."

Though I should have been elated, I was too tired to

feel anything but relief. But I wasn't too tired to notice that this was the second time Falco had referred to "our friend" in the legislature. *Why*, I wondered, *didn't he use the person's name?* I would find out soon enough.

13.

A couple of months later I received another surprise call from LeBlanc. Becky answered the phone and listened for a moment before handing it to me. She didn't look happy.

When I took the phone, the first thing I heard was, "Whatever plans you have for tonight, cancel them. I have a meeting that I want you to attend."

My initial instinct was to tell him I had plans that I couldn't change. I didn't really have anything on my schedule, but I was pissed at LeBlanc for thinking I was someone he could order around. I also had a gnawing feeling the whatever he was calling about was something I shouldn't get involved with. I didn't realize it at the time, but I had become addicted to being associated with powerful players, and doing business with Falco was the ultimate fix. "Who's the meeting with?"

"One of the people I work with in Baton Rouge."

"Who?"

"You'll find out tonight."

I didn't like the way the conversation was going. I'd grown accustomed to the mystery surrounding LeBlanc's requests for meetings, but he sounded more cryptic than usual. I considered declining the invitation, but his tone implied that refusal was not an option.

"I'm tied up, so you'll have to drive yourself to the club."

"What time?"

"Make it eight."

§

LeBlanc met me at the club door and beckoned me to follow him upstairs.

"When are you going to tell me what this meeting is about?" I asked as I followed LeBlanc.

"You'll find out soon enough."

"Well, will you at least tell me why I'm here?"

"You're just here to listen."

"To what?"

"We're going to talk about some business. You just need to listen. We'll talk about what I need from you after the meeting."

I followed him to the same room where we'd had our first meeting. The door was closed, but I heard laughter coming from inside. LeBlanc opened the door and, with a wiggle of his index finger, signaled for me to follow him.

Inside, Falco was chatting and laughing it up with someone whose face was familiar. I'd seen it in the newspapers but hadn't read the articles and couldn't remember his name. I did, however, remember that he was someone high in the agency that regulated gambling. Neither of them looked at us when we entered. LeBlanc took a seat on the sofa beside Falco while motioning me to a chair in the corner of the room. No introductions were made.

The meeting appeared to have been going on for a while before I arrived. Both Falco and the other man, whose name I was still trying to remember, were holding nearly empty glasses. A third glass, which I assumed was LeBlanc's, was sitting on the coffee table beside what remained of a bottle of Old Rip Van Winkle bourbon that must have cost about what I take home in a month.

Old-friend chitchat continued for a few minutes until Falco finally said, "I guess we better get down to business."

The stranger nodded. LeBlanc didn't move. This was obviously going to be Falco's meeting. I still couldn't imagine why I was here, and to be perfectly honest, I was starting to wish I weren't.

Falco began. "You know I have a license application pending."

The stranger nodded again.

"Well, there's a holdup."

"I'm aware of that. But what you want is something new. The statute providing for it was only enacted last spring, and the regulations aren't polished yet."

"I understand that, but there must be something you can do. Time is money. I've been generous with the latter, and I'm running out of the former."

"And…" The stranger hesitated and, with a slight tilt of his head, glanced in my direction.

"It's okay. He's my lawyer. Fact is, he drafted the amendment that got me what I wanted."

The stranger shifted his position on the love seat I'd once occupied. "As I was about to say, your generosity is appreciated, but there's only so much I can do. The proposed regulations have to be approved by the legislature."

Everyone but me seemed to know what the last statement meant. Falco responded with a derisive snort. LeBlanc lowered his head and sighed.

For the next half hour or so, the three of them engaged in a discussion that I now wish I hadn't heard.

Eventually, the business of the evening concluded. Falco and LeBlanc shook hands with the stranger, and Falco escorted him from the room. LeBlanc resumed his position on the sofa and waved me to the love seat.

"Do you want a drink?" he asked. I'm sure that for him the meeting had been just a routine business meeting, but for me it was a step deeper into a world I wasn't sure I was ready to enter. I admit that I coveted a taste of the bourbon, but I didn't want him to see my hands shaking so I declined.

"Can you find a way to do what we were discussing?"

"I don't know. I don't know anything about campaign finance laws."

LeBlanc chuckled. "You didn't know anything about gambling laws before we gave you that project, and look what you did."

"That was… different."

"What's the problem? All we need is a way to make campaign contributions that nobody can trace to us."

§

By the time we left the room, LeBlanc was again the friendly, somewhat jovial man I'd come to know. As we wandered toward the stairs, he put his arm over my shoulder. "Don't worry. I have confidence in you."

Falco and the other man, whose name I was still trying to recall, were saying their good-byes on the porch of the club when we came out. Falco looked toward LeBlanc, who nodded once and said, "We're good."

As I started down the steps, a black Chevy Suburban pulled away from the curb and sped down the street. Just realizing that I noticed such a thing made my heart beat a little faster.

14.

I didn't have to research the issue to know that there was no legal way to accomplish what Falco wanted to do. I already knew that all I could do was find the least illegal solution to his problem.

As I drove back to the French Quarter bungalow that Becky and I called home, I considered what I would tell her about my latest project for Sonny Falco. She was already begging me to end my relationship with him. I continued to assure her that it was just business, but even I knew that my argument lacked merit. I toyed with the idea of not telling her about my new project—I could have said that everything was subject to the confidentiality requirements of the attorney-client privilege—but that wouldn't have changed anything.

Becky was already in bed when I arrived home. She was reading a book when I bent down to kiss her. She turned away. I was about to ask her what was wrong, but there wasn't any point—I already knew.

"You're going to do something else for *him*, aren't you?" she said. Her voice was a mixture of disappointment and angst.

"I can't talk about it."

"I *know* you can't talk about *what* you're going to be doing. I just want to know—"

I knew what she was about to say, but I didn't want to

discuss it. "I'm drained. Can we talk about it in the morning?"

Becky rolled away from me and wrapped the blanket tightly around herself. "What's the point?" Her voice was cold enough to freeze helium. "You're going to do what you want the do."

"What the hell do you want from me? The guy pays me twice my usual rate—in cash. I don't even have to pay taxes on it."

She spun over to face me. "That's not the point and, damn it, you know it. We were doing just fine before you started working for him."

I crawled into bed and propped an elbow on my pillow as I looked at her. "What is it that concerns you? I mean, *really*."

Tears formed in the corners of her eyes, and she wiped them away with the back of her hand. "I don't want some policeman coming to the door to give me bad news. I don't want to have to go to your funeral."

I reached out and she moved into the crook of my arm. "I won't let that happen. Besides, that's not how Falco does things."

She wiped away another tear.

"Of course, I might get a leg broken."

She sat up and looked at me. I was grinning. She hit me with a pillow.

§

I spent most of the next day at the Tulane law school library reading everything I could find on Louisiana's campaign finance laws and regulations. Then it was back to the office to research cases. To be as thorough as I could, I also examined federal case authorities. By midnight, I decided that I'd covered everything I needed. There wasn't any way, no *legal* way, to do what Falco and LeBlanc wanted to do. I hadn't expected to find a solution to their problem, but at least by then I knew my initial conclusion was correct.

I was about to leave my office when something that had been nagging me all day drew me back. I returned to my computer and began researching the penalties for violating campaign finance laws. There was an abundance of cases on the subject, and none of them brought me comfort. At a minimum, violators faced stiff fines. I suspected that this alone wouldn't deter Falco or LeBlanc. But knowingly violating these laws could also result in prison time for both the donors and the recipients of illegal contributions and those who assisted them.

When I arrived home at close to three, Becky was sound asleep with her arm wrapped around a pillow. As I slid into bed, she rolled over, snuggled close, and draped her arm across my chest. For a while, I thought about her and our life together, but my thoughts inexorably turned to what she'd said the night before. Then I started thinking about the problem Falco and LeBlanc had given me.

I couldn't sleep.

15.

I met Falco and LeBlanc at their club at four the next afternoon. I suppose I could have racked up a few more billable hours before I gave them the bad news, but I knew that no amount of research would change my conclusion.

LeBlanc was waiting for me at the door. "Sonny's taking care of some business. He'll be with us as soon as he's finished."

I followed him into the... I don't know what to call it. Lounge? Card room? Game room? He took a seat in one of the dozen or so high-backed burgundy leather chairs. He didn't indicate where I should sit, so I claimed a matching chair opposite him. Immediately, a smallish man in a white shirt, dark pants, and a matching vest entered the room.

"I'll have my usual, John," LeBlanc said.

"Of course."

The waiter turned toward me. "And you, sir?"

I debated the wisdom of having a drink. On one hand, I didn't think it was very professional, and we hadn't reached the point where I could call LeBlanc a friend. On the other hand, I felt the time had come to establish that I wasn't a supplicant. I suspected that some of the things I'd been asked to do were tests of my skills. Whatever their agenda was, they'd had sufficient opportunity to decide what our future relationship would be, so I had nothing to lose.

"I'll have a Cutty Sark... neat."

"Very well, sir."

LeBlanc and I chatted about nothing in particular. When our drinks arrived, LeBlanc tipped his glass toward me in a way that I took to be a toast. I responded in kind.

A few minutes later, I heard muffled voices and footsteps on the stairs. Falco and a man of Latin heritage emerged from the stairwell and strode across the vestibule to the door. They hugged in a European way, and the Latin man left.

I followed Falco and LeBlanc up the stairs and into Falco's office. LeBlanc closed the door.

"What do you have, counselor?" Falco said.

"Mr. Falco," I began. I was determined to establish my status in our professional relationship, but calling him Sonny without being invited to do so would have been going too far. "The simple fact is that there's no way you can legally do what you want to do, but there are some things you can do to minimize the risk of detection."

"Give me the whole story."

I told them everything I'd done to research the issue and why I'd concluded what I did.

They didn't show any surprise at my conclusion. They didn't even react when I explained the penalties they could incur. They just looked at each other. As I glanced from one to the other, I had the feeling that there was some unspoken communication going on. I sensed that I'd somehow failed to discover something they already knew. If my research was deficient, I had only myself to blame. If they already knew of a better solution than I'd suggested... well, I guess I'm not as smart as I think I am.

Falco withdrew a cigar from his jacket pocket and lit it. Then he put my report in the shredder under his desk and took a couple of puffs on his cigar before returning his attention to me. I expected him to be frowning, but instead he smiled. "You have balls! I appreciate that."

I must have looked confused.

"My attorneys usually just call when they have bad news."

It felt good to have scored some points with Falco, and I decided not to spoil the moment by pointing out that I didn't have his number.

Falco leaned back and rubbed his neck. "What do you know about corporate law?"

The sudden change of topics took me by surprise. "I've formed a few corporations."

"What kinds?"

He could have been asking what kind of business I had incorporated, but I surmised that he was asking about the type of corporations I had formed. "Regular corporations, S corporations, professional association, limited liability companies."

"Do you know about something called a personal holding company?"

I nodded.

"My accountant says I can save a bundle on taxes if I form one of them."

"It's possible."

"Do you know anything about tax laws?"

"I studied accounting as an undergraduate, and I clerked for a boutique tax law firm when I was in law school."

What Falco wanted me to do was reasonable, and it was possible that a reorganization of his business could provide him with some significant tax advantages. But that depended on the tax and financial features of the businesses to be merged into his holding company.

Falco chewed on the inside of his cheek. "I want you to meet with my accountant. He'll give you the tax returns for my businesses. You two can see what we can work out."

"The tax returns alone won't be enough. I'll need to see the business's articles of organization, financial statements, and the profit-and-loss statements."

"My accountant can give you all of that," Falco said.

"Just one more thing, Mr. Falco."

He frowned. "What's that?"

I hadn't intended to say what I had, but I'd gone too far to turn back now. If what they say about kindred spirits sensing what was on each other's mind, somewhere Becky was having a warm feeling about me.

I sucked it up, as they say, and said, "About your businesses..."

"Yes."

"I'll need to see *both* sets of books."

16.

I didn't actually need to see the second set of books to do what Falco wanted me to do. I didn't even have any reason to think his businesses *kept* two sets of books, and I dimly hoped they didn't. I was sure that would be news that would make Becky happy. (Okay, it wouldn't have made her happy, but it might have made her less concerned about my work for Falco.)

I was ready for, and hoping for, an indignant response from Falco. Instead, he merely nodded and said, "The accountant can get whatever you need."

"There's one other thing."

Falco gave me what I thought was the beginning of a scowl. "That's what you said when you asked for the books."

"This really is the last thing—for now."

Falco gave an ambivalent sigh. I hoped that, in time, I would learn to interpret his expressions, but he was good at hiding his emotions. "Yeah, what do you need?"

"I need a list of the owners of each of the business, what percentage of the business they own, and how much they paid for their interest."

Falco frowned and narrowed his eyes. I didn't have any difficulty interpreting *that* look. "What do you need that for?"

"It's a tax thing."

He eyed me suspiciously.

"It is important." I wondered why the release of this information was of concern to Falco, and then it occurred to me. I wanted to slap my forehead. Falco had business partners he didn't want me to know about—or who didn't want to be known to anyone but Falco. I couldn't believe I'd been so stupid.

Having committed the faux pas of the month, I hurried to recover. "We can do some things to skirt around the edges of the law, but tax evasion shouldn't be one of them." I conveniently ignored the fact that I hadn't planned on reporting Falco's cash payments on my tax return. I put the thought aside as I pressed ever further into the land of tar pits. "Did you know that more crime bosses get convicted of tax evasion than for any other crime?"

That's right. I all but accused Falco of being a crime boss. I tried to avoid thinking about how it would feel when the bullet entered the back of my skull.

Maybe he hadn't heard me. Or maybe what I'd said just hadn't registered with him. Or perhaps he didn't mind hearing the truth. Whatever it was, his only response was a snort and the suggestion that the IRS perform an act that could have been accommodated by one of his associate's prostitutes.

§

I met with Falco's accountant the following day. I'd expected that our meeting would be strained—no professional likes it when a client wants his work or advice reviewed by someone else—but Saul Weinberg was only too happy to have me involved. I told him right up front that I was going to defer to him on the tax aspects of any transaction we might recommend. We quickly agreed that we were, in some respects, entering uncharted waters, and he was more than willing to let me be responsible for the purely legal aspects of our effort.

We spent our first afternoon going over the books and records of Falco's various businesses. I suppose I shouldn't have been surprised to learn that most of them had to do with the tourist industry. In addition to ties with riverboat gambling, he had interests in several small hotels, half a dozen restaurants of varying degrees of renown, liquor distributorships and a couple of linen cleaning enterprises. In some of the enterprises, he was the controlling shareholder or partner. In others, he only had minority interests.

As we went through the documents, I decided I liked Saul, and I think the feeling was mutual. When I mentioned that I was doing a lot of work for Falco and his associates, Saul allowed as to how he, too, had a limited and "very select" clientele. The way he said it made me curious about his practice, but I knew better than to ask any questions. I also suspected that I would be better off not knowing.

At some point, I noticed that his one-man office didn't have any file cabinets. When I mentioned my observation, I expected him to tell me that one of the doors in his office led to a file room or that his files were in another room down the hall, but he was shocked at my assumption.

"What!" he said. "At what they charge for rent in this building I should pay to store paper? Here I keep only what I am working on. It's better that I should schlep out to the warehouse when I need something."

Saul's explanation struck me as reasonable, and I stored the idea away for when I became more successful and could move my office to a more exclusive location. My question did, however, give Saul an opportunity to brag about his computerized record-keeping system with its advanced file encryption software and sophisticated access coding. Since my computer skills are limited to using my legal search programs and browsing the Internet, I was impressed. It also raised some questions about the nature of Saul's very select clientele, but who was I to talk?

We ended the afternoon with an agreed-on to-do list and division of labor. Saul printed me copies of the latest tax records and the records of enterprise ownership and I headed for my office. I wasn't in any hurry to start on the tax issues on our to-do list, but I wanted to look into the list of Falco's investment partners.

Some of the names I already knew and, with a little help from the Internet, was able to match the names with faces, mostly front and side views. If I'd thought about it, I might have been concerned that the discovery of their criminal records didn't surprise me. Or I might have admitted to myself that I was working for a bunch of criminals, just as Becky had repeatedly warned me. But I couldn't, or didn't want to, acknowledge any of that. I was getting pretty good at lying to myself.

The next time I looked at my watch it was almost nine. I knew I was in trouble for not calling to let Becky know I'd be late. After I dialed, the phone rang five times, and the call went to the answering machine. It was worse than I'd expected. Either she was home and, seeing that the call was from me, not answering the phone, or she was out with her girlfriends. Either way, it wasn't good for me.

I stuffed the papers on my desk into a file and tossed it into a drawer. I could give it the attention it needed tomorrow. I only hoped it wasn't too late to give Becky the attention she needed tonight.

17.

I spent the next day holed up with my computer and a slightly out-of-date copy of the Internal Revenue Code and Regulations. What Saul Weinberg had proposed was going to involve a lot of paperwork, but since I billed by the hour that didn't bother me. What did bother me was the nagging feeling that I didn't know as much as I should about Falco's businesses.

I knew that the answer was somewhere in the documents Saul had given me, but I'll be damned if I could find it. Once again, I painstakingly paged through Saul's documents. Nothing. Nada. Zip. Unless...

I turned to my computer, pulled up the Louisiana secretary of state's website and began searching for any filed documents for the businesses in which Falco had an ownership interest. I still wasn't sure what I was looking for, but I knew I would recognize it when I found it.

And there it was. All the businesses in which Falco had an interest had the same officers, directors, and partners—and none of them were the owners of record. I didn't know what it meant, but I knew it was significant. I called the only person I knew who was likely to give me a straight answer.

It took forever for Saul to answer the phone. When he did finally pick up, he was out of breath.

I said hello and he sighed. "I thought you were my

wife. If I'm late getting home, I'll hear about it all evening. What a kvetch."

"I wouldn't want you to offend the missus," I said, and I meant it. "But I need to take a look at the other books."

"Is there a problem?" His tone suggested he was concerned about my interest.

"No. I only need to look into something. It has to do with how we have to structure the transfers of Falco's interests." I wasn't being completely honest with him, and I felt bad about that, but he was agitated and that made him vulnerable. If I could get what I needed without having to explain myself, my life would be infinitely easier.

I could visualize Saul debating what to do. Falco had told him to give me whatever I asked for, including the second set of books. I could justify my need to Falco only because he knew nothing about the taxation of business organizations, but Saul was a different matter.

"I know Rosh Hashanah starts tonight, Saul, and I wouldn't be asking if it wasn't important. I can meet you at your warehouse, make copies of what I need and you'll still be home by sundown."

He reluctantly agreed, and I wrote down the address as I grabbed my coat.

§

Saul was waiting when I arrived. His warehouse was a unit in a self-storage facility on the edge of an industrial park. The facility itself was small, not more than fifteen units, but it was the most secure facility I'd ever seen. It was surrounded by twelve-foot fences topped by razor wire, and *Caution—High Voltage* signs were affixed to the fence at regular intervals. I don't know if the fence was or wasn't electrified, but I wasn't interested in finding out the hard way.

The storage facility didn't have an office and I mentioned this fact to Saul. "What? Do you think I'm meshugge? I own the place. Of course, the title is in my cousin's name, but he's dead, so I don't think he'll mind. And all the units contain my client's files."

I said something about his having a lot of clients to need so much file storage space.

He shook his head. "I've got a *few* clients. *They've* got a lot of files—and I keep them all. They don't even know where I keep them."

I looked at him with what must have been an expression of surprise.

"It's the way they want it."

"All of them?"

He shrugged. "Who am I to ask questions? They do their business together, and I keep everything straightened out the way they want."

I followed Saul to Unit 12. He spun the dial of a combination lock that could have survived a grenade blast then stepped back and opened the door. Banker's boxes covered the shelves on two sides of the room and part of the third. A square wooden table and two chairs occupied the middle of the room. A copy machine and a coffeemaker sat on a shelf nearby.

Saul knew precisely where everything was. He put his coat over one of the chairs and went directly to a solitary box which he removed from the shelf and placed on the table. "There you are. Three years of the end-of-year financial statements for each of Mr. Falco's businesses—including, I might add, the distributions to his partners."

I picked up the box and took a step toward the door.

"No! No!" Saul said. "*First* you make copies. The original records never leave this room. And I have to leave now. Just be sure you lock up."

I finished making copies of the second set of books, stored the originals in their banker's box and returned it to the shelf. As I started to leave, I saw a box labeled "campaign finance." Even as I reached for it, I knew I didn't want to know what it contained. (The thought that I *shouldn't* be looking at the contents came and went with hardly a notice.)

The first file in the box included the names of political candidates and other public officials along with a list of dollar amounts and matching names I didn't recognize. Under that was a file containing bank statements for out-of-state banks.

Of all the things that could have come to mind at that moment, I thought of Becky and the many times she'd advised me not to get too involved with Falco. My second thought was that I was about to vomit.

18.

When the phone rang a few minutes after nine the next morning, I pulled the pillow over my head and waited for Becky to answer the call. But the phone kept ringing.

Finally, I gave up, rolled over, and answered in a groggy, Sunday-morning-hangover voice—even though it was only Wednesday.

"Counselor," a voice I didn't recognize began, "our mutual friend from the club gave me your number."

Usually, when I received calls from a potential new client, it was for something simple like prostitution or a minor drug offense. But those callers always identified some referrer by name.

This caller's vague reference to 'our mutual friend' and 'the club' were not entirely new to me. What was new was the tone of his voice.

Before asking his name, I asked what he had been charged with. It was a habit I had picked up early in my venture into criminal law. If the caller was charged with something that was clearly outside my zone of competence, I knew that I wouldn't be taking the case and I didn't even want to know the caller's name.

"They've charged me with murder, but I didn't do it." The second part of the statement was unnecessary. Nobody admits to committing a murder, because there are no murders. People may die when guns discharge accidentally and when knives get swung carelessly. As any criminal defense attorney will tell you, those are unfortunate incidents, but certainly not murder.

I was about to tell the caller I was too busy to take a new case when he continued.

"Our friend said to tell you I was referred to you by Jolly Roger." That was the name LeBlanc had told Falco's associates to use when calling me. He thought it was a clever reference to the pirate costume he was wearing when we first met. I thought it was stupid, but the reference did get my attention.

"Did anyone tell you when you'll be arraigned?"

"This afternoon, I think."

"All right. I'll be there as soon as I can. By the way, what's your name?"

I wrote it down on a pad I kept on the nightstand and headed for the shower. I must have been very hungover because I was still standing under the shower when the water started turning cold.

After I got dressed, I did a quick check to make sure that my socks matched and headed for the jail.

§

I drove into the parking lot at the police station, pulled my Porsche into a visitor's parking spot and headed for the main entrance. I stopped at the front desk to get a copy of my client's booking sheet and then headed across the parking lot to the jail. At the reception desk, I showed my bar membership card, signed the register, and handed my briefcase to the desk sergeant for inspection.

"Who you here to see?" the sergeant asked without looking up.

I gave him my client's name—André LaForrette.

The sergeant mumbled something unintelligible and consulted a three-ring binder before picking up the telephone.

"Lawyer's here to see LaForrette…. Yeah, I'll tell him." The sergeant made a note in the visitors' log. "Take a seat. Someone will come to get you."

I retreated to a plastic seat in the featureless waiting area. The only interruption in the monotony of the pale gray walls was the cork bulletin board containing job postings and a half-dozen wanted posters. I had just closed my eyes, hoping to grab a few extra winks, when I heard the door to the inner sanctum open.

"Are you waiting for LaForrette?" the jail deputy said.

"That's me."

"I'm Deputy Burandt. LaForrette's in the interview room."

Burandt led me through the door to the wing of the jail where the interview rooms were located. The ominous clang of steel on steel as the door closed reverberated down the sterile gray hallway.

The interview room could have been on the back lot of any television studio. Two chairs faced each other across a scratched steel table that was bolted to the floor. Bars covered the high window at one end of the room, and the walls were the same gray color as the chairs, table, and floor. Two lights in wire-protected fixtures hung from the ceiling just out of reach of anyone in the room.

André LaForrette sat upright in the metal chair on one side of the steel table. He had dark eyes and bushy eyebrows that didn't move when I entered the room. His narrow face wore a two-day stubble, and his medium brown hair was pulled back in what passed for the beginning of a ponytail.

I sat down opposite him. After we shook hands, I pulled a legal pad from my briefcase and got straight to business.

I read my copy of the arrest report aloud while occasionally glancing at my prospective client. I was as surprised as my client to learn that a grand jury had indicted him before he was arrested. The victim's name was Anthony LaRouche aka Tony LaRouche aka Harold Newburg.

I got right down to business. "How did you know the man you are accused of killing?"

"I didn't. Not personally."

I waited, wishing that I had an aspirin and a glass of water.

"He was sort of... Let's say he did business with someone I know."

"What kind of business?"

"What does that have to do with anything?"

I put down my pen, crossed my hands on the metal table, and stared coldly at LaForrette.

"What?" LaForrette demanded.

"André," I said, trying to sound calm but stern. "Right now, I'm the only person standing between you and life in the state penitentiary. If you want to cop an attitude, that's fine with me. But if you do, you'd better get used to bending over for someone named Big Bubba. Now, the next words out of your mouth are going to determine whether you get represented by me or some public defender who graduated from law school last week and already has fifty cases on his desk. He may get around to you the second Thursday after hell freezes over. So, what's it going to be?"

LaForrette glared at me.

After a few seconds of silence, I picked up my legal pad, put it in my briefcase, and stood to leave.

"Wait."

I paused and looked at him.

"I'm sorry. What do you want to know?"

I remained standing and leaned on the table with my

arms extended. "First of all, I don't care what you did or didn't do. It's not my job to judge you. My job is to keep you from being convicted."

LaForrette seemed to relax.

"In fact," I said. "I don't even want to know what you did."

LaForrette gave me a confused look. "Why?"

"When your case goes to trial, I may have to let you testify. You're going to want the jury to let you off, and you may be tempted to lie."

"But—"

I held up a hand. "Hear me out. If I know you're going to lie, I can't let you testify. That's why it's sometimes better if I don't know the truth."

He looked confused.

"I know it may not make much sense, but you're going to have to trust me."

He nodded but said nothing.

"Right now, I'm going to represent you for your bail hearing *only*."

"And then?"

"I doubt if the judge will let you out on bail, so it's a moot question. But before I agree to represent you, I have to do some investigating."

As I had expected, the judge denied bail. I told LaForrette I'd see him the following day and reminded him not to talk to anyone about his case.

19.

LaForrette's arraignment had taken about two minutes. Sitting on my ass and waiting for his case to be called had taken about two hours. By the time it was all over, it was too late to do anything productive at the office, and I knew Becky would be working late, so there was no sense going home.

A rumbling in my stomach reminded me that I hadn't eaten all day, and I wanted a drink. Who was I kidding? I was going to have more than one drink—possibly quite a few more. It depended on how my next call went.

LeBlanc answered on the second ring. "LeBlanc."

"I met with your friend André LaForrette this afternoon."

After a moment of silence, LaBlanc said, "He's more like an acquaintance of a mutual friend."

"Whatever!" I said. "Why in God's name did you send him to me? I've never handled a murder case before. Hell, the only felony cases I've handled are drug cases."

"I'm sure you'll do fine."

I didn't share LeBlanc's confidence, and he had to have known it.

"How much do you know about him... and the charges against him?"

There was a long pause before LeBlanc said, "Not on the phone." His voice was unusually wary.

"Then we need to meet. Can you make it to the French Market Restaurant?"

"Why do you want to meet there? Why not come out to the club?"

"I'm hungry, and the food's good. Besides, they know me there, and it's within walking distance of home."

"It's not a good idea to talk in public."

"Like I said, they know me there. We'll have all the privacy we need."

LeBlanc hesitated before finally agreeing.

He knew something. That much I was sure of. The question was, how much of what he knew was he willing to share?

§

I was ensconced at a corner table, working on my second drink and waiting for my order of crawfish when LeBlanc arrived. I could have been polite and waited for him before starting, but to tell the truth, I was pissed. I thought that referring an accused murderer to me without asking was a little presumptuous. I realized that LeBlanc and Falco still thought of me as a high-priced employee—which was fine with me—but I had a feeling that the matter of André LaForrette was going to change things.

LeBlanc stood by the door looking into the dining room. I could tell he'd seen me, so he must have been looking for something, or someone, else. Whatever or whoever it was, he must have been satisfied with the results of his survey and strolled to the table where I was sitting. He and my crawfish arrived at the same time.

LeBlanc sat and ordered a Jack Daniels, black label,

and soda from a passing waitress. I offered him some of my crawfish, but he declined and began to peruse the menu. When his drink arrived, he ordered a half dozen oysters then turned his attention to me.

"Now, exactly what do you want to know about André LaForrette?"

I detected some displeasure in his voice. I took a step back from the brink and softened my tone. "Start with the basics. How do you know him?"

"He does some work for us from time to time."

Us, I thought. There was that plural again. What was it about Falco and LeBlanc and the few of their associates I'd worked with that made them think of themselves as part of a singular unit?

Of course, I had thought about all the Mafia movies I'd seen and how they distinguished members and non-members with different pronouns. Jack Crowley had been quite specific when he called Falco the godfather of the New Orleans Mafia, but I hadn't found any evidence that supported his conclusion.

"What kind of work?"

"It depends on what we need done."

"You're not being very specific."

"You're not asking specific questions."

The conversation was not going at all as I had hoped. "His arrest report says he's from New Iberia."

"Could be. We're not that close."

"But you use him to do… what?"

"He's what you might call a fixer. He straightens out problems. Occasionally he finds missing people."

I suspected that, in addition to finding missing people, he caused some people to disappear. That would at least explain why LeBlanc was being so vague.

"Damn it, if you want me to represent this guy, you're going to have to give me something."

LeBlanc swallowed a raw oyster and took a sip of his drink. "I sent André to you because he's not guilty and I'm sure you can get him off."

"What's your interest in getting him off?"

"Like I said, he does some work for us from time to time. Sonny wants to make sure he doesn't do something stupid like making a deal with the prosecutor. I figured you'd be the guy to look out for our interests."

"It doesn't work that way. If I represent him, I have to look out for *his* interests, not yours."

A few heads turned toward us. They were far enough away that I knew they couldn't hear what I was saying. Nonetheless, just the fact that I was concerned about having our conversation in such close proximity to anyone else made me nervous.

LeBlanc raised his arms in mock surrender. "That's fine, but you have to know that André isn't guilty."

"How do *you* know that?"

LeBlanc stared straight at my eyes. "Are you sure you want to know?"

"If I'm going to defend him, I *have* to know."

"I know because he has an alibi. He was a hundred miles away taking care of a problem for us at the time of the murder."

I didn't take solace in the news. Whatever other business LaForrette was taking care of was probably also illegal. I didn't even want to know what it was. My only question was *How am I going to get out of this mess?*

20.

I was returning to my office from lunch a few days later and enjoying the cool breeze when LeBlanc's limousine pulled to the curb beside me and the driver got out.

"Sonny wants to see you immediately. You need to come with me."

My first instinct was to tell Falco he could shove it. For all he knew, I already had appointments for the afternoon. (I didn't, but that's not the point.) If he wanted to see me, he could make an appointment like everyone else. Then the left hemisphere of my brain kicked in and rational thoughts took over from my initial emotional response.

I got in the limo and we sped toward St. Charles. I was sure the driver didn't know what Falco wanted me for, but the way he drove left no doubt that Falco wanted me in a hurry.

§

LeBlanc was waiting for me at his club. I knew something important was happening when he trotted from the veranda to the limo to collect me. "Come with me," he said as soon as he'd opened the door.

I wasn't sure whether to just continue to feel annoyed or start feeling frightened. "What's going on?"

"We have a problem." The way he said it left no doubt

that whatever had happened was of grave concern to Falco, and maybe to LeBlanc.

LeBlanc took the stairs two at a time. I hurried behind him—up the stairs and down the hall to Falco's office. The door was closed, and this time LeBlanc didn't just go in. I heard Falco's voice through the door. What little I could make out made me think I was overhearing one side of a telephone conversation.

"Of course I know what it means!… We'll find them!… He already knows!… When I know, you'll know…. He should be here any minute."

The last snippet I overheard got my attention. I dearly hoped Falco was referring to someone else, but in my pounding heart I knew better.

I heard Falco drop heavily onto his desk chair, and that's when LeBlanc knocked and opened the door. I followed LaBlanc inside and took a seat in one of the chairs opposite Falco's desk.

Falco looked up with a strained attempt to smile. There was a hint of moisture on his forehead and dark patches at the armpits of his maroon shirt. He was wearing suit pants but no matching jacket and his vest was unbuttoned. It was the first time I'd seen him when he wasn't wearing a closed vest and suit coat.

I expected some kind of outburst, although I couldn't imagine what the subject would be. Instead, Falco spoke in a matter-of-fact business tone. "Are you making any progress on the business reorganization thing with Saul?"

I took a deep breath and exhaled as I considered how to respond. "That's something I need to talk to you about."

"Why's that? Is there a problem?" I'm not sure what it was, but something—maybe the way he sucked in his breath—told me that his business reorganization had something to do with the call I had overheard.

"No. No problem. Saul's plan looks feasible, but he needs to look into some questions that came up when we were talking. They don't represent any problems, but I need some more information before I can finish drafting the transfer documents."

"When can you have the documents done?

"I can finish them in a couple of days after I hear from Saul. But that's not where the hold-up may be."

Falco reached into his desk drawer and withdrew a package of chewable anti-acids. He opened it and popped three into his mouth. "Where's the holdup?"

"Some of the organizational documents for your businesses require the consent of the other owners to transfer your interests to a new entity."

Falco swallowed, and his jaw tightened.

"That won't be a problem, will it?"

Falco didn't answer. Instead, he changed the subject. "How much money can I save if I do what Saul suggested?"

"That will depend on each year's business income. But if the years Saul analyzed are representative, you can save a hundred thousand or more a year."

"That's what Saul said." Falco patted his stomach and burped. "This thing Saul was still looking into… was it important?"

"It's the key to making the whole plan work. We're dealing with an arcane provision in the tax code. The regulations are ambiguous, and there aren't any rulings on their application. Nothing by the IRS and nothing by the courts."

Falco took a deep breath and let it out slowly. "This thing… this provision. How important is it to the plan?"

I shrugged. "Saul's plan is very aggressive. It'll save you a lot of money, but I can almost guarantee that it will trigger an audit. I think Saul's capable of handling that, but I don't know many accountants who could."

Falco muttered a virtually inaudible "Fuck." He pushed himself away from his desk, stood, and began pacing in small circles in the confined space between the desk and the walls. After half a minute, he leaned forward with his weight on his outstretched arms resting on the edge of the desk.

"Can you finish the work without whatever you were waiting for Saul to get you?"

I thought for a minute before responding. "Yes. I can do what *I* have to do. But we still have to get the agreement of the other owners."

Falco slumped into his chair. His hands gripped the armrests so tightly that his whole arm shuddered.

I sensed there was something important that I didn't know, but I tried to alleviate the last of the concerns Falco might have been harboring about the deal. "Saul said that all the people you are investing with are also his clients, so getting their consent shouldn't be a problem."

Falco frowned and his eyes took on a hollow, empty look. For the first time, LeBlanc spoke. "Saul Weinberg is dead. He was shot in his office this morning."

21.

I wish I could say I was surprised by the news of Saul's death—I really do wish that. Maybe then I could continue to tell Becky that my representation of Sonny Falco and his associates was just business. I think I had known better for longer than I was willing to admit. But it all came together for me, slow learner that I am, when I went to Saul's private warehouse to collect his files on Falco.

I didn't actually need to see what was in the files to do what I had to do, but I wanted to know more about Falco and his businesses. I suppose I could say that Falco was still an enigma, and to some extent that was true. I didn't know anything about him personally, and that was fine with me. What concerned me was that I didn't know enough about what made him tick. Jack Crowley had painted him as some sort of a criminal kingpin, but others had drawn a much more benign picture. I was sure—or, at least, I tried to convince myself—that the truth lay somewhere in between. That changed with Saul Weinberg.

As I said, I liked Saul. He was funny in a way that only a New York Jew can be, and his accent reminded me of my law school years. (Did I mention that I went to law school in New York? NYU to be exact. I don't make a big thing out of it, and I'm sure NYU doesn't take any particular pride in having me as an alum.)

As I was saying, I liked Saul's personality and didn't

give much thought to his business until the night we met at his warehouse. What was it he had said? The files for each of his clients were all kept in separate storage units. And he had maybe fifteen units. That's a very exclusive practice. Maybe it wasn't as exclusive as the lawyer's one-client law practice in the *Godfather* films, but just the fact that I was thinking in those terms made me sweat. Or it could be that I was sweating because of what happened after I heard the news of Saul's untimely demise.

I knew that Saul had the original records of the transactions his clients were involved in. There was nothing particularly unusual about that. Most attorneys and accountants keep the originals of client documents. But the documents are normally kept at the lawyer's or accountant's office and the client can claim them at any time. I knew that Saul's practice was a little unorthodox—no pun intended—but I didn't know the most important part until Falco asked if I knew where Saul kept his files.

I don't know why, but I told him that I had no idea. I expected him to see through me right away and I was already thinking about how to explain that I'd misunderstood the question. But instead of asking me anything else, he pounded his desk with the side of his fist.

"We have to get those damned files before the cops find them," Falco said as he pounded his desk again.

I wasn't sure whether he was talking to LeBlanc or me. I hoped he was addressing himself to LeBlanc because I couldn't come up with any response to his pronouncement.

LeBlanc muttered something—I think it was a French profanity—before standing, taking a step back and leaning against the wall. "There's nothing we can do right now. His office is a crime scene. It will be crawling with cops."

Falco frowned. Or maybe it was a scowl. With Falco I could never be certain.

From behind me, I heard LeBlanc continue, "They're probably going to take his computer for analysis."

Falco made a *harrumph* sound. "Good fucking luck with that. Saul's computer is protected with military-grade encryption software. He claimed that *no one* could get into his files."

Because LeBlanc was behind me, I don't know if he did anything to communicate with Falco. I can only assume he did because the next thing I heard was Falco saying that I could leave and that LeBlanc's driver would take me back to my office.

I don't think I was ever so glad to leave a meeting.

§

At four o'clock I was back in my office. I still had a few hours to kill before Becky would be home. Under normal circumstances, I would have headed for one of my favorite drinking establishments, but these weren't normal circumstances.

About that time, I heard the mail being fed through the slot in the door. I hadn't sent out any bills lately—my fees now being paid mostly in cash—so I wasn't expecting any checks.

Even from across the room I recognized that two of the envelopes were from utility companies. There wasn't any urgency to them. But the third envelope was equally familiar and justified expending the energy to retrieve it.

As I thought, it was from the disciplinary committee of the State Bar Association. Probably just another complaint from a client who had been found guilty and blamed me. What the hell. The absurd reasons felons came up with for blaming their circumstances on their lawyer's incompetent representation were legendary. Maybe I could at least end my day with a laugh.

Whatever measure of pleasure I felt as I opened the letter melted away when I read the subject line of the letter: "IN RE: DISBARMENT PROCEEDINGS AGAINST…"

It took me a few seconds to catch my breath. To be perfectly honest, I'd expected to receive such a letter for some time. My drinking had increased, and I'd begun to miss hearings and wasn't prepared for the ones I made.

The letter contained all the charges against me and the whys and wherefores for them. It went on for nine pages. As I read the charges—all of which were true and accurately documented—I concluded that my days as an attorney were numbered, and it was a small number. The fact is, if I'd been on the committee that decides such things, even I would have voted to disbar me.

I know I should have felt downhearted, but there was one bright side. I had, as I've previously mentioned, won my aunt and uncle's wrongful death case and I was set for life. And I was never particularly happy practicing law. I only did it because that's what my family expected of me. Now I had my way out.

No more hookers or junkies. No more night-court appearances. And best of all, no more Sonny Falco, Louis LeBlanc or any of their associates. What better excuse could I give them? Sorry, fellows, but I'm not a lawyer anymore.

§

I was certain Becky would be pleased when I gave her the news, and I was right—mostly. As expected, she professed sadness over the impending loss of my law license, but she knew that, for the most part, I wasn't happy practicing law and was only doing it because I didn't have any other skills. The fact that I was financially able to "retire" wasn't enough for me, though. I had to have something to do; some way to keep my mind occupied and challenged. For better or worse, representing Falco had given me a reason to stretch my intellectual muscle. Becky understood all of this. She didn't say it in so many words, but I knew what she was thinking. Finally, we could start making plans for our own life.

It's too bad that destiny had something else in mind for me.

22.

The day after I learned of Saul Weinberg's death and my pending disbarment, I had an early-morning motion hearing. I don't remember the subject of the motion or the result of the hearing, but I must have lost because I always try to forget the ones I lose. That's probably not the best way to practice law. We should all remember our mistakes and learn from them, but in my case, that would have consumed too much of my gray matter.

After the hearing, I wandered over to the jail to give André LaForrette the news that I would be unable to represent him. I couldn't predict when I would become officially disbarred, but I was confident it would happen before his case would come to trial. I couldn't justify getting involved in something that I knew I couldn't finish. Besides, I didn't want to take on a murder case.

§

Two men in dark suits, white shirts, solid ties, and utilitarian black shoes approached me as I came out of the jail and headed for my car. There was no mistaking who or what they were.

The taller of the men flashed his FBI badge and identification. "Sir, please come with us."

I could have objected. They hadn't said I was under

arrest, and I wasn't under any obligation to go with them, but refusal would only have delayed the inevitable.

Half an hour later, I was ensconced in a room at the New Orleans office of the Federal Bureau of Investigation. I assumed it was a conference room. There was a six-person table with matching chairs in the middle of the room. Against one wall there was a small settee and an end table with a lamp and telephone.

I could say I wondered what was going on and why I was there, but I thought I already knew the answers to those questions. No one had read me my rights, so I was sure I wasn't under arrest... and reasonably sure I wasn't there as a suspect in anything. Nonetheless, my thoughts went to the many times Becky had warned me about my growing association with Sonny Falco.

There was a mirror on a narrow wall of the room. I assumed it was a two-way mirror and that someone was watching me. I tried my best to remain calm and feign a lack of concern while I waited for whatever was going to happen next.

I didn't have to wait long.

Five minutes later, the door opened and there stood Lawrence Hitchens, U.S. Attorney for the Eastern District of Louisiana. The big cheese himself, and he wasn't smiling. But he also wasn't frowning the way I would have expected him to be if he had his sights on me. I really couldn't imagine what I'd been brought in for. Well, that's not entirely true. I could imagine what his interest in me might be, but I didn't want to think about it.

He introduced himself—as if I didn't know who he was—but didn't offer to shake hands.

He closed the door and, rather than take a seat, he leaned against the wall, paging through a file. It was a thicker file than I would have expected him to have on me. For several minutes he remained standing silently.

I understood the game. I'd used it often myself. Remain silent and let the witness, or whatever I was, sweat over what might be coming next. I did my best to remain calm, but acid was assaulting my stomach by the time he spoke.

"How long have you been representing Sonny Falco?"

The acid spigot opened wider, but I think I was able to retain my composure.

"I'm not sure what you're asking."

"I said—"

"I know what you *said*. I simply don't know what you *meant*." Sometimes the best defense is a good offense. "Until I know what this is all about, I'm not going to say anything about my client."

Hitchens seemed prepared for my gambit. He casually took a seat opposite me. We were so close that I could smell his aftershave—Brut, I think.

"All right," he said. "Then let's talk about *you*."

He opened his file and began laying photographs on the table. They were all of me with either Falco or LeBlanc, sometimes both, and one or another of the state agency officials or politicians I'd met during the preceding months. He gave me a few minutes to think about the significance of the pictures.

"Do you want to read the transcripts of your meetings?"

I know it's a cliché, but I felt my sphincter slam shut. I'm also sure Hitchens was aware of my reaction. For a minute he remained silent. I'm certain he was only giving me time to think about my situation.

When he finally broke the silence, his voice was flat and unemotional. "Tax evasion, aiding and abetting a money-laundering scheme, aiding and abetting a scheme to violate campaign finance laws, aiding and abetting a scheme to bribe public officials… and let's not forget your role in Falco's violations of the RICO Act. Shall I go on?"

I bent forward, crossed my arms on the table and lowered my head. "No. I think I get the picture."

He sat back with his hands clasped behind his neck. "Am I under arrest?"

"No. At least not yet."

I'm no genius, but it doesn't take a whole lot of brainpower to see where he was going. "You want Falco."

Hitchens leaned over the table, putting his weight on his elbows. His face was only inches from mine. "I want his whole organization. And you can give me what I want."

A woman silently entered the room, took a seat on the settee and crossed her legs. She had a nice pair of legs, and the rest of her wasn't half bad either. Five-six, maybe five-seven and a little overweight at about one-forty. Her dark hair was pulled back in a bun, and she had a severe, no-nonsense expression.

I returned my attention to Hitchens. "What's in it for me?"

The woman on the settee stood up. "That depends on how helpful you decide to be," she said.

She glanced at Hitchens. "I think I can take it from here, Larry."

As he headed for the door, Hitchens said, "Stop by my office later. I need an update on that other thing."

She nodded as she began collecting the photographs that were spread across the table and putting them back in the file that Hitchens had left behind. She took her time ordering the photographs, giving me time to start worrying about what was coming next. Without looking at me, she mumbled an introduction. "I'm Barbara Blain. I'm with the office of the United States attorney for the Eastern District of Louisiana. And you…" She paused while she raised her head and fixed her eyes on mine. "You're in deep shit." It wasn't the kind of language I'd expected, but I couldn't argue with the substance of her statement.

I'm sure she expected some kind of response, but I'd been through enough interrogations to know how the game is played. I'd always told my clients to keep their mouths shut and answer questions only after conferring with me. Since I didn't have anyone to confer with, I just kept my mouth closed and waited.

She slid the file out of the way and rested her elbows on the table. Her forearms were raised and her fingers intertwined and resting against her lips. She looked at me with cool, confident eyes. "Yessir. You are in big trouble.

I tried to reciprocate with the eyes bit, but my shaking hands would have cost me whatever bargaining position I had, so I kept them in my lap.

"However," she said, my heart fluttering, "you *may* see the light of day as a free man in this lifetime."

Even without my help, she was following the script. Start the bidding high and negotiate your way down. Now she waited for me to say something.

I thought about what Hitchens had said and wondered just how badly he wanted my help. I suspected he had a hard-on for Falco, but I couldn't imagine why and didn't try. All I knew was that I was holding some good cards.

"You can't do anything to me. Whatever you think you have on Falco, I was working as his attorney, so I'm protected by the attorney-client and work-product privileges. Nothing I've said to him, or done for him, can be used as evidence against him—or me."

"Ordinarily, you would be right. But when you started helping him plan how to break the law in the future, you became a co-conspirator."

I hate it when the prosecutor is right.

"Besides, we don't need you to get Falco and his crew. We have all the public officials who have been on the receiving end of Falco's favors. I'm sure they'd rather be witnesses for the prosecution than co-defendants."

I didn't doubt that she was right. Everyone who watches crime shows knows that the first one to talk gets the best deal.

"*Assuming*, without admitting, that I know anything that can help you, what do I get out of it?"

Blain shook her head. "Don't play games with me, counselor. We've got you dead to rights. It's just a question of how much time you serve. But in the larger scheme of things you're just a little fish—a guppy. We want the whale, and we want all the public officials who have gone swimming with him."

I was reasonably certain that the part about having me dead to rights on anything was a bluff, something she said to scare people into helping her. I might have bent a few laws. I may even have fractured some. But I was reasonably sure I hadn't actually broken any.

What got my attention was the rest of what she'd said. I knew she was talking about Falco, and maybe LeBlanc, and the people they did business with. I did a quick mental review of the projects I'd worked on for Falco and concluded that the only thing she could be referring to was the work I had done on political contributions. I knew I hadn't done anything wrong, and I didn't have any personal knowledge of what Falco might have done, but the federal statutes on aiding and abetting criminal activities cast a wide net. It was time to rethink my position.

The letter from the Bar Association floated down into the front of my mind. I wasn't going to be a lawyer for much longer, and I had to think about what I would do after my license was revoked. Being surrounded by bars and picking up roadside trash didn't strike me as desirable ways to occupy my time. But becoming part of the roadside trash was an even less desirable alternative.

I looked at Blain and tried to decide what she had in mind.

Her expression was cold and grim. It's possible she was bluffing, but I didn't think so. It was more likely that there were a couple of U.S. Marshals outside the door waiting to take me into custody if she didn't get what she wanted. But she was obviously willing to make me a deal. The only question was how good a deal I could make.

"I'll tell you what I know, and I'll name names, but I won't testify—and I don't have to turn over any of the documents I collected while acting as Falco's attorney. And my girlfriend, Becky, and I get into the Witness Protection Program if we want to."

Blain laughed. "You don't want much."

"That's my offer." I didn't expect to get everything, but I figured there was no harm in trying. I'd represented enough clients in plea negotiations to know how the game works. Ask for the universe and settle for a small planet and a moon or two.

Blain's response was quick and unequivocal. "Here's the deal, and it's not negotiable. You plead no contest to one count of aiding and abetting a scheme to evade taxes, and you agree to a five-year suspended sentence. You answer all of my questions truthfully and name all the names you know, and you agree to testify at the trial of Sonny Falco if it becomes necessary. You also get immunity from prosecution for anything you tell me. For that, *you* get put in the Federal Witness Protection Program."

"Where are you going to send me? I don't want to go anywhere that's cold."

"That will be up to the Marshal's Service. They're in charge of witness protection."

"Do you think I really need to go into the program? I mean, Falco already knows I won't be able to represent him after I'm disbarred, and I'm not going to testify. Maybe he won't even know I'm working with you."

"If you don't want to go into the Program, that's fine with me. But you can't count on Falco not finding out about your cooperation. Whether you testify or not, he'll know there are only a limited number of people who could provide us with the evidence we will be using at trial."

"And what about Becky"

"What about her?"

"We have a life together. I want her to be able to come with me."

Blain leaned back while tapping her pen on the edge of the conference table. I knew enough about the Witness Protection Program to know that it's usually limited to a witness and his or her immediate family. Either Blain was desperate for my testimony or she had a soft spot for lovers, because she finally said, "She can go into the program after Falco is convicted."

"I want to see it all in writing."

"Sit tight," she said as she left the room.

A few minutes later, another woman opened the door and asked if I would like some coffee or a soda. I passed.

After a half an hour, give or take, Blain was back with a folder containing several sheets of paper. "Sorry it took so long," she said. "Hitchens took some convincing."

I knew that was bullshit. She'd known what they were willing to give me before they brought me in.

Now that we were, or were about to be, on the same side, she was all smiles. She came and sat on my side of the table and together we went over the written agreement. We corrected a typo or two, and she agreed to some wording changes I wanted. In retrospect, I don't think she was fully aware of the significance of the changes she agreed to, but that wasn't my problem.

A final draft of the agreement was typed, and we both signed it. All things considered, on my celestial scale, I'd gotten a couple of medium-size planets and at least one moon. That was fine for the moment, but there remained the problem of telling Becky what had happened.

I knew I wouldn't hear an "I told you so." Becky wasn't that type. Besides, she would have known that I was beating myself up for not listening to her. I'd like to think that if I could have done it all over, I would have listened to Becky and never have become involved with Falco at all. That's what I'd *like* to think, but I'd just be kidding myself.

PRESENT DAY

23.

An hour south of Knoxville, I was out of the rainstorm and traffic had thinned markedly. It was just me and, pardon the metaphor, a truckload of eighteen-wheelers. I still didn't have a plan for saving my sorry ass, but I knew what I had to do now.

By early the next morning, I was in Florida and it was time to find out if my hopes for assistance were even viable. I rummaged through the pocket of my coat, located my iPhone and dialed the number for Horse McGee. It was answered in the deep baritone befitting the monster of a man to whom it belonged.

"McGee."

"Horse, this is Harris Masters."

There was a long pause as if Horse were analyzing why someone he only knew as a drinking buddy would be calling him. When he eventually spoke, his voice was a mixture of surprise and concern. "Hey, Masters. How's life in Tennessee?"

I hadn't really thought through my answer to what I should have anticipated would be his initial response. A few preliminary pleasantries would have been appropriate, but my anxiety compelled me to get right to the point.

"All hell has broken loose, and I need your help."

There was another pause as Horse apparently covered his phone and spoke with someone else.

"I'm with Lucius. I'm going to put you on speaker-phone."

The next voice I heard was Lucius White's. He spoke, as I expected, with the hesitation of someone who barely knew me and was uncertain why I would be calling. "What kind of trouble are you in?"

I briefly described the circumstances that had caused me to abruptly leave Tennessee, but I omitted the fact that I was in the Witness Protection Program. That would have required too much explanation. I knew I'd eventually have the get into that, and the circumstances that got me into the program, but this didn't seem to be the time. I didn't know White well enough to even guess at what he might be thinking or how he was reacting to my call. I only hoped he'd be willing to hear me out.

"Where are you?" His tone was somewhere between neutral and skeptical. It wasn't a hopeful sign, but at least it wasn't entirely negative.

"Somewhere just south of the Georgia line."

I envisioned Horse and White engaged in some kind of nonverbal communication. Like I said, I didn't know White at all well, but Horse had told me enough about their relationship that I knew they didn't always need words to share their thoughts. I tried to control my breathing as I waited for some response. I guess I hadn't thought about the possibility that they wouldn't be willing to help me. Now I feared that they'd think that I was too presumptuous on making the decision to come to Florida without confer-ring with them first.

"Do you know how to get to my office?"

For the first time since laying eyes on my ransacked cabin, I relaxed. The back of my skull found the Porsche's head rest and a gusting sigh left my chest. At least I'd get an audience. "I have the address on Horse's business card."

"Come straight here. We'll talk more when you get here." He sounded as if he was at least interested in my predicament but wasn't committing to anything.

I did a quick check of the mile marker signs on the side of the interstate and calculated the driving time to Fort Myers. "I can be there in about six hours."

"We'll talk then," White said before hanging up.

The next six hours were the longest hours of my life.

§

When I arrived at the first Interstate exit for downtown Fort Myers, I called Horse and he gave me directions to his location. After the second wrong turn, I again swore that I was going to get a navigation system. It ended up taking me an hour instead of the half hour it should have taken me to get there, and when I finally arrived, it wasn't a moment too soon. I don't know how much longer I could have kept my eyes open.

All the spots in White's parking lot were full, so I pulled into the lot in the small shopping center across the street. Horse was waiting at the door of White's office. When he saw my Porsche pull into the lot, he trotted across the street and greeted me with a bear-hug. I took that to be a good sign. It was going on seven hours since I'd called and outlined my situation, and if they were going to turn me down, I was sure the greeting wouldn't have been so warm.

For the first time, I really looked at Horse. In all the time we'd spent together in Tennessee, I don't think I'd ever really considered what he looked like. It's not as if I judge people by their appearance, but now that I was about to put my life in his hands, I felt justified in being socially incorrect.

I knew he'd been a starting tackle at the University of

Florida, but I'd never paid attention to how big he really was. I mean, he was *big*. I'm not the best judge of such things, but I'd say that six-foot-six and a gym-rat three-ten was pretty close. I did a little math with the few facts I knew and figured him for between thirty-five and forty, but his boyish smile made him look much younger. If I hadn't known better, I would have pegged him for a bouncer at some club instead of the investigator and computer wizard I knew him to be. More important to me now was that he was a friendly face. Even though exhaustion had its hooks in me, seeing him gave me a lift that I was sorely in need of.

I commented on the building that housed White's apartment and the offices of Lucius J. White & Associates, and Horse launched into a story of its history. He seemed to take pride in the story, almost like it was his own, and that was okay with me. I'm a little bit the same way when people visit me in New Orleans. As tired as I was, the story of White's offices and apartment in the converted nineteenth-century warehouse fascinated me. The warehouse had been built late in the eighteenth century to store goods transported by ship to the small community on the site of what had once been a frontier fort maintained by the Union Army during the Civil War. In the 1920s, the railroad arrived in Fort Myers, and ship-borne trade began an immediate and precipitous decline. Over the next sixty years, the waterfront warehouses slowly succumbed to the ravages of time, neglect, and decay. By the early 1980s, only the warehouse that now housed White's offices and apartment still stood. Eventually, it had become the property of the city, seized for unpaid property taxes, and was scheduled for demolition as a public nuisance. The city had been more than happy to sell the derelict building to Lucius White.

After more than a year of restoration, the warehouse

had been completely gutted and refurbished. All that remained of the original structure were the red brick walls and the giant oak beams that supported the original floors and ceilings. The remainder of the building had been painstakingly restored using the same tools and construction methods used to build the original. No detail had been overlooked. A blacksmith's furnace had been built on the site to make nails as they had been made in Florida's early frontier days, and floor planks had been cut on an original steam-powered saw that White acquired for the project and later donated to the city historical museum.

When Horse finished his story, we crossed the street and went directly to one of the two elevators inside the lobby. The elevator we took was marked "private," and I assumed it went directly to White's office. Instead, it opened in the foyer of what had to have been his apartment.

I've seen some opulence in my day, mostly in the open-house tours of the Uptown mansions in New Orleans, but I wasn't prepared for what greeted my eyes.

The room was sixty feet long if it was an inch. Through the picture windows on the far end of the room, I could see all the way to the Gulf of Mexico. To the right, I saw a row of French doors that opened onto a wide wooden balcony overlooking the river. The row of doors was broken in the middle by a fieldstone fireplace that was big enough to cook a cow on a spit. The opposite wall, all two stories of it, was the red brick of the original warehouse and covered by an eclectic collection of art. I had never seen such a variety in one place—everything from African carvings to Native American blankets shared space with modern works of art and the stuffed heads of deer and elk. A tubular brass sculpture that defied description dominated the center of the room.

I was jolted out of my trance by a voice to my right. "Leslie is my decorator."

I recognized Lucius White's deep, gravelly voice and turned toward it. He was standing over the island stove in his restaurant-quality gourmet kitchen. "I assumed you'd be hungry by the time you got here, so I've made you something to eat. I hope elk burgers are okay."

I was suddenly aware of the hunger I was feeling and thanked White. I'd never had an elk burger or any other kind of wild animal burger, but I was up for anything.

White lowered the flame under the grill and flipped a lone burger. Apparently, I would be the only diner.

"Is sourdough bread okay? I also have some nice prosciutto and goat cheese."

For a brief moment, I thought about how many times I'd bragged about the uniqueness of dining in New Orleans. "That all sounds great," I said, and I meant it.

I pulled a stool out from under the granite breakfast bar and sat down. The stress of the break-in at my cabin and the strain of my twelve-hour drive began to overwhelm me, and I fought the urge to lay my head on the bar and doze off.

Horse wandered into the business end of the kitchen and retrieved two beers and a can of Diet Pepsi from the Sub-Zero. I knew from Horse that White was a recovering alcoholic. He'd had his share of relapses, but I admired him for making the effort. Many have been the mornings that I've also taken the pledge, but I've yet to act on it.

Horse put the beers on the bar and slid onto a stool beside me. White served my burger on a wooden plate and asked if I needed any condiments. The burger smelled so good that I couldn't imagine how anything could improve it, so I declined. I took a massive bite and concluded that

I'd made the right decision. The combination of elk, prosciutto and goat cheese was perfect.

White popped open his Pepsi and took a swallow, and Horse did the same with his beer. No one said anything while I devoured a few bites of my sandwich. I hadn't realized how hungry I was until I thought about the fact that I had last eaten a day and a half ago.

After a few bites, I took a break and a swallow of beer. "I guess you want to know why I'm here."

"You gave us the short version when you called this morning, and Horse has been checking some parts of your story on the Internet. But I'd like to hear it from you."

I finished the final bite of my burger, and, as White cleared my plate, the elevator opened and Leslie Halloran stepped out. I remembered her as hot, and she was everything that I remembered. Five-foot-six, a hundred and twenty well-toned pounds, hazel eyes, shiny brick-red hair that cascaded halfway down her back. She had the legs of a tennis player and a pair of hooters that… let's just say they were very nice.

She greeted me with a cheery "Nice to see you again," ruffled Horse's shoulder-length hair as she passed, and planted a big wet one on White. He patted her on her shapely ass as she turned away and faced me.

"You must be exhausted. Go lie down in the guest room. Batman and Robin will still be here when you get up."

White—who I assumed was Batman in Leslie's scenario—nodded. "Go ahead. I want you to be alert when we talk."

I was definitely in need of at least a short nap, but I really didn't want to impose. "No, I'll survive."

"Isn't that the point of your trip?" White said.

I must have looked confused.

"Isn't assuring your survival the reason you're here?"

24.

I don't even recall going into the guest bedroom. The next thing I remember is rolling over and looking at my watch. It was almost nine o'clock. I must have been more fatigued than I thought.

I heard the sounds of John Coltrane and voices and smelled the aroma of something that I couldn't identify but that instantly had my taste buds ready and waiting.

I heard a light knock on the door and mumbled a groggy, "Yes."

Leslie stuck her head into the room. "How did you sleep?"

"Great! Thanks for asking."

She smiled. "We're just about to have something to eat. I hope you're up to joining us."

I bent over and put on my shoes. "Thanks. It smells great."

"Don't thank me. Lucius is the cook around here. When it comes to the kitchen, I'm what you might call domestically impaired."

I chuckled and followed her into the main room of the apartment. "Look what I found in the guest bedroom."

White nodded a greeting from his place at the island stove, and Horse dipped his beer mug in my direction. "Can I get you a cold one?"

"That would be great." I was beginning to feel like an old friend.

I had no doubt that my arrival, and the brief pre-nap discussion of my predicament, had been the topic of further conversation. But now I was feeling more like a guest than a... I'm not sure what I was hoping to become. Anyway, I left it to White to decide when we were ready to talk about my future.

We adjourned to a four-person brass and glass table between the kitchen and the deck overlooking the river. Dinner was something I'd never experienced: blackened chicken served over angel-hair pasta with a light sauce that was something between a béarnaise and a hollandaise. Damn, it was good!

During dinner, we mostly talked about Leslie's day. She's a social activist attorney who spends most of her time suing the government for funds for local clinics. Considering my own circumstances, and the conduct that had gotten me where I was, I had quite a bit of admiration for what she was doing.

After dinner, Leslie brought us coffee. Real chicory coffee. I wondered if it was what they usually drank or if it was something they'd gotten for my benefit. Either way, it tasted great.

With the arrival of coffee, White slid back from the table, stretched his legs, and clasped his hand behind his neck. "Suppose you tell us about what got you into the Witness Protection Program." If there was judgement or pity in his voice, it was buried too deep to recognize.

I was surprised that he knew about my participation in the Program. I was fairly sure I had never mentioned it. I guessed that, during my nap, Horse had been investigating me, but the names of people in the Program are closely guarded. My admiration for his investigative skills took an abrupt turn upward.

I hardly knew where to begin. The fact is, I still don't know exactly when the FBI and the U.S. Attorney started looking at me as a potential witness. I decided to tell them everything and hope they could find something that would be useful.

For the next hour or so, I took a walk down memory lane. I started with my first meeting with Louis LeBlanc and continued through the meeting at which I learned about the killing of Saul Weinberg. When I told them about our last meeting, the one where I told Falco about my pending disbarment and my inability to continue to represent him, I felt an inexplicable pang of remorse. I ended with a short summary of my various meetings with the U.S. attorney and my opinion of the case that she was pursuing.

White, Horse and Leslie all remained silent, listening intently during my monologue. Occasionally they nodded and exchanged glances, but I was too focused on my story to try to interpret their actions. —

When I finished speaking, Leslie left the table and went into the kitchen where she started loading dishes into the washer. White and Horse remained. For a minute, neither of them said anything, and I grew increasingly nervous. What if they didn't think my situation was deserving of their help?

When he finally spoke, White asked the question I'd most feared, the one to which I had no answer. "What do you want us to do?"

I suppose I could have given some bullshit answer, but I couldn't come up with anything even remotely plausible. So I fell back on the adage that has served me best: "When in doubt tell the truth." I leaned forward with my forearms crossed on the table and looked at White with all the earnestness I could muster. "I have no idea. None whatsoever."

White showed a controlled smile and Horse laughed. I think I may have blushed, but to my credit, I persevered.

"I hoped that *you* could see a way out of my problem."

White nodded. "I appreciate your honesty. I don't know what we can do for you, but I have some thoughts."

I took his statement as a sign that he was willing to help. That was a long way from actually solving my problems, but it was enough that I felt a wave of relief. At least I wasn't alone.

He quoted me a daily rate and I faked a cough. It was better than choking. I agreed but pointed out that all the funds I had were still in accounts in my pre-witness protection name. He acknowledged that this presented a problem but added that we would make getting my money the first order of business. He didn't seem to have any doubts about his ability to get my funds, and that pleased me. In the right hands, unabashed confidence is a wonderful quality to behold.-

I realized that I'd allowed my mind to wander when I heard White saying, "You'd better stay here for a few days. Until we know more about what's happening out there, we need to keep you under wraps."

Horse was already on his feet and heading for the elevator. "I'll help you with your things."

I stood and followed him. He had to have known that whatever I could have packed in my Porsche wouldn't require two people to carry. I assumed he wanted to talk with me in private, and I was happy to do so. When we left the building, he confirmed my suspicions.

"Lucius made a few calls while you were taking your nap."

"I expected as much. I guess he found something he liked."

"Lucius hates government prosecutors."

If there was a segue in there, I must have missed it.

"I assume you know Barbara Blain."

"Of course. She's the U.S. attorney I was working with. She's the one who prosecuted Falco."

"Well, now she's after you. She issued a material witness warrant this afternoon. Now the good guys and the bad guys are both looking for you."

25.

I waited silently on the sofa opposite White's desk as he examined my plea agreement. Horse stood behind him, reading over his shoulder.

My agreement was four pages long. My experience hadn't given me anything to compare it with, so I didn't know whether it was long, short or just about the normal size for such agreements.

White slid the papers to the side of his desk, leaned back and ran the fingers of both hands through the long graying walnut hair on the sides of his head. Horse remained standing but was now resting his butt on the edge of the credenza behind White's desk.

"Interesting agreement," White said. Horse made what I can only describe as a mini-nod.

White rocked back and forth slightly. His eyes had the far-away look of someone who was deep in thought.

I couldn't imagine what White's comment meant, and I wasn't certain that I wanted to know. I mean, I *did* want to know what he meant, but I feared that it was something I wouldn't like.

As White's silence continued, my respiratory rate increased. I tried to remain calm but failed miserably. I found myself thinking about White and his reputation as a trial attorney. If he could have a client feel this anxious in his office, I could only imagine how he could make an opposing witness feel in court.

Finally, he leaned forward and rested his elbows on the desk. His forearms were raised, and the fingers of both hands were intertwined. There was no apparent urgency to his movements, and when he spoke his voice was devoid of emotion. Somehow, I found that comforting, and I think my breathing slowed.

His eyes held mine as he began. "This isn't a typical plea agreement."

I wasn't sure how to respond. "Is that good or bad?"

He took a deep breath and exhaled slowly. "A lot of that depends on what you actually told the U.S. attorney. If you told her everything you know, then I'd say you're in good shape."

I raised a hand and displayed what I remembered was the sign of the Boy Scout oath. "I swear. I answered all of her questions as completely as I could."

"That's not the same as telling her everything you know."

I knew what he meant, and he was right. I could even remember specific times during the hours of interrogation by Barbara Blain when I wondered why she wasn't asking certain questions. I tried to justify my silence by concluding that she already had all the information she needed. I think that even then I knew better, but I wasn't her co-counsel, and it wasn't my job to help her prepare her case. I was doing what my plea agreement required me to do and no more.

"She'd already decided what charges she was going to bring. As far as I was concerned, she'd made a deal to get what I knew about those charges."

White wrinkled his nose. "I don't think she'd agree with your interpretation of the plea."

"Then I suppose that's something else we'll have to deal with."

"We should know soon enough. Her filings for the material witness warrant should tell us what she wants you for. We may be able to argue that the terms of your plea agreement were satisfied if you gave her everything you knew about. Come to think of it; what were the charges she was going to bring?"

"The only things she charged anyone with before the last trial concerned bribery of a public official and violation of campaign finance laws."

White looked me straight in the eye. "Did you have anything to do with that?"

I took a deep breath. Admitting that you helped a client break the law isn't something lawyers, even ex-lawyers, take any pleasure in. I took the coward's way out and said, "Sort of."

White leaned forward with his arms spread out on his desk. "If I'm going to help you, I have to know everything. You already admitted to being disbarred, so nothing you say is going to affect what I think of you."

I wasn't sure whether he was expressing disapproval of my conduct as a lawyer or as a client. I don't suppose it made much difference. Either way, I felt like shit.

"Now," White said, "I'll ask you again. Did you have anything to do with Falco's actions?"

So this is what it's like to be on the other side of this, I thought. I swallowed hard before responding. "I was in one meeting where it was being discussed… and I may have given them a plan for doing what they may have done."

"What do you mean by 'what they may have done?'"

"I don't know what they ended up doing, and I don't know what evidence Blain used."

White nodded and scribbled a note on his legal pad.

Horse stood and headed out of the room. "I'm going to check the docket for any updates."

White sat up, leaned back in his chair, and began clicking his pen open and closed. I felt like a schoolboy waiting for the principal to mete out punishment for some transgression. For a minute White remained silent. I watched his chest heave as he breathed, deep and slow. His narrowed eyes and furrowed brow suggested that he was concentrating on some idea. I was afraid to ask what he was thinking about.

My bout of temporary anxiety was saved when Horse returned with two sheets of paper.

"Fresh off the docket," he said as he handed the pages to White.

"You might have dodged a bullet," White said. "You're only wanted as a material witness relating to the bribery and campaign finance charges. She probably can't do anything to you for withholding what you know about anything else."

I slumped. "I hate it when a lawyer says 'probably.'"

"It's all I can tell you for now."

"Yeah, I know. But it really doesn't make much difference what I go back to testify about. If Falco finds me, I'll be dead all the same."

26.

I woke up at about nine the next morning. That was early by the standard I'd grown accustomed to during my year in exile. I grabbed a quick shower and put on the one pair of clean jeans and the shirt I'd packed when making my getaway from purgatory.

Leslie was pouring herself a cup of coffee when I came out of the guestroom. She asked how I had slept and whether I wanted a cup of coffee. I'm sure I was on my best guest behavior and told her I had slept well and would love some coffee. I didn't even care if it wasn't Chicory as long as it was strong. Sleep or no sleep, I need a caffeine fix to get me going in the morning, which for me is any time before noon.

I took a seat at the breakfast bar. Leslie brought me a big mug of coffee and asked if I wanted cream and sugar. I shook my head as I took my first shallow sip.

Leslie leaned on the breakfast bar and offered me some cereal, which I declined. I haven't had a meal resembling breakfast since the last time I'd been with Becky. That would three hundred forty-seven days and—I looked at my watch—three hours ago.

I found myself cursing Barbara Blain. Why the hell couldn't she have gotten a conviction? Then at least Becky and I could have been together. It probably wouldn't have been in New Orleans—there's no way I would have been safe there—but Becky didn't have any family, and there were numerous places we'd talked about moving to. The only thing that really kept us where we were was the fact that I only had a license to practice law in Louisiana and couldn't bring myself to retake the bar exam in some other state. But now that I'd been disbarred, I couldn't get admitted in another state anyway.

My mind must have drifted off because the next thing I remember is Leslie shaking my shoulder and telling me Lucius and Horse wanted me to come down to White's office. I headed for the stairs in the corner and the certainty that I was still in big trouble.

White was on the phone when I approached his office. He gave me a sweeping arm gesture and pointed to a chair at the conference table. Horse must have heard me arrive because he came into the office a minute later. I'm not sure what I was hoping for, but whatever it was I didn't see it in Horse's eyes.

Horse leaned toward me and whispered, "Lucius has been on the phone about you all morning. Don't get your hopes up, but we may have a lead that will be helpful."

White concluded his phone call and joined Horse and me at the conference table. He was shaking his head, and I'm fairly sure he was laughing. It was one of those closed-mouth chuckles that might have indicated anything, but I needed to believe he had good news, so I interpreted it as a laugh.

He looked at me and continued making his laughing sound, but now I could see that he was genuinely enjoying whatever he'd learned. "You must have said something that really pissed off Barbara Blain."

That didn't sound like an opening phrase that would be followed by good news for me. My heart started beating faster. "What's she pissed about?"

"Well, to begin with, you vanished without telling any-one what your plans were."

"That's right. I told you why I had to do that. My cabin had been broken into, and I was afraid that Falco had tracked me down."

"*We* know that, but she doesn't. She thinks you ran because she needed you to stay lost for a while longer and then testify at Falco's next trial."

I shook my head. "How do you know this?"

"I've worked with some attorneys in New Orleans over the years. I had one of them call Ms. Blain to find out what she was doing about you."

I think I gulped, or at least I swallowed hard.

"Don't worry. My friend didn't tell her anything about us or where you are. He told her he just wanted to know if there was a reward for bringing you in."

I don't know if I wanted to know the answer, but I had to ask the next logical question. "And is there? A reward, I mean."

White smiled. "I hate to disappoint you, but you're not that important. At least not yet."

"But there's still a material witness warrant out for me."

"*Oh yeah*. She wants to be sure you're available for trial."

"But that could be months away."

White nodded. "At least two or three. But you'll be in protective custody."

"You mean I'll be in jail, in a cell by myself, and iso-lated from the other prisoners."

"That's how it generally works when you're testifying against a gangster."

"*Jesus*. I'll go bonkers if I don't get killed first."

"Don't worry. I think I can arrange something that will satisfy both of you."

I wanted to ask what he had in mind, but I was afraid

I already knew the answer. I was going to have to disappear again. Just the thought of starting over with another new identity was so painful that it took me a few seconds to realize that White was still talking.

"I'll have to square it with the Department of Justice, but I have a ranch in Idaho where you can stay. This time of year, all the roads and trails are snowed in, and the only way in or out is by plane."

If White was trying to make me feel better, he wasn't doing a very good job of it. I'd still have all the joys of being in witness protection but without a bar to go to. At least in Tennessee I had The Red Rose, Delores, and her beautiful hooters.

White may have been reading my mind, or maybe he'd just been through this game before. Whatever the reason, he had a sweetener for his proposal. Unfortunately, it wasn't the kind of sweetener I would have hoped for.

"My friend in New Orleans also did some asking around."

White's tone suggested that whatever he had found out didn't bode well for me.

"There's a contract out on you."

I closed my eyes and rubbed them with the heel of my palms. This day just kept getting better and better. I didn't even open my eyes when I asked, "How much am I worth to Sonny?"

"Right now, five thousand. But it will get higher when we get closer to the date of the next trial."

I thought how fortunate it was that White was a great lawyer because as the deliverer of encouraging news he sucked.

27.

I knew Horse was some kind of genius when it came to doing things with a computer. I'm not talking about simple things like searching for general information. Every eighth-grader knows how to do a Google search. What Horse is good at is doing things that are—how can I put this politely—frowned on by law enforcement authorities. Oh, what the hell. Horse knows how to hack other people's computers.

My first priority, after staying alive, was getting my hands on some money. Like I've said, I had a comfortable nest egg as a result of my aunt and uncle's wrongful death case. I never got around to investing it, and I'm glad I hadn't because the stock market had since made a significant "correction." That's how the financial people described it—a "correction." What it really means, in layman's terms, is that investors took a bath. But that's not my point.

My point is that all that money was sitting in an account in my "old" name, and I suspected that Falco had someone in the bank who was keeping an eye on it. I confess that I had no reason to *know* that anyone in the bank was on his payroll, but I knew enough about how he conducted his business to think it was a distinct possibility.

I sat in a midnight-blue velour recliner in Horse's office while his fingers danced across the keyboard of his computer. Occasionally he paused to ask me a question, but mostly he sat hunched over the keyboard and studying the plasma screen on his desk. Every once in a while, the screen flashed as a page full of computer code was replaced with a recognizable image. Each time that happened, my heart beat a little faster.

I suppose it would have been easier on me if I'd known more about what Horse was doing. He'd started the morning by trying to explain how he was going to check on the current status of my bank account, but beyond that was all gibberish to me. I suppose I could have taken solace in the fact that White also found Horse's explanations incomprehensible. I could have, but I didn't.

By noon, my frustration over Horse's apparent lack of progress was giving me a headache. No matter how much I thought about it, I didn't see that I had any choice. One way or the other, I was going to have to change my identity again.

I couldn't go back to who I'd been before I went into witness protection. Even if Falco was convicted at his next trial, his associates were going to be looking for me. And I didn't see how remaining "Harris Masters" was a better option. The break-in at my cabin was evidence enough that my new identity had been compromised. Besides, if another change of identity was inevitable, I wanted it to be a clean break—so clean that even the U.S. attorney couldn't find me. I was sorry that I'd ever agreed to help convict Falco, but Blain hadn't given me much choice. I suppose I should consider myself lucky that she hadn't made cooperation in the investigation of everyone in Falco's organization a part of my plea deal. But as long as any of them remained free, I was in danger.

My contemplation about my future was interrupted when Horse's intercom sounded. "No progress so far,"

Horse said. "Hacking into a bank's computers is almost as hard as breaking into the Pentagon."

"That's too bad," I heard White say. "But that's not what I need. Send Masters up to my office. There have been some developments."

"You heard him," Horse said without looking up from his computer. "I'll let you know as soon as I find anything."

§

I don't claim to be very good at reading people's expressions, but it didn't take much to know that White didn't have good news. On the plus side, he didn't try to soften the news. That's one of his qualities I've come to admire most. I didn't realize it at the time, but he's a no-holds-barred, tell-it-like-it-is kind of guy.

"The Idaho option we discussed yesterday is off the table."

I wasn't disappointed by the news. The prospect of spending the winter is some isolated compound in Idaho had never appealed to me, but I did want to know how the change of plans had come about.

"I have a… friend… in the Department of Justice. Graham Brochette. He used to be the U.S. Attorney for this district, and we do each other favors from time to time. I called him this morning and proposed letting me keep you under wraps until Falco's next trial. He called the attorney in charge of the case—"

"Barbara Blain."

"Yeah. She demanded that I turn you in."

I can't say that I was surprised. She'd been pleasant enough when we were negotiating my plea deal, but when it came to disclosing what I knew, she'd turned into a real bitch. No matter how much I gave her, she wanted more.

The fact that I didn't have all the information she wanted didn't seem to matter, and every time I told her I didn't know the answer to a question, she threatened to revoke our deal. My only source of satisfaction came from the fact that she wasn't as smart as she thought she was. She had already made up her mind about what she wanted to charge Falco with, and the only things she asked about were related to those charges. If she'd been a little more decent when she first approached me, I might have told her about all the other things she could charge him with. But she wasn't, and I didn't.

I realized that I'd let my mind wander and returned my attention to White. "If your friend is with the DOJ, couldn't he order her to let me stay in your custody?"

"Under ordinary circumstances he probably could. But there are some other things going on that he has to consider."

"So what are we going to do?"

"Right now, nothing. I never told my friend that you were with me, or even that I knew where you were. I only told him that you had contacted me and that I was trying to help you out."

"Do you think he believed you?"

"Probably not. But he didn't tell Blain anything about me, so I can be sure that *she* doesn't know where you are. At least not yet."

"So what am I expected to do now?"

"You're going to take another little road trip."

"To where?"

"I can't officially know. You're going to go to Tampa and get off at an exit where there's a gas station and a convenience store. Someone will meet you there."

"Who?"

"I can't tell you, because I can't know—not officially. I can't know anything more than that you left here."

"But—"

"You're going to have to trust me. We can stay in touch through a third party. But we need to cover as much as we can in the next few days."

I didn't know how I felt about White's plan, but I didn't see that I had any good alternatives. Barbara Blain wasn't stupid. One way or another, she would eventually find out it was White who had called Brochette—and that would lead her to me. Ready or not, it was time to run again.

28.

White put down the receiver and glared at the phone. Eventually, he turned to me. "What did Blain tell you about the first trial?"

"She said she thought Falco had gotten to a juror."

"That's all?"

"That's what she said. Is there something else?"

White shook his head.

"What's the matter? *Was* there something else?"

"I'll say. The judge tossed most of her documentary evidence."

"On what grounds?"

"Some of it was tossed under the 'best evidence rule.' She tried to get copies admitted, and Falco's attorneys objected because they weren't originals. Other evidence was tossed when she couldn't get it properly authenticated."

"How does that affect me?"

"Blain says you told her about original documents you could locate."

"I told her I *thought* there were some documents that I *might* be able to find."

"Well, she expects you to produce them."

"What documents is she looking for?"

"She didn't say. She said you couldn't, or wouldn't, tell her what the documents were."

"That's because I don't know what all the documents

say. I just knew there were documents that would help her case."

I knew I'd slipped when I said I didn't know what "all" the documents said. I bent forward with my elbows on my knees and eyes on the floor and hoped he wouldn't have realized what my statement suggested. No such luck.

"You said you didn't know what *all* the documents say. Do you know what *some* of them say?"

I nodded. "I worked on some of them. But nothing I worked on had any connection to Blain's case. She was trying to make a case for bribery and public corruption. The only documents I knew about had to do with Falco's businesses and a reorganization I was planning."

"Who else knows about those documents?"

"His accountant knew. But he was murdered before I met Blain."

White mulled this fact over for a minute before continuing. "What do you know about the location of the documents?"

"Not much. I met Saul Weinberg at his storage place one night to collect some papers I needed for the business reorganization work we were doing."

"Exactly where did you meet?"

"Saul owns, or used to own, a self-storage facility where he keeps all his client files."

Without looking away from me, White jotted a note on a legal pad on the corner of his desk. "You said that the accountant kept *all* his files at this storage facility?"

I nodded. "That's what he said."

"Were they all in one storage unit?"

I couldn't understand what the question had to do with me, but I answered anyway. "No. The files for each of his clients were kept in separate units."

"How many units were there at the storage facility?"

I was about to ask what this could possibly have to do with my situation. But I was still getting to know White and had to trust him to be thinking about something relevant to my case. "About fifteen."

White made another note on his pad and changed the topic.

"If we're going to negotiate anything with her, we're going to have to figure out what she needs and what we have to offer."

"How do you propose we do that?"

He handed me four large binders. "These are copies of the trial transcripts. You need to go through them and find out what you know that could help her."

"How can I do that without knowing what documents I may be able to locate?"

"Suppose we start by figuring out what documents you think *might* be available."

"What I *think* can be located are the financial records for all of Falco's businesses."

"How do you know about them?"

"One of the last projects I did for Falco involved a reorganization of his businesses. His accountant keeps the originals of all his financial records. When I was negotiating my plea agreement, I told Blain that I thought there were some documents that could be used to convict Falco, but I didn't know exactly where they were."

White nodded. "That's close to what Blain assumed. They didn't come up with anything when they raided Falco's offices. She figured the records would be with his accountant—maybe in an off-site storage facility. But there must be at least a hundred of them in the New Orleans area. And he probably didn't rent the unit under his own name. That would make our job too easy. Besides, if he had, I'm sure Falco and the feds would have found the documents by now."

"According to his accountant, even Falco doesn't know where the documents are located. The accountant owns the mini-storage facility where he keeps all his client files."

"Why doesn't Blain know about that?"

"I didn't tell her about the accountant. By the time I was cooperating with her, the accountant was already dead. She didn't ask about him, and I didn't volunteer anything."

"But you know where the warehouse is."

"I don't know the address, but I'm sure I can find it. My question is, who do we give them to? If I give the files to the feds and Falco is convicted, I'm a dead man. If I give the files to Falco, he might stop looking for me."

"Do you really believe Falco will leave you alone?" What White was asking was not a question.

I couldn't bring myself to respond right away, even though the answer was obvious. Falco wouldn't stop until I was dead.

29.

It was starting to drizzle when I pulled out of the parking lot at White's warehouse. I admit that my sample size was small, but I was beginning to think that rain and running for my life had something in common for me. I still hadn't done anything about the leak in the roof of my Porsche, but I was starting to get the hang of the running part.

For the two-hour drive from Fort Myers to Tampa, I debated the wisdom of my decision to put my future in the hands of some complete stranger. The fact that White trusted him weighed heavily in his favor, but the fact that he wouldn't tell me the stranger's name made me more than a little apprehensive.———

As I approached the Tampa exit from I-75, I was still thinking about skipping Tampa and heading north and fending for myself. I didn't have any idea what I would do, but being pawned off on a stranger wasn't what I had in mind when I went to Horse and White for help. I had about decided that I had to take control of my situation when I found myself on the Selman Expressway heading into Tampa.

I pulled off the expressway at the designated exit and parked in front of the convenience store. After half an hour, no one had arrived to get me, and I was growing nervous. Was I at the wrong spot? Had the plan been changed?

TRIPLE CROSS

I went into the store to get a soda, but as I was checking out, my old urges overtook me and I bought a pack of cigarettes. What the hell—if Falco was going to kill me, I might as well have a smoke.

I was sitting on the fender of my Porsche when a motorcycle pulled up beside me. Without raising his dark visor, the rider asked if I was waiting for someone to guide me somewhere. When I said I was, he handed me an envelope and sped off. *Oh, Christ. What now?* I tore open the envelope and removed its contents: a map and a page of directions.

The directions I'd been given took me directly to my destination, although what I saw when I arrived there wasn't what I expected. I thought the homes in Uptown New Orleans were quite grand, but they weren't much more than guest houses compared with what I was facing.

The twelve-foot high wall along the street went on for a couple of New Orleans-size lots before I came to a pair of wrought iron gates. On top of the wall, cameras turned slowly as I approached, but I didn't see any way to announce my arrival. I was debating what to do when the gates swung open. I drove in and was immediately faced with another choice — turn right to the small parking graveled area or left toward the portico that fronted the main entrance and the pair of paved parking spots beyond.

My decision was dictated by a small mountain in a black suit standing in the middle of the drive. With a wiggle of his index finger he signaled for me to follow him. He walked surprisingly rapidly toward the portico and came to a halt by the steps to the entrance. He didn't say anything, but I assumed I was expected to stop there.

I extracted myself from my Porsche and stretched before heading for the front doors of the mansion. The mountain didn't move as I climbed the steps. As I reached for the ornate brass knocker, the door opened and I had my first look at Manuel "Manny" Rodriguez.

I don't know what I expected, but whatever it was, Rodriquez wasn't it. White had given me a short history of his relationship with Rodriguez, but it was mostly about his past representations and why he'd agreed to be my host until we figured out what to do next. I'd been left with the impression that Rodriguez was a larger-than-life figure, but to tell the truth, the man standing in from of me was something of a disappointment. He couldn't have been more than five-nine, and that may have been a stretch. He was of average build and dressed in casual attire: gray slacks, a light blue open-collared shirt, and black loafers. His hair was dark but not quite black. Aside from obviously being Hispanic, his features were remarkably average. What I was most drawn to were his eyes. His thick eyebrows formed perfect arches over a pair of black eyes that made me feel like he could see into my mind.

He stepped toward me, smiled, and extended his hand. "Good morning, Mr. Masters. Welcome to my home." His voice was deeper than I'd expected from a man of his stature, but it was warm and sounded genuinely inviting. I took his outstretched hand. His grip was firm and confident.

"Come," he said. "Lunch is about to be served."

I couldn't avoid gawking as he led me down a paneled hallway covered with oriental carpets and past a formal living room, a family room, a library, a game room and a few other rooms whose doors were closed. At the end of the hallway, we came to a set of open French doors that led to a spacious patio and a swimming pool that could have been used for the Olympic trials. Beyond the pool, the manicured lawn sloped gently to the seawall and a pier where a yacht, a medium-size fishing boat, and a ski boat rocked gently in the waters of what I guessed was Tampa Bay. Around the yard were topiaries trimmed into animal shapes.

Rodriguez led me to a table that was already set for two, and we took our seats.

"Lucius tells me you are from New Orleans."

"That's right." My thoughts immediately went to questions about how much White had disclosed about my situation. Having too many people know too much was not in my best interest.

"Don't worry," he said as if reading my thoughts. "That's all Lucius told me about you. That and the fact that you were in need of a secure place to stay until he made other arrangements."

"I appreciate your hospitality, Mr. Rodriguez."

"Please, call me Manny. Any friend of Lucius and Horse is a friend of mine."

"Thank you… Manny. Most people just call me Masters."

Rodriguez gave me a faint smile and a slight nod. "I have taken the liberty of ordering some oysters and shrimp gumbo for lunch. I hope it's to your liking."

I was instantly salivating. It had been almost a year since I'd last had oysters and shrimp gumbo, and my thoughts flashed to my last meal with Becky. I could still see the sadness in her eyes as we shared our final meal together before I was to leave for wherever the Marshals Service was going to take me until Sonny Falco's trial was over. *How ironic,* I thought. *Here I was, hiding out from one gangster in the home of another.*

Lunch was served by an attractive Hispanic woman in her early thirties who asked what I would like to drink. I was tempted to ask for a Hurricane but thought better of it and asked for an iced tea. Rodriguez requested the same, and we settled into a brief but awkward silence. What do you talk about with someone when he isn't supposed to know anything about you and you aren't sure how much you want to know about him? I *already* knew more than I wanted to know. I knew he'd been one of White's clients, so that narrowed things down a bit. And he obviously had money, but he was home on a workday, so that narrowed things a little further. More than that, I didn't want to think about.

I don't remember, but I think we just made chitchat about the weather, his boats and our common interest in fishing. It relaxed me, but only slightly. It was chatter for the sake of noise, but his voice was pleasing to my ears.

As we ate, I surveyed what little I could see of the property. For the first time, I noticed the security cameras located on each corner of the house and the razor wire on top of the high brick wall that ran down each side of the property. I began to feel safer already.

I was just finishing the last of my gumbo when the walking mountain approached Manny and whispered something in his ear. Manny nodded and turned to me as he stood.

"Jake will take you and your things to the guest quarters. I'm wanted on the phone. Lucius says there have been some developments he needs to discuss with me."

30.

Considering that "my things" consisted of two changes of clothes, a jacket, and my computer, the move into Manny's guest quarters didn't represent a burdensome undertaking. The move was made especially convenient by the fact that my Porsche had been moved into one of the bays of Manny's five-car garage and an elevator in the front of the bay led directly to the guest quarters. My only problem was that the quarters didn't come with a map. Okay, that might be overstating things a little, but what I had pictured as a large bedroom with maybe a kitchenette and sitting area was, in fact, significantly larger than the bungalow I shared with Becky in New Orleans. It consisted of two spacious bedrooms, each with a full bath, and an enormous open-plan combination kitchen—fully stocked—separated from the living room and dining area by a granite-topped breakfast bar. A wine rack over the wet bar in the living area was stocked with a collection of bottles that Becky and I would have only ordered on special occasions. Whatever else anyone might say about Manny, he knew how to treat his guests.

Having nothing else to do, I laid down on the leather sofa and started thinking about what I had to do next. Horse, White and I had only discussed our plans in the most general terms, but the one thing we had agreed on was that I was going to have to change my identity—again.

I never considered how difficult it is to create a new identity. In my first and only experience, the officials at the Witness Protection Program had taken care of everything. But, of course, they have some experience in such matters, and they are the government.

In principle, creating a new identity is easy enough, so easy that there are dozens of sites on the Internet with step-by-step instructions. Find a death certificate for someone of the right age and get a certified copy of their birth certificate from the appropriate state agency. Parlay that into a state-issued ID card or driver's license and you're well on your way, at least for most purposes. But the do-it-yourself approach is fraught with problems. How do you know that the person whose identity you assumed didn't have lousy credit or a criminal record or had an ex-spouse and children who have claims for support?

I needed a fresh new identity. Getting false identification documents—drivers' licenses and the like—is simple enough if you know the right people, but manufacturing a completely new identity is something else entirely. Creating a credit history, a driving record, a voting record, a social security record, and employment history aren't things that a layman can do. Only the government can create that kind of thing, and I didn't see any help coming from that direction.

I was still thinking about my identity problem when there was a knock on the door that I assumed connected the guest quarters to the main house. When I opened the door, a man I hadn't seen before said Rodriguez wanted me to join him in his study. I assumed it had something to do with the call he'd received from White, and I was anxious to hear about the new developments in my case.

Rodriguez was seated behind a modern glass-topped table that apparently served as his desk. He glanced up and gave me a half-smile as I entered, but he didn't stand. I took a seat in one of the two chrome and black leather chairs in front of him. He tapped his index finger on a pad that lay to the side of his desk. His eyes were narrowed, and there were shallow furrows on his forehead.

My heart was pounding. It would have been impolite to come right out and ask what White had called about, so I waited for him to speak. It seemed to take forever, although it couldn't have been more than a few seconds, before he looked at me. His face didn't reveal anything about what he was thinking. Only his eyes, which were still slightly narrowed, suggested he had something serious on his mind.

"Lucius tells me you're a lawyer."

The statement, which didn't have any obvious relevance to my present circumstances, startled me. I didn't know where he was going or how important the fact was, so I merely said, "That's right." Telling him that I was a disbarred ex-lawyer would have taken too much explaining. Besides, if White had told Rodriguez I was a lawyer, he must have had his reasons.

"I assume Lucius told you that he's my lawyer."

"He mentioned that." I still couldn't figure out where Rodriguez was going. "He also said you were friends."

"I suppose you could say that."

I had the feeling Rodriguez was trying to size me up. Whatever the relationship between White and Rodriguez was, it had to be more than a friendship—and certainly more than just lawyer and client. I still knew it was better if I didn't know too much about either Rodriguez or his relationship to White. Nonetheless, my curiosity was in overdrive. But understanding their relationship wasn't my highest priority. I was aching to know what new development White had called about. I didn't have to wait long.

"Lucius said you need help moving some money out of your bank in New Orleans."

I rubbed the back of my neck. "I have to pay his retainer."

Rodriquez considered my response before continuing. "But it's more than just that, isn't it?"

I didn't know whether he was fishing or testing me. I sensed that the development White had discussed with Rodriguez had something to do with what Horse had been working on. I didn't want to disclose any more information than White had thought was necessary and I tried to be noncommittal.

"I'm a little low on cash."

"And you can't just withdraw money from your bank." The way he said it made it clear that he was making a statement and not merely implying a question.

I didn't see any reason to play games. There were some things I wasn't about to disclose—chief among them being my status as a protected witness and that I was now the subject of a material witness warrant. But as long as we were only talking about money, I was willing to go along with whatever plan White had come up with. I just had to figure out what that plan was, and there was only one way to do that.

"Just how much did Lucius tell you?"

For a fleeting moment, Rodriguez stifled a chuckle. It was as if he'd won a bet he made with himself about how long it would take for me to ask about White's call.

I had tried to make my question sound ambiguous. White had been very circumspect in telling me about his arrangement for my sanctuary, and I assumed he'd been the same when discussing my situation with Rodriguez. But of course, from White's perspective, I was still a largely unknown quantity while Rodriguez was... I still didn't know enough to complete that thought. My mind went back to our luncheon conversation where Rodriguez professed that he only knew I was from New Orleans. I was beginning to wonder if that was all he knew.

I don't know how long I had been reflecting on these facts. It couldn't have been more than a second or two, but it felt much longer. My contemplation was abruptly ended when I heard Rodriguez begin to answer my question.

"I know the money is in an account that isn't in the name of Harris Masters."

I swallowed hard and coughed.

Rodriguez's face didn't show any emotion.

I regained control of myself and said, "It's still my money." I had intended it to sound assertive, but even I heard the defensive tone in my voice.

"I don't doubt that. But you can't just walk into Hibernia National and get it, can you?"

I tried not to show my surprise that he knew the name of my bank. I must not have been very successful, but this kind of conversation was new to me.

"Lucius wanted me to tell you that Horse found a way into the bank's computers and was able to confirm that your account is intact."

I nodded but didn't say anything. I think I was able to disguise my excitement at the news.

"There have only been a few withdrawals by…" Rodriguez paused and referred to his notes before continuing. "Becky Edwards." He stated Becky's name as if he was asking me to confirm his information.

"That's my… girlfriend." I don't know why I felt it was necessary to explain my relationship to Becky. I had added her to the account so that she could use it to supplement her income from the gallery where she worked. I knew she didn't use the account often. In fact, I'd forgotten about it until that moment. But being reminded that she had access to the funds opened up some possibilities that I hadn't considered.

The challenging look in Rodriguez's eyes suggested that he was thinking the same thing that had just occurred to me. *If Becky had access to the funds in my account, why couldn't she just send money to me?*

I knew the answer. There was too much potential that a large transfer from my account would come to Falco's attention. But I couldn't tell Rodriguez about my concern without telling him my whole story.

31.

I felt an intense uneasiness over my lack of knowledge about Rodriguez. The fact that White trusted him to protect me was no longer enough. If he was going to be the intermediary in my communications with White, he would have to eventually learn my whole story. I trusted White to decide how much to tell Rodriguez, and when to tell him, but I needed to know more about Rodriguez before I would be comfortable.

My first inclination was to do the easy thing: get on the Internet and search for anything I could find there. I don't know what I expected to find, but I had to try.

When I returned to the guest quarters, I unpacked my laptop and began searching for a Wi-Fi connection. That's not normally a difficult process. I've had done it dozens of times when staying at hotels and motels around the country. Just press a few buttons and the computer searches out a wireless connection. But after half an hour I hadn't found one.

That's when it occurred to me that I hadn't seen a computer in Rodriguez's office. There could only be one reason for that and my failure to find a Wi-Fi connection: Computers can be seized as evidence, and a Wi-Fi connection can be used by anyone within range of its signal. Just knowing that Rodriguez was taking precautions against such things added to my queasy feeling and made me determined to learn more about him. I remembered passing a truck stop just outside Tampa and decided to go there to do my research.

When I went to tell Rodriguez I was going for a drive he was nowhere to be found. One of the members of the household staff told me he'd gone to a meeting and wouldn't be back for several hours.

In the hour or so it took me to reach the truck stop I tried to think through what I was really looking for. I'd put my life in the hands of someone I knew almost nothing about, and what I did know—that White had represented him on more than one occasion—didn't give me any comfort.

I pulled into the truck stop; drove around to the back where the big rigs were parked and pulled into the first open spot I could find. It wasn't near any meal time, but the lot was almost full. I surmised that most of the drivers were probably just sleeping or doing something else to kill time during the break they were required to take after racking up their allotted number of daily driving hours.

I grabbed my laptop and headed inside. As expected, the dining area was mostly empty. A couple of tables in the "drivers only" section were occupied, but only one table in the rest of the restaurant had anyone sitting at it. I headed for a booth as far from the entrance as I could get and opened my laptop. I was still waiting for my computer to connect with the Wi-Fi signal when the lone waitress on the afternoon shift came and asked what I would like. I was tempted to say that what I would like would be to be anywhere but where I was, but I settled on a request for a burger and coffee. Then I went to work.

I started by looking for anything that included "Lucius White" and "Manuel Rodriguez." A couple of dozen newspaper articles came up and I started reading. As I'd expected, most of the stories were from local papers chronicling the progress of cases in which White had represented Rodriguez. Two of them were cases in which Rodriguez had been charged with money laundering, one case of tax evasion, and one count of illegal transfers of money to offshore banks. I also learned that Rodriguez owned more than three hundred laundromats and self-service car washes—all of them cash businesses where receipts weren't recorded. I chuckled to myself at these businesses bringing a whole new meaning to money laundering, for which they were the perfect front as long as you paid the taxes. All the cases had resulted in acquittals—which isn't the same as innocence.

I think I was happy to find that none of the cases involved drug trafficking, illegal gambling or violent crimes. Of course, that didn't eliminate the possibility that Rodriguez had ever participated in these activities—it just meant he hadn't been tried on any such charges.

I suspended my search while I ate my burger and thought about what I had learned. If Rodriguez was involved in money laundering, he must be doing it for someone, and if it wasn't for himself, then who? Since he hadn't been charged with any of the crimes that usually provided the sources of money to be laundered, he could be merely providing a service to those who were.

I had only eaten half my burger when I returned to my computer and searched only the names Manuel Rodriguez and Manny Rodriguez. Most of the hits were the same newspaper articles I'd already read, but there was one new one. It was a general story about organized crime and made only one reference to Rodriguez and the cases I'd already read, but I read the whole article anyway. However, about midway through the article I came to another reference that made my heart stop. It was only one sentence and didn't provide any details, but it did identify as a suspected underworld kingpin someone I knew all too intimately: Salvatore "Sonny" Falco.

I read the whole article again, looking for anything I'd missed. I took a little solace in the fact that there were no references to any connection between Rodriguez and Falco. Did Rodriguez even know it was Falco I was hiding from? Supposedly, White hadn't told Rodriguez any of the particulars of my situation, so it was possible he didn't know. But just the thought that there might be a connection between the two scared the hell out of me.

Another half an hour of searching didn't turn up anything noteworthy, and I decided to call it a day. On the drive back to Rodriguez's home, I kept considering the possibility of a relationship between him and Falco. I had to trust White's judgment in sending me into hiding with Rodriguez, but maybe he didn't know of a connection between my pursuer and my protector. I desperately needed to talk to White.

Rodriguez was already home when I arrived. He didn't ask where I'd been, and I was glad he didn't. I was ready to tell him I'd just taken a drive to see what Tampa was like, but I suspected he was a master at seeing a lie for what it was. For a moment, I even considered the possibility that one of his people had followed me and that he knew exactly where I had been. Obviously, my paranoia was in overdrive, and I was relieved when he merely invited me to join him and his family for dinner. I didn't think I could make it through an entire meal without showing any of my concerns, so I declined as politely as I could by saying I had a splitting headache. Apparently satisfied, he started back toward what I now considered to be the main house, but then he stopped and returned his attention to me.

"I hope you feel better tomorrow. We're going to do some boating."

I said that sounded like fun, but my mind was picturing me in cement shoes. I needed to do something about my paranoia—and remember to wear a life jacket.

32.

When I stepped onto the patio of Rodriguez's mansion the next morning, I heard the muted rumble of the diesels on his yacht. It was a perfect day for a cruise: sunny with a cloudless sky and a light cooling breeze. On any other day, I would have looked forward to spending time on the water, but that wasn't what today was about.

The fact is that I didn't know the purpose of our outing. All Rodriguez had said was that we were going to discuss the plans for my immediate future. Whatever reason there could have been for not doing that at his home eluded me, but I had grown accustomed to his ways. Before I'd researched him, I would have thought his penchant for obfuscation was a sign of paranoia, but now I knew better.

Rodriguez, who was wearing white pants and a multicolor shirt with no discernable pattern, was standing at the helm of his boat. The ever-present Jake was standing on the dock beside the boat with his legs slightly spread and his arms crossed over his chest. As usual, he wore a dark suit. I wondered if he owned anything but dark suits.

When he spotted me, Rodriguez waved for me to join him, and I strolled out the pier and climbed aboard. Rodriguez nodded to Jake, who released the last of the mooring lines and followed me onto the boat. As we powered away from the pier, I asked Rodriguez where we were going. Rather than answer, he suggested that I get something to drink and enjoy the ride. I was all in favor of the first; the second was beyond the realm of possibility.

We cruised south for about an hour before turning into a channel that led to a large marina. Rodriguez guided the boat effortlessly to the visitor's dock and honked the horn twice. I had no idea where we were, but I assumed that whatever was going to happen would happen there. I was only partly right.

White and Horse emerged from the shadows by the dockside bar and came aboard. I was now more confused than ever but was happy to see familiar faces. I shook hands with White and exchanged hugs with Horse as Rodriguez advanced the throttles and we headed back to Tampa Bay. White climbed the ladder and greeted Rodriguez with an exchange of hugs while Horse guided me to a seat in the lounge area at the rear of the boat. Jake brought us two bottles of beer and returned to his position by the doors that led to the salon.

Horse got right to the point.

"We've been going over your situation and think we have a plan."

I knew the "we" included Horse and White, and I suspected that it also included Rodriguez. Though it's not uncommon for attorneys to formulate plans for the conduct of a case without involving their clients in everything, I was a little pissed that I'd been excluded. I didn't say anything, but Horse must have sensed what I was feeling.

"I'm sorry you had to be kept out of it, but some of what we were discussing involved other clients. We couldn't let you in on those discussions without breaching the attorney-client privilege. We had to protect their interests as well as yours."

I couldn't understand why my situation called for discussions with any other client, but I understood and accepted their reasoning. "Okay, so what's the plan?"

"First, let's talk about your money."

Getting at my money wasn't my biggest concern, but it ranked high enough for me to be willing to hear about their plan before getting to what concerned me most.

"How sure are you that your cabin was broken into by one of Falco's people?"

I wasn't prepared for the question and had to think about it.

Horse took a swallow from his beer and waited patiently.

"I guess I'm not sure. Nothing of value was taken, but the place was ransacked. If it was an ordinary robbery, they would have at least taken my stereo and television, but they were still there. And I had a few dollars on the dresser that were also still there."

Horse nodded. "Then your assumption about Falco makes sense."

"Why is that important?"

"If Falco knew enough to know where you are, he knows you're alive, and we can assume he also knows the name you're using."

"Yeah. Probably." I still didn't know where Horse was going, but he seemed to have a plan based on his assumption.

"Is there *any* way he could have discovered those things if he didn't have a source in the U.S. Attorney's office or the Marshals Service?"

"I don't know how," I said. "I've stayed in touch with Becky through e-mails. We both set up accounts in false names and only send mail from public places—Internet cafes and libraries."

As Horse thought about this, my anxiety grew until I couldn't hold back. "So! What's your plan?" I hated being so publicly panicked. It felt undignified. Then I remembered the particulars of my position and realized there was very little dignity left in any of this. Panic it was.

Horse took another drink. "If whoever is after you knows enough to have found your cabin, we have to assume they also know the name you're using in the Witness Protection Program. Since there's no longer any reason for trying to hide your identity, we think you should move your money to an account in your new name. We don't know if Falco has any way to know about any transactions in your old account. But just in case, the account should be somewhere that will make Falco look for you where you aren't."

"I have a small account in a bank near where I was living in Tennessee."

"Does anyone know you're no longer in Tennessee?"

"The U.S. Attorney must know. That's why she issued the material witness warrant. But she obviously doesn't know where I am now."

"Then your old account would be perfect. All we have to do is send wiring instructions to your bank in New Orleans. Lucius thought this is what we'd be doing, and he's already gotten the necessary forms." Horse pulled some papers from inside his jacket pocket and handed them to me. "Just sign these, and we'll take care of the rest."

I was signing the forms when I realized that White was standing beside me. "Are we good?" he said.

I finished signing the forms and returned them to Horse. "So, far," I said. "What happens now?"

"That's what we're here to discuss."

33.

Plans had been progressing more rapidly than I'd anticipated. White said that nothing had been decided because I had the final say, but I'm now sure he was just trying to make me feel a part of the planning process. I had no doubt that things had gone beyond the mere planning stage and that arrangements for our next steps had already been made.

I suppose I shouldn't have been surprised. When I was still practicing law, I frequently made plans for presenting a case without consulting with my clients. That's not the way it's supposed to work. Attorneys are expected to maintain regular contact with their clients, and clients are supposed to have the final say in how their representation is handled. That's all fine in theory, but that's rarely how things are done. Clients who know too much get too hung up on details. They want to know why a lawyer is doing one thing and not another, and they second-guess everything. For attorneys who bill by the hour, that's not a concern. But criminal representations are generally fixed-fee arrangements, and time spent explaining legal strategies and the nuances of legal principles doesn't add to the bottom line.

Having lawyers as clients is, as I'd learned from experience, the worst of all worlds. They think they know the law and want to know the whys and wherefores of every proposed action and they question every decision and recommendation. That's why I stopped representing other lawyers early in my career. But now I, a lawyer, albeit a disbarred one, was the client and I was inclined to exhibit all the behaviors I detested in other lawyers/clients. Notwithstanding my urges to interrupt with constant questions, I listened patiently while White explained what he intended to do. It was really quite simple, and it didn't take long to explain.

White had already contacted Barbara Blain, told her that I had retained him and arranged a meeting to discuss her demands concerning my continued participation in her case against Falco. Not surprisingly, she asserted that there was nothing to discuss; my plea agreement was clear, and she intended to enforce it to the fullest. Just for good measure, she pointed out that I would be fair game for a criminal complaint against me if I failed to comply with all the terms of the agreement. But she had, nonetheless, agreed to a meeting the following week. It looked like I was finally going back to New Orleans.

As White described the position Blain had taken, I couldn't help thinking about what she was getting herself into. White never discussed it with me, but Horse explained that White had an abiding hatred of government law enforcement agencies in general and prosecutors in particular. I don't remember all the details, but it had something to do with his father having been arrested on arguably trumped-up charges and tried and imprisoned when he wouldn't cooperate with the government's investigation. His father's death at the hands of another prisoner had set White on a path that fell only slightly short of vengeance against all prosecutors who he thought were abusing their power. In my own way, I was glad to hear that Blain was being intransigent because I knew it would bring out the best in White.

White must have realized that I had allowed my mind to wander because he was waiting silently when I returned my attention to him. "What do you intend to do if Blain sticks to her unreasonable position?" I said.

"We're ready to file a motion for a judgment determining that Blain's position is inconsistent with your obligations under the plea agreement. We're also going to move to quash her material witness warrant."

The plan sounded good on paper, but the lawyer in me wanted to know what arguments he was going to make to achieve his objective. I was about to say something when I realized that I'd be acting like that typical lawyer/client I despised. Besides, I knew there would be opportunities to discuss things like that another time. Right now, I needed to know the rest of his plan. I hated to be blunt, but there really wasn't any other way.

"What's your Plan B?"

White seemed to have expected the question. "Falco's retrial has already been docketed for two months from now. That means Blain has a limited time to get anything else from you and prepare for the trial. If we don't get the ruling we want on our motions, we'll file an immediate appeal. She'll know that an appeal won't be ruled on until after the trial, and I'm counting on her to back off on her demands. Something is better than nothing, and without your help she has nothing."

"But Falco also knows that. He knows that Blain couldn't get all her documents into evidence in his first trial. And he knows that I can solve her problem because I know where the original documents are."

"And that's what we'll offer to tell her in exchange for your not having to testify. You'll have fulfilled your obligation by telling her where the documents were the last time you saw them, but by now Falco has probably moved them somewhere else."

I shook my head. "No, he can't have moved them. Saul told me that even his clients didn't know where their files are stored."

White's eyes opened wide. "You're kidding!"

"That's what he told me."

"Why wouldn't he want his clients to know where their files were stored?"

"I can't be sure, but I think it's the other way around. I think his clients agreed that no one but Saul was supposed to know where the files were stored."

"How did you reach that conclusion?"

"I didn't work with Saul very long, so I don't know all the details, but I do know that his clients did business with each other. At least they had a financial interest in each other's businesses. He didn't have that many clients, so he must have done a fair amount of work that involved more than one client. The more I've thought about it, the more convinced I am that his clients weren't all upstanding citizens, and they probably didn't completely trust each other. The only way any of them would be safe would be if none of the others could disclose anything about their business dealings. That could only be done if none of them knew where any of the files were. That also explains why Saul didn't keep any of the files in his office, where they could be found by any tax or law enforcement authorities."

White shook his head and seemed to chuckle. "The cold war among criminals. Mutually assured destruction. They had it arranged so that if anyone tried to make a plea deal, they'd all go down."

It took a few seconds for what White had said to sink in, but when it did, I had a sudden burning in my gut.

White must have seen me grimace. "What's the problem, Masters?"

I was having trouble breathing. "What you just said," I said between gasps. "If I lead Blain to the documents, she can follow the trail to all of Saul's clients. If they think that could happen, they'd *all* want to see me dead."

34.

For most of a year, I had thought about the day I would return to New Orleans, but it had never occurred to me that it would happen like it did.

For most of the flight from Fort Myers, I was alone in the passenger cabin. White, who was doing most of the flying, came back to check on me a couple of times, but mostly I was alone and lost in my thoughts.

Horse and Rodriguez had left Florida a few days earlier and I had moved back to White's apartment. White had spent most of his time in his office preparing for what I knew was going to be a judicial challenge to the requirement of my plea agreement and, I presumed, following the progress of whatever Horse and Rodriguez were doing.

I had spent most of my first day at White's apartment alone with Leslie. Mostly we talked about her work as a social activist attorney and some of the work she'd done for White on other cases. I found her work interesting and was happy to be talking about anything but my own situation. But the day before White and I were due to fly to New Orleans, she'd left to go somewhere I wasn't told about, and my thoughts returned to my own plight.

I was still thinking about what lay ahead when I heard the sound of hydraulics and felt the thump of the landing gear of White's Lear 45, the *Legal Eagle*, being lowered and locked in place. As I tightened my seat belt, I looked out the window and watched as we closed in on Lake Pontchartrain. The plane turned to the west and began the long arc that would put it on its final, easterly approach to the Louis Armstrong New Orleans International Airport.

I don't remember what I thought about during the final minutes of the flight, and it probably isn't important. There was a strange feeling of calm though. I missed Becky and the city. I missed a life that didn't include lonesome cabins in the woods. There was a warmth here. It was good to be home, even if I was only returning to be finished off once and for all.

The next thing I remember was the jolt of the plane touching down and the screaming of the reverse thrusters as they slowed the plane and it turned and taxied toward the private aircraft terminal.

I felt my heart beat faster. It was too late to turn back. In another few days, either I would be free or I would be dead.

The *Legal Eagle* came to a stop in front of the private aircraft terminal and a black Ford Expedition pulled away from its parking spot beside the hangar and headed our way. As I watched it approach, I could see the faint shimmering of the heat waves rising from the tarmac.

The door to the flight deck opened, and White entered the cabin. I heard the captain as he congratulated White on his near-perfect landing before returning to the radio and his final communication with the control tower.

White released the latch on the cabin door. I'm sure he knew the apprehension I was feeling, and without saying anything, he signaled for me to follow him. The Expedition was waiting at the foot of the stairs as I descended and felt the blast of hot, humid air. During my year of exile in Tennessee I'd forgotten how oppressive the air in New Orleans could be.

The driver of the Expedition greeted White, and they spoke for a few minutes before I joined them. The driver was wearing a black suit, which I thought was odd considering the heat, but when his coat fluttered open I understood. He was wearing a shoulder holster containing what I immediately recognized as a .357 SIG Sauer.

Sweat was already running down my face as the driver opened the rear door of the Expedition. Without waiting for him, I hustled to the other side of the car and got in. The blast of the air conditioner was a welcome relief from the stifling heat outside, and I leaned close to the vent.

While the driver stowed our luggage in the rear of the Expedition, White entered the car, opened the manila envelope that was waiting on his seat and removed several sheets of paper that were stapled together. I was curious about their content but waited for White to finish reading them before asking about the status of our plan. I could see that they were mostly forms that had been filled in, some by hand and some with a typewriter.

As he read, White pursed his lips and nodded several times but didn't say anything. The face he made was completely opaque. Waiting was my only recourse. When he completed his perusal of the papers, he returned them to the envelope. I waited for him to speak, but he merely looked out the window while rubbing his chin.

After a minute, I couldn't contain my curiosity. "What do they say?"

White turned to me. "Huh?" he said as though my question had interrupted his thoughts.

"What do the papers say?"

He sucked on his lips and seemed to think about the question. "It's better if you don't know. At least not yet."

I was pissed and about to tell him what I thought about all the secrecy that surrounded his plans, but thought better of it. As a lawyer, I was accustomed to having to withhold certain information from my clients. Usually it was because explaining the legal basis for what I was doing would only confuse them. But I was a lawyer, at least I had been, and I was perfectly capable of understanding anything White might be planning. I concluded that whatever was in the papers White had been reviewing had something to do with what Horse and Rodriguez had been doing. That could only mean that White's reluctance to share whatever was in the papers didn't bode well for me.

The driver started out of the airport and, speaking over his shoulder, asked White where he wanted to go. White looked at me. "Where to?"

We'd already agreed that the first thing we had to do was locate Saul's storage facility and identify Falco's unit. That would give White something to bargain with when he met with Barbara Blain.

When we'd made our plan, I was certain I'd be able to find the storage facility, but now that the time had come, I wasn't so sure. I had only been there once, and that had been more than a year ago. In spite of the chill from the air conditioner, I felt beads of sweat forming on my forehead as I strained to remember how I'd gotten to Saul's warehouse.

I leaned forward and told the driver to take us to the Ochsner Medical Center, which was the nearest major landmark I could remember. Saul's facility was somewhere in that general vicinity, and I hoped I would recognize enough to get us where we needed to go.

From the airport, we took the access road to I-10 and headed east toward the Pontchartrain Causeway. The rush hour traffic was already starting to build as we passed through Kenner and entered Metairie. As usual, there was a long backup at the causeway exit, and it took us two changes of the light to get off I-10 and start heading south on Causeway Boulevard toward the Mississippi. At U.S. 90 we turned east and I started looking for anything familiar. I don't know why I bothered—I knew we'd have to go past Ochsner before I would recognize anything meaningful— but my stress level was rising and I needed to do something to occupy my mind. White seemed to understand what I was feeling and remained silent.

When we passed Ochsner, my search for anything that would remind me of the night I'd met with Saul intensified. My problem was that I'd been to the area many times when I was still living in New Orleans, and I couldn't separate what I recognized from previous visits to the area from clues to the location of Saul's storage facility. When we came to a Lowe's store, I realized we'd gone too far and told the driver to turn around. He swung through the Lowe's parking lot and got back on 90 heading west.

I was beginning to panic. Our whole plan, and maybe my life, depended on finding Saul's facility. I had been certain I could do that. How hard could it be? If I couldn't find this, then…well, I wouldn't let myself finish that thought.

White must have sensed how I was feeling and instructed the driver to pull onto a side street. When we were stopped, I realized I was hyperventilating and beginning to feel dizzy.

White reached out and gripped my forearm.

"Calm down," he said. "Take a minute to get hold of yourself."

I started to say something when he tightened his grip.

"Don't try to talk. Just relax and hold your breath."

I did as he told me, and the dizziness began to dissipate. Finally, I was able to breathe normally and I said, "I'm okay now."

He released his hold on my arm. "Are you certain?"

I nodded. "I know we're close."

"Think. How far off the highway is it?"

"I'm not sure. I don't remember passing any cross streets, but that doesn't mean there weren't any. It was night, and I was concentrating on addresses."

"Was the street perpendicular or parallel to 90?"

I closed my eyes and tried to visualize my first trip to Saul's warehouse. "Perpendicular."

Without being given any instructions, the driver pulled away from the curb and started up the street. After a hundred yards, it came to a dead end. We turned around and returned to 90, where we took a right and another right onto the next intersecting street. That also came to a dead end. After we followed the same procedure of trial and error a couple more times, I was ready to give up. Maybe if I slept on it, what I'd seen so far would remind me of something and we could try again the next day. White agreed, and we were about to head for… I didn't know where we were going next. The driver had already turned onto another street and White was about to give him new instructions when I had a hair-standing-up-on-the-back-of-my neck feeling that I'd been on that street before. We passed several storage facilities and a couple of warehouses and my sense of familiarity increased.

Then there it was.

35.

I'm not sure how I felt about locating Saul's storage facilities. Part of me was elated. Knowing its location was critical to White's plans, and now they could proceed. But we had no way of knowing if Falco had also discovered where his documents were stored and removed them.

Saul was dead, so he couldn't have told Falco. But all of Saul's client files were stored in the units at his facility, and I couldn't be certain that none of the others had discovered where it was. If they knew where Saul kept their records, they would surely have removed their own files and advised Falco to do the same. If that had happened, our whole plan would fall apart. I'd be left with nothing to give Blain, a position that had zero appeal to me.

White left me in the car while he went to the gate and studied the security system. He was only gone a few minutes, but when he returned he looked as if he was concerned about what he'd seen. I'd learned that asking him what he was thinking was a wasted effort. I knew he had his reasons for keeping me in the dark about some aspects of his plan—but it continued to frustrate me.

White leaned forward and said something to the driver, who nodded. He put the car in gear and we pulled away, heading back the way we'd come. I didn't know where we were going, but that was something I was becoming bitterly accustomed to.

As we approached I-10, I expected the driver to take the interstate toward downtown New Orleans, but instead he continued on Causeway Boulevard. In a few minutes we were over Lake Pontchartrain and heading for Mandeville.

I'd like to say I just sat back and enjoyed the ride, but that would be giving myself too much credit. The fact is, my guts were in knots. We had just achieved some critical successes, but it didn't seem to matter. The tension remained regardless of our good fortunes. Every once in a while, I glanced at White. I hoped he'd see how I was feeling and tell me what he was thinking, but he was too preoccupied to even notice.

Traffic was light, but each of the twin bridges was only one lane wide, and drivers tended to drive more cautiously over water. We made the twenty-four-mile crossing in about thirty minutes.

Mandeville, with its population of only around twelve-thousand, is mostly a commuter community with little in the way of a business district. Its major claim to fame, if you can call it that, is that it's home to the Seven Sisters Oak, which is estimated to be 1,500 years old and is the largest certified southern live oak in the country.

I quickly lost track of where we were, but the driver appeared to knew the way even without using the Expedition's navigation system. I wondered if it had been turned off so that I wouldn't know where we were. My paranoia was running rampant. I took a deep breath and let it out slowly.

Eventually, we were driving down a street that paralleled the lake. Between the houses, I could see the water and the dim lights of Metairie to the south. All the houses were large, not mansion large, but big enough that I knew we were on the better side of the tracks. Most of the homes were surrounded by iron fences with security gates.

There weren't any cars parked on the street, and I didn't see any traffic ahead of us. For some reason, I turned and looked out the rear window of the Expedition. All I saw were the headlights of a car about a half a mile behind us. Otherwise, there was nothing.

We'd driven for a mile or two when we approached a house set particularly far back from the road and surrounded by a dense growth of live oaks with a thick covering of Spanish moss. The driver pressed a button on the visor, and the gate slid open just as we arrived. Tall, manicured bushes flanked the driveway, which, after about fifty yards, widened in front of a three-car garage.

My Porsche, which Horse and Rodriguez had driven from Florida, was parked in front of one of the garage doors, and a small sedan whose license plates I recognized as those of a car rental agency sat beside it. I expected to see my Porsche but was confused by the presence of another car with a rental car agency sticker on the trunk.

As White and I slid out of the Expedition, the door to the house opened and Horse emerged. I was about to say something when he was pushed aside by a woman in tight jeans and a green halter top tied beneath her breasts.

I gasped as Becky bounded down the steps. She wrapped her arms around me and showered my face with kisses that ended with her lips planted firmly on mine. My heart beat faster as I held her tightly and we kissed and probed each other's mouths with our tongues. After what had to be at least a minute, she pulled her head away and pressed it against my shoulder. I heard her sob and felt her tears on my cheek.

I glanced toward the door and saw that Leslie had joined Horse and was smiling. Even Horse, who I'd never seen demonstrate any emotion, was grinning.

I felt White's hand on my shoulder as he pulled me

toward the house. "You two can celebrate later, but right now we need to get inside. There's no telling who may be watching us."

I glanced toward the street. Most of my view was obscured by the hedges along the driveway, but about a hundred yards away I saw the brake lights of a car as it pulled to the curb.

I turned toward White whose eyes were focused on the same car I had observed. He was frowning.

36.

Becky and I walked into the house with our arms wrapped around each other. Leslie, whose idea it had been to get Becky and have her waiting for me, was particularly pleased with herself.

Rodriguez was seated on one of the sofas when we entered. He didn't stand but tipped his raised glass in what I took to be a greeting and said something about how charming Becky was. He may have said something else, but I wasn't paying attention. I was too happy to see Becky and feel her arm around me.

After Horse and White brought our luggage in from the car, Leslie handed Horse a beer and gave White a glass of something I assumed was Diet Pepsi. He kissed her and summoned us to the seating area around Rodriguez's sofa.

Knowing that I had a lot of questions, he got right to the point. "Just so you know, this house belongs to an associate of Manny's." As happy as I was feeling, I didn't miss his use of the term 'associate' rather than 'friend.' My research into Rodriguez was incomplete, but I'd learned enough to know that he probably had many "associates" with whom he exchanged favors without questions being asked.

"Our business here shouldn't take long, but I've been assured that we should be safe for the time being." The fact that he had referred to "the time being" suggested that our long-term safety was far from certain, but for Becky's sake,

I did my best not to react, and I didn't ask any questions. My hand swallowed Becky's and squeezed gently.

White turned to Becky. He didn't exactly frown, but his expression no longer held any hint of pleasure. "I assume you know you have to stay here."

"Leslie and Mr. Rodriguez have explained all that. I've already called the gallery and told them my mother is ill and I have to be out of town for a while."

"That's good. Whatever you do, don't call anyone and don't leave the house unless one of us is with you."

Becky's grip on my hand tightened. I was certain she hadn't been told any of the details of our plans, but she's a bright woman. I'm sure she'd already concluded that whatever we were doing was going to be dangerous. I felt her shudder as she quietly said that she understood.

White continued to watch Becky until he seemed certain that she understood the gravity of the situation. Leslie must have sensed Becky's anxiety because she chose that time to announce that they'd picked up takeout dinners and it was time to eat. The two of them adjourned to the kitchen while White filled Horse and Rodriguez in on our successful search for Saul's warehouse. He had no sooner finished than Leslie reappeared to announce that dinner was ready.

I had no doubt that Becky selected the food for the evening repast. Everything—the crawfish, barbequed shrimp and gumbo—was from one of our favorite restaurants. I had forgotten how much I missed the cajun classics and attached the fare with a gusto I had not felt for more than a year.

§

While Becky and Leslie cleaned up after dinner, White,

Horse, Rodriguez and I adjourned to the study. Rodriguez opened the door to the patio, where he remained standing while he lit a cigar. I was sure White had been in contact with Horse and Rodriguez from the plane and probably knew what they'd been doing and what had, or hadn't, been accomplished and that the pending discussion was probably for my benefit.

Rodriguez began with a quick summary of what he had done before coming to New Orleans. He and Falco had never met, but they had business dealings with some of the same people. The nature of their common dealings wasn't mentioned, and I was happy about that. I already knew more than I wanted to know about both of them and was acutely aware of what could happen to people who knew too much. But just to be sure that we all knew where we stood, I clarified that Rodriguez and I were both White's clients and that Horse was present in his capacity as White's investigator. That way, attorney-client privilege covered everything that was said—even if I wasn't present.

Rodriguez told us their common business associate had arranged for him to talk with Falco. They hadn't met yet, but Rodriguez emphasized he'd made it clear that I was now under his protection. I'm certain there was more to their conversation than that, but I was relatively sure I knew what being under Rodriguez's protection was intended to mean. Again, I was making some assumptions, but I think we all knew that being too explicit wasn't in anyone's best interest.

According to Rodriguez, Falco wanted to know where I was and what my intentions were, but Rodriguez had only said he would disclose more of what he knew when they met after he'd talked with me. He said the subject of the break-in at my cabin hadn't been addressed, but it had been agreed that my safety was assured until after they'd met in person. Just when that would happen was anyone's guess, but we all knew that events would be happening fast.

We'd been talking for about an hour when Leslie interrupted and suggested that we call it a night and pick up our conversation in the morning. She was quite insistent in pointing out that Becky and I probably had some catching up to do. She was right, and I was grateful for her suggestion.

After adjourning to our designated bedroom, we had so much to tell each other that neither of us knew where to begin, but we both knew that it would have to wait. We tore each other's clothes off and crawled naked into bed, where we, as Leslie had so politely put it, got "caught up" repeatedly before we eventually dozed off in each other's arms.

37.

Even by New Orleans standards, it was an oppressively muggy day, and most of the men entering the federal courthouse carried their coats slung over their shoulders. Fortunately, the trees that filled the sidewalk courtyard in front of the modern gray building afforded me some relief from the heat. It probably wasn't a good idea for me to be there. Scratch that. It *certainly* wasn't a good idea for me to be there. There was a warrant out for my arrest and I was taking a big chance coming to where someone in authority might recognize me. Both White and Becky had urged me to stay behind in Mandeville, but my whole future was at stake and there was no way I was going to miss this hearing.

White arrived about a half an hour before the scheduled five o'clock hearing and moved quickly from the coolness of the Expedition to the courthouse without acknowledging my presence. Regardless of how much he wished I hadn't insisted on being there, it was too late to do anything about it. Any further discussion we might have in public would only draw attention to me, and that was the last thing either of us wanted.

I waited until a few minutes before the hearing was scheduled to begin before I entered the courthouse. I handed the guards my old driver's license and bar card and prayed that they hadn't been alerted to the material witness warrant that was out for me. There were few others entering the courthouse at what was normally the end of the judicial day, and I passed quickly through the metal detector and headed for the elevator and the courtroom where my hearing was to be held.

My pleadings had, as expected, been put on the motion calendar, which is always crowded and rarely concludes on time. Inside the courtroom, White was seated alone in the gallery, and, as I had hoped, Barbara Blain was at the prosecutor's table arguing another motion. I had counted on that and felt a sense of relief on discovering that I was right. The last thing I needed was for her to recognize me, although I was fairly sure my loss of seventy-five pounds and my new long hair, ponytail, and mustache would be enough to keep her from recognizing me as I slipped into the room and took a seat in the last row. My palms sweat aggressively. Having Blain occupied with other cases was a definite plus.

As I took my seat, a defense attorney was in the middle of his argument for the suppression of evidence of the possession of cocaine. My mind flashed to the first time I had represented Louis LeBlanc, and I listened intently to the arguments being put forth. I hadn't heard the whole argument, but what I did hear seemed to make a compelling case for suppression.

When Blain rose to present the government's argument, she gave every impression that she was having a bad day. Her movements were slow and labored. Of course, it had been almost a year since our last interview, and maybe my memory was playing tricks on me. I wasn't particularly impressed by her argument, and apparently the judge wasn't either. When he announced his decision to suppress the evidence, I saw her shoulders sag. The other person at the prosecution table put a hand on her arm in what I interpreted to be an act of consolation. Blain hung her head before reaching for a copy of what I recognized as the afternoon docket sheet. My case was the last hearing scheduled for the day, and the deep breath she took made me think she was glad her day was about to be over.

White moved from the gallery to the defense table to the left of the podium as the clerk called the next case. "*John Doe v. The United States*. Emergency motion for declaratory judgment regarding the terms of a plea agreement and motion to quash material witness warrant."

In spite of the fact that it was the end of what had been a grueling day—motion days always are—I think I detected a hint of pleasant expectation on the judge's face. He had to know that something unusual was coming. Emergency motions are themselves rare, and issues involving plea bargains are even rarer.

The judge leaned forward and pulled his microphone closer. "Please enter your appearances."

Blain stood slowly as if the action required substantial effort. "Barbara Blain, the office of the U.S. attorney, for the United States." Her voice was flat, almost bored. I wondered how many times she'd said those words over the years. Certainly hundreds, probably thousands.

The judge turned to White.

"May it please the court," he began with the time-honored statement drilled into the head of every first-year law student, "Lucius White, counsel for the movant."

The judge gave a hint of a smile. He probably hadn't heard the formal introduction by an attorney in many years. I'd always used it, and I was secretly pleased that White had followed the tradition that most attorneys had abandoned.

"All right, Mr. White, suppose you begin by telling me why you filed an emergency motion."

White spent the next ten minutes providing the judge

with a history of the circumstances surrounding the nego-
tiation of my plea agreement; the charges asserted and facts
adduced in Falco's earlier trial; the demands for additional
assistance that Blain was now making; and the contention
that requiring more of me would place my life in danger.

Blain started to stand to rebut what White had said,
but the judge waved her to her seat and continued to
address White. "What makes you think his life would be in
any greater danger if he complied with the U.S. attorney's
request?"

I was heartened to hear the judge acknowledge that I
had put my life in danger as a result of my initial plea agreement.

The judge leaned even closer to his microphone. Or
maybe he was just moving closer to White. "Isn't the
movant in witness protection?"

Blain bolted to her feet and glared at White before
addressing the judge. "That's just the point, your honor.
The movant *is* in the Witness Protection Program, and his
identity and location are secret. And furthermore—"

The judge raised a hand, and Blain stopped speaking.

The judge lowered his head and let his glasses slide
down to the end of his nose. He looked at White over the
rim of his glasses and let his eyes ask the next question for
him.

White wasted no time in responding. "What counsel
says is what was agreed to and was initially true. But my
client believes that his identity and location have been
compromised. Furthermore, my client's contention is that
he has fully complied with the terms of his plea agreement,
and as a matter of simple contract law, he is not obligated
to provide the government with any information he has
not already disclosed."

The judge inhaled and sighed. "Have you tried to work this out between yourselves?"

"Yes, your honor," White said. "We met yesterday, but we were unable to reach a mutually satisfactory compromise."

The judge put his hand over his microphone and wiggled a finger at his clerk. The clerk hustled to the judge's side and they exchanged a few words before the clerk withdrew and left the courtroom.

"Mr. White, I understand you have filed a memorandum of law in support of your emergency motion."

"That's correct, Your Honor. But we believe an evidentiary hearing is necessary for you to fully understand the basis for my client's motion."

The judge's eyebrows both rose. "What evidence do you intend to introduce?"

"I intend to examine the U.S. Attorney, Barbara Blain."

38.

The judge's head snapped toward Blain as she leaped to her feet. "Your honor, I object to being called as a witness in this matter. My testimony cannot have any possible relevance to what Mr. White has alleged in his pleadings. Besides, I was only served with a subpoena this morning, and there hasn't been enough time to prepare anyone in my office to act as my counsel if I am to be examined as a witness."

"Do you intend to file a motion to quash the subpoena?" he asked. If Blain's words had impacted him, he certainly didn't show it.

"I do, Your Honor."

The judge rubbed his chin and frowned. "Mr. White, why is Ms. Blain required as a witness?"

"The motion at issue is a motion for a judicial determination of my client's obligations under his plea agreement. In particular, there are several conditions of the agreement that are unquestionably ambiguous and require a determination of the intent of the parties. Ms. Blain negotiated the agreement with my client and is the only person who can offer evidence of her intent."

"What about your client? Do you intend to examine him regarding *his* understanding of the terms of the agreement?"

"No, your honor. We don't believe his testimony is necessary. The government is arguing for an expansive interpretation of the terms of the agreement, so it is up to them to justify their position."

The judge took off his glasses and bit on one of the earpieces. After half a minute of silence, every excruciating second of which I believed he would trash White's argument, he turned to Blain. "I'm going to treat your representation as an oral motion to quash the subpoena and deny the motion. I believe that your testimony is both relevant and necessary. On the other hand, you *are* entitled to be represented by counsel, so I am going to continue this hearing until…" The judge paused and looked in the direction of his courtroom deputy. She opened what appeared to be the judicial hearing calendar and laid it in front of the judge. He put his hand over his microphone and exchanged words with the deputy. Finally, the judge said, "two o'clock tomorrow afternoon."

"Judge," Blain said, a plaintive tone in her voice, "I don't think we have any attorneys available to prepare for an examination on such short notice."

"I can't do anything about that. Mr. White has told me enough to convince me that there is a need for this matter to be considered on an emergency basis. I'm not willing to delay any longer than absolutely necessary."

"In that case, your honor, the government demands that the movant be made available for examination."

"Mr. White?"

"Your honor, we're prepared to accept the court's ruling based on evidence adduced from Ms. Blain alone. Besides, Ms. Blain has issued a material witness warrant for my client's arrest, and he fears for his life if he is incarcerated. The validity of that warrant is the subject of a motion to quash that must also be heard."

The color in Blain's face moved into the crimson tones.

"If Mr. White knows where his client is, he is obligated, as an officer of the court, to disclose that information. Until the court rules otherwise, the warrant must be deemed valid on its face, and he must disclose what he knows about his client's whereabouts."

My whole body stiffened. I was tempted to try to slip out of the courtroom. That way, White could at least say he didn't know my *exact* whereabouts, but I was afraid that any movement would draw Blain's attention. I prayed that White had a plan for dealing with what he had to know would happen if Blain made my testimony an issue.

"Mr. White, do you know where your client is?"

"I am assured that my client is safe from harm where he is, and I will see to it that he turns himself in if the court denies the motion to quash."

It wasn't really an answer to the judge's question, but it also wasn't exactly a lie. I suppose it might be called a lie of omission, but I didn't have time to consider the issue. We hadn't discussed anything about turning myself in if we lost on our motion to quash, and now White had promised that I would do just that.

Two feelings of equal intensity arose in me. I was livid that the stakes had just been raised without my consent or input. In jail I would be as good as dead, and now that was exactly where I could end up. On the other hand, I feared that so much as whisper would give me away. To find me, all Blain would have to do is turn around and look. I held my breath and tried hard to turn invisible.

The next several minutes of arguments are a blur. I was terrified that the judge would see through White's response and did my best not to make any movement that would draw his attention. As I sat there, I realized I was the only person in the gallery and feared that the judge would call attention to me by asking me what I was doing there. Fortunately, the judge was fully engaged in the arguments being made and didn't give any indication that he even noticed me.

The last words I remember hearing were, "We're adjourned."

I quickly stood and left the courtroom while Blain was gathering her papers. I wanted to run from the courthouse but knew that would have drawn too much attention in what was now a virtually empty building. My chest was pounding, and I did everything I could to remain calm as I passed the security guards at the door. They bade me a polite, "Good evening." I nodded but couldn't bring myself to say anything.

I was still trying to decide what to do next when I spotted the black Expedition waiting across the street. The driver must have realized that something was wrong and called to me. He opened the rear door open as I darted crossed the street. I ducked inside and huddled down on the backseat.

After several minutes, the driver opened the door again and White climbed in. He didn't say anything as we pulled into the remnants of rush hour traffic on Poydras and headed for I-10.

"I didn't have a choice," White said when we merged into I-10.

I knew what he meant. His promise that I would be present for the next day's hearing had been unavoidable, but it was my own damned fault. If I hadn't insisted on being in court, he wouldn't have had to be so circumspect in responding to Blain's arguments. Once again, I knew that the mess I was in was of my own making. It was like a sickness or a tic. I put my head in my hands and closed my eyes.

We didn't speak again for the rest of the drive to our Mandeville home away from home. It was just as well. I knew White was already planning how to handle the matters that needed to be addressed at the hearing the next day and didn't want to interrupt his thoughts. Besides, I was already thinking about what I would say to Becky about my potential incarceration.

39.

When we arrived at the house in Mandeville, White went directly to the study, followed by Horse and Rodriguez. I wasn't invited, nor did I want to be. I felt bad enough about my own stupidity and didn't want to relive it with the others.

Becky and Leslie were sitting on the patio and chatting like old friends when I came out. Becky stood and ran to me. "How did it go?"

I tried to force a smile but must not have been very successful.

"That bad?"

"Not really. The judge didn't rule on anything. We have another hearing tomorrow afternoon."

"But?"

She had a sour look. We had been together for so long that she could sense my every mood. I took her hand and led her inside. Leslie must have sensed that we needed privacy and headed for the study.

Becky and I sat on the sofa. She had her legs curled up under her and her lips quivered and tears formed in the corner of her eyes as I told her about the hearing.

"Does this mean you'll be going to jail?"

"It's possible, but I don't think so. White has some good arguments, and I think the judge will quash the material witness warrant." I wished I felt as confident as my words.

Becky relaxed and leaned against me. "Leslie is really nice."

The sudden change of topics caught me by surprise, and it took a moment for me to process what she'd said.

"Yes, she is." I put an arm around her and held her against me.

"It was her idea to come and get me," Becky said. "I'm glad she did. You shouldn't have to go through this alone."

I was already thinking about how I would tell Becky about what could happen if things didn't go our way, but all I could say was, "I'm glad she did, too."

We held each other in silence until I mustered the courage to broach the subject of our future. "How would you feel about leaving New Orleans?"

Becky moved away and looked at me.

During my exile in Tennessee I had hinted at the possibility of relocating somewhere together. Now that we were nearing the end of the ordeal, the question was looming large in my thoughts.

Becky only hesitated for a moment. "If that's what it takes, I'll do whatever's necessary to be with you."

My heart skipped a beat. "Are you sure? I mean *really* sure?"

She leaned over and kissed me. "Do you really have to ask?"

Our conversation was interrupted when our driver opened the front door and entered carrying packages that immediately filled the room with delicious aromas. I suddenly realized that I hadn't eaten all day and was famished.

"It's time to take a break," Leslie called from the study. "You can finish your work after dinner."

"We'll be there in a minute," White said.

"Now!" Leslie said insistently. "You had a busy day, and you need some nourishment."

Becky went to help Leslie set the table as White, Horse, and Rodriguez came out of the study. White was continuing his discussion with Rodriguez as Horse came and sat beside me. "How are you feeling?"

"Compared to what?" I said. Even I heard the frustration in my voice.

"Things could be worse."

I didn't see how, but I muttered some sort of thanks for the encouragement.

"If it makes you feel any better, Lucius is still optimistic about your hearing tomorrow."

"Did he say anything about me?"

Horse looked at the floor for a moment before returning his attention to me. "Everything is about you."

I knew he understood what my question meant, but I was grateful for his evasive response.

"You have to understand. Lucius is a 'what's done is done' kind of guy. Today is done, and we only talked about what has to be done tomorrow."

I wasn't sure whether he was merely trying to make me feel better or build my confidence in White. I just knew that I had to stop feeling sorry for myself and do what I could, whatever that was, to help White prepare for the upcoming hearing. My whole future depended on it.

§

We all adjourned to the dining room where we feasted on the best barbeque ribs I had ever had. Leslie had made it clear that there was to be no discussion of my case at dinner, and that was fine with me.

Mostly, the meal was spent with Leslie and Becky talking about their day. I was relieved by the respite from any talk about my case and was soon engrossed in their discussion. For two women who didn't appear to have anything in common, they had obviously found something to bond over. I was reminded of better times when Becky and I had spent our evenings just talking about our days and thinking about what our future life together might be like.

After dinner, Rodriquez excused himself, saying he had some business to attend to, but I suspected it was just an excuse to let White, Horse and me meet alone.

The three of us went to the study and White closed the door before taking his seat at the owner's desk. Horse and I sat on the sofa and waited while White paged through a legal pad filled with notes. I still didn't know what was expected of me, but I finally felt relaxed and ready to do whatever White asked.

Finally, he took a copy of my plea agreement from a file and began asking me questions about my negotiations and what Blain had asked me after it had been signed. I answered his questions as completely as I could but was surprised at how little I could recall with the specificity that I knew he wanted. The only things I had a clear recollection of were the changes I'd made to the draft agreement and my near-shock that Blain had agreed to them.

I remembered, as clearly as if it had happened only yesterday, how we had dissected the provisions of my agreement. Blain was a criminal lawyer, and the only thing she cared about was the provisions of the agreement that related to the information I could provide to help her make her case. But I had retained enough of my wits to think of my plea agreement as a contract. In that regard, I had an advantage. She tried cases, and I knew she was good at it. She was so good, in fact, that the possibility that a mistrial might occur and that she might need more from me if that happened had apparently never occurred to her. I can't say I'd anticipated what would eventually happen, but I knew more about contract law than she did. Now, as White continued to question me, I could see where he was going. Maybe, just maybe, what I had done was going to save me.

40.

I didn't sleep well the night before my hearing. The evening meeting with White and Horse had given me an increased sense of confidence in our chances, but I was biased. Maybe I had only heard what I wanted to hear.

I was still thinking about the upcoming hearing when I crawled into bed, desperate for the sleep that I feared wouldn't come. Becky snuggled next to me and tried to comfort me with words of optimism, but it didn't help. Finally, I turned on the bedside lamp and leaned against the headboard. Becky rolled onto her stomach and propped herself up on her elbows, waiting for me to say something. I didn't know what to say.

After a few minutes of silence, she started to talk about what would happen after we won the hearing, and I was temporarily buoyed by her optimism. She came to me and laid her head on my stomach. I think we talked about the future we hoped to have together, but I don't really remember. At some point, she fell asleep curled around me. I couldn't help wondering if this was the last time we would sleep together. The thought that it could be our last night together wore heavily on me and I couldn't get to sleep.

Night was beginning to surrender to dawn when I slipped out of bed and stumbled into the bathroom. I turned on the light, closed the door, and grabbed my robe. I steadied myself against the sink and studied my face in the mirror. I looked as bad as I felt. My eyes were bloodshot and there were dark circles under them. I splashed some cold water on my face and reached for a packet of Alka-Seltzer. Even the bubbles emitting noise from the dissolving tablets made my head hurt.

I needed something to eat and headed for the kitchen. As I crossed the living room, I noticed that the door to the study was closed, but the light was on. I went to see who else was up, or still up.

Horse opened the door when I knocked. He held the tip of one finger to his lips then, with a flip of his hand, signaled for me to enter.

White was sitting on the edge of the desk with his cell phone to his ear. I couldn't imagine who he could be talking to at this hour. Even considering that we were in the central time zone, it was still before seven on the East Coast. Whoever he was talking to was either an early riser or a damned good friend.

I joined Horse on the sofa and tried to make sense of the one side of the conversation I could hear.

"Yes, it's that important!… I know you don't have any authority over it, but you're Horse's only hope… I don't know what I expect to find… I'm sure you will. Call Horse as soon as you have anything… No, I'll be in court…. Okay. And thanks, Graham."

White put down his phone and, ignoring my presence, looked at Horse. "Graham is going to see what he can do about getting you access to the rest of the file on Saul Weinberg."

Horse responded with a muted nod. "You know that I don't even know what I'm looking for."

White shrugged. "I don't either. I'm not even sure there's a connection. But we have to look into everything."

Horse sighed and stifled a yawn. "We've done more with less. Your hunches are usually pretty good."

As I listened to them, I realized they were both wearing the same clothes they'd been wearing the evening before. They'd obviously been up all night. I knew that whatever they'd been talking about was probably none of my business, but I was desperate for anything to take my mind off the upcoming hearing. "What file are you talking about?"

Horse and White exchanged looks in the kind of silent communication that can only take place between people who have the kind of history that Horse and White shared. Their silence was deafening.

"Will someone please tell me what's going on?"

White made a sound that I can only describe as a half sigh and nodded.

Horse turned to me. "I'm looking into Saul Weinberg's death?"

"Saul? Why?"

Horse hesitated before looking toward White. "We might as well tell him."

White hesitated before speaking. "That was Graham Brochette I was just talking to."

It took me a minute to recognize the name. "Isn't he the guy at the Department of Justice who wouldn't let you send me to your ranch for my protection?"

"That's right."

"What does he have to do with my situation?"

White hesitated for a long moment before continuing. "There's a federal task force looking into organized crime in the Southeast. Sonny Falco and his organization are of particular interest to him."

"What does that have to do with me?"

"The operation is being run out of Washington. The local U.S. Attorney's office doesn't know anything about it. That's why he couldn't tell Blain that he might have an interest in what you could tell him about what you and Saul Weinberg had been doing for Falco."

"I still don't understand what that has to do with me."

"He may want you as a witness."

"*Oh shit*! Agreeing to tell the feds about Falco it what got me into this mess."

"Don't worry. I've already negotiated an agreement on your behalf. You have absolute immunity for anything you may have done. I saw to that."

"That's what Blain promised me, and look where it got me!"

"But you said it yourself. Blain didn't know how to negotiate a plea agreement as a contract, but I do. Besides, I know I can trust Graham."

My head was spinning and my guts were rumbling. "Then why are we fighting my agreement with Blain?"

"The agreement I negotiated with Graham has a few contingencies. His hands are tied by DOJ policy. Your new agreement doesn't take effect as long as your agreement with Blain is in force *and* you've been interviewed by his task force."

"So, I could win in the challenge to Blain's agreement and still be subject to prosecution by the new task force. And either way I still have to worry about Sonny Falco coming after me. Any way you look at it, I'm screwed."

41.

We arrived at the federal courthouse an hour before our scheduled hearing. Horse and White went inside while I stayed with our driver as we headed for a parking lot up the street. I wasn't about to set foot in the courthouse until I was assured that I wouldn't be taken into custody immediately. That was the reason for our early arrival. White needed to meet with Blain to ensure that I would remain free until the judge had ruled on our motions.

Fifteen minutes later, the driver's cell phone rang. He spoke for only a few seconds before turning to me. "You're good. Horse is waiting in front of the courthouse."

Two minutes later, I entered the courthouse with Horse at my side. I was already sweating profusely, and not just because of the heat.

Outside the courtroom, White was talking with Barbara Blain. As we approached, she turned toward us. I watched as her eyes grew wide and her face began to turn red. It was obvious that she recognized me as the lone occupant of the gallery at the end of the previous day's hearing. It didn't take a mind reader to know what she was thinking. I gave her my best taunting smile and entered the courtroom, but not before hearing the start of her next utterance to White. "You son of…"

§

White and Horse joined me in the back row of the gallery.

Blain continued to glare at me as she walked to the prosecutor's table in the well of the courtroom. After taking her seat, she said something to one of the men sitting at the table and I saw him stiffen as he turned toward us.

We sat quietly watching the proceedings as final arguments were made in the case that preceded us. The judge took the case under advisement and promised a ruling by the end of the following day. When my case was called, White stood and walked confidently to the defense table.

White and Blain entered their appearances, and the man Blain had spoken to at the prosecutor's table entered a special appearance as Blain's attorney. The judge seemed to be oblivious to the statements by the attorneys as he accepted a file offered by his clerk. He studied the file for a moment before speaking. "I've read the motions filed by the parties, and unless someone has anything to add, I'm ready to proceed."

The new man at the prosecutor's table stood. "Your honor, the government reiterates its objection to this hearing. As the court has noted, the issues have been fully briefed and the government contends that there is nothing relevant to be gained by taking any further evidence. The movant's plea agreement is unambiguous. It is valid and binding, and nothing that the movant can offer through an examination of my client can change these facts. We ask that the court find that the movant is obligated to continue to assist the government and order him to surrender himself immediately."

"Is the movant here today?"

White stood and addressed the judge. "As I promised you yesterday, he is present and prepared to fully comply with the ruling of the court."

"What do you have to say about the government's contention?"

"Obviously, we disagree. We don't believe the court can make an informed ruling without hearing evidence. The Fifth Circuit has recently reversed a decision by this court in a case that is factually indistinguishable from the matter now before you."

White handed the bailiff copies of the decision to which he was referring, and the bailiff distributed the copies to the opposing attorneys and the judge. The judge lowered his glasses and read the opinion. "This opinion is on point," he said. "The government's request is denied." As he spoke, he rotated his chair to face White. "Call your first witness."

"The movant calls Barbara Blain."

Blain went to the witness stand and was sworn in. Without being asked, she stated her name and position as White took his place behind the podium in the middle of the room in front of the judge. He removed a copy of the plea agreement and gave it to the bailiff for distribution to the judge, opposing counsel, and Blain.

"Please identify the document you have just been handed."

"It's a copy of the binding agreement signed by your client and me."

White faced the judge. "Your honor, I request that the word *binding* be stricken from the witness's answer. It's a conclusion of law, and that's what we're here to determine."

"Granted," the judge said without waiting to hear any argument from Blain's attorney and turned his attention to the witness. "You know better than that, Ms. Blain. Please limit your answers to the facts."

White requested that the document be entered into evidence. There was no objection from the government's attorney and the document was accepted.

"Ms. Blain," White continued, "in the second line of the third paragraph there is a highlighted passage."

"I see it."

"Please read it aloud."

Blain's attorney jumped to his feet. "Objection. The document speaks for itself. There is no need to have any portion of it separately read into the record."

The argument made in support of the objection was technically correct, but White was ready for it. "Your honor, I simply want the record to properly identify the portion of the document I will be examining the witness about."

The judge studied the document for a moment before announcing, "I don't see how the government can be prejudiced by having a portion of the document read into the record. The objection is overruled."

"Ms. Blain—," White said.

Blain put on her glasses and reviewed the document. "The highlighted section says, 'The witness will provide the government with all assistance necessary to prepare for the trial of Salvador 'Sonny' Falco et. al.'"

"And 'the witness' referred to in this passage is my client. Is that correct?"

"Yes."

White stepped to the side and rested his arm on the podium. "And has the government tried Mr. Falco?"

"You know that it has, and it ended in a mistrial."

"Do you intend to try Mr. Falco a *second* time?"

"Yes. The trial is docketed for two months from now."

A woman who I assumed was the judge's secretary entered the courtroom and climbed the steps to the judge's bench. He turned toward the woman and bent over as she whispered something into his ear.

White ignored the action and continued his examination. "My client's agreement calls for his assistance in the government's preparation for '*the* trial.' Where does it require him to assist in your preparation for *more* than *one* trial?"

Before Blain could answer, the judge said. "I'm sorry, but a matter has come up that requires my immediate attention. We need to take a short recess."

42.

Fifteen long minutes later the judge returned to the bench and instructed the court reporter to read White's last question.

Blain's attorney was immediately on his feet with another objection. "Your honor, the question can't have any possible relevance. It's clear that the intent of the plea agreement was that the movant would provide all assistance to the government's efforts to try Mr. Falco. The relevant issue is the *subject* of the prosecution to be assisted, *not* the number of actual trials involved."

The judge swiveled to face White. "Counselor. Any rebuttal?"

"Yes, your honor. A plea agreement is a contract, and it is black letter law that an unambiguous term in a contract is not subject to alteration based on any evidence of the intent of the parties. It is also relevant that the Fifth Circuit has expressly held that the terms of a plea agreement must be narrowly construed."

As he spoke, White opened another file and handed copies of the relevant Fifth Circuit opinion to the bailiff for distribution to the judge and opposing counsel. The judge spent a minute reviewing the ruling White was relying on before announcing, "I'm going to take the matter under advisement. For now, the objection is overruled. You may continue, Mr. White."

White returned his attention to Blain. "Would you like the question to be reread?"

"No. I understand the question, and I agree with my attorney that the agreement was intended to cover all trials of Mr. Falco."

I couldn't see White's face, so I don't know how he responded to the answer. Whatever he was considering during the minute of silence that followed Blain's response, his next question represented a sudden change in direction.

"In Mr. Falco's first trial, were all the documents you offered admitted into evidence?"

Blain fidgeted with her hands as she changed her position in the witness chair. "No. Some documents were excluded."

"Why weren't they admitted?"

Blain adjusted her position again. "Because they couldn't be properly authenticated by my witnesses."

"Had you previously reviewed the excluded documents with my client?"

"Yes," Blain said very softly.

"You need to speak up so that the court reporter can hear your answer."

I had heard her original answer, and I'm sure the court reporter had also heard it. I assumed White was only asking her to repeat her answer for the sake of emphasis. *Come on,* I thought. *Twist that knife.*

Blain cleared her throat. "Yes."

"And what had my client said about the documents?"

"He said that they were copies of documents he had seen."

"Did you ask him if he had ever seen the original documents from which the copies had been made?"

"Yes. And he said that he had."

"Then why didn't you call him to authenticate the copies?"

"If you read the plea agreement, you'll see that he was only required to testify if his testimony was *necessary*."

White thumbed through his copy of the plea agreement. "That would be in accordance with the highlighted provision in paragraph five, right?"

Blain, the judge, and opposing counsel all examined their copies of the agreement.

"Yes," Blain finally said.

"Why was this provision included in the plea agreement?"

"I don't remember. I think it was a provision your client wanted."

"But you agreed to it, didn't you?"

Blain again shifted in her chair. "Yes."

"Who made the decision that my client's testimony regarding the documents was not necessary?"

"I had other witnesses who had seen copies of the documents."

"That doesn't answer my question. I asked, 'Who made the decision that my client's testimony regarding the documents was not necessary?'"

"There were several of us working on the case."

White looked toward the judge. "Your honor, I ask that the witness be instructed to give a straight answer to the question I asked."

The judge glowered at Blain. My heart soared. "You know the rules, Ms. Blain. Answer the question that Mr. White asked."

Blain hesitated, taking a moment to study the floor, before responding. "I suppose that I made the final decision."

When he next spoke, White's voice was loud and accusatory. "So, you had a chance to call my client as a witness, and you chose not to!"

It wasn't a proper question and could have been objected to, but opposing counsel didn't say anything. White had seized control of the room. My palms sweat, but I was starting to believe.

Blain was clearly flustered and her face drifted toward the color of smoked ham. "I suppose that's correct."

White slapped his hand on the podium and boomed, "And isn't it true that you now want my client to testify at Mr. Falco's next trial to make up for a tactical mistake *you* made?"

"Objection," Blain's attorney shouted. "Mr. White is badgering the witness."

The objection was sustained, but I could see from the judge's expression that White had made his point.

"Was the lack of proper authentication the only reason your documents were not admitted at Mr. Falco's first trial?"

"No. Some were excluded because we couldn't produce any of the original documents."

"What did you do to try to obtain them?"

Blain hesitated before reluctantly responding. "There wasn't anything we could do. Your client said he didn't know where they were."

"Did you believe him?"

"Yes."

"Has anything changed to make you think he now knows where the original documents are?"

"Not that I know of."

"So as far as you know, nothing has changed that will enable you to overcome the objection that kept the documents out of evidence in the first trial. Is that right?"

"We'll have a different judge."

I watched as the judge's face grew taut. Even I knew that judges bristle at the suggestion that another judge might admit evidence that had been excluded by the judge at Falco's first trial.

White had apparently seen what I saw and decided to end his examination on that note.

"I have no further questions for the witness."

The judge asked Blain's attorney if he had any questions for the witness. He asserted that White's examination had not elicited anything that was not addressed in the government's pleadings and that a cross-examination would not be of any benefit to the court.

The judge shuffled through some papers on his desk. "Am I correct in understanding that a ruling on the motion to quash the material witness warrant will be determined by my ruling on the interpretation of the plea agreement?"

White and Blain agreed that it would be.

"Then unless anyone wants to add anything that hasn't been covered in their pleadings…" The judge paused and waited for anyone to speak. No one did.

"Then we're adjourned. I'll have a ruling by the first thing in the morning."

43.

As we prepared to leave the courtroom, I realized that Horse was no longer there. I assumed he had simply gone to call our driver, but when we left the courthouse, only the car was waiting. I looked around and didn't see any sign of Horse. White must have sensed my concern and said that Horse had gone to the police station and we were going to pick him up on our way home.

Horse was waiting by the curb when we reached the station. He had a thick file under his arm and a concerned look on his face. He got into the car without saying anything, and we headed for I-10 and home.

"Did you have any trouble getting the file?" White asked.

"Graham's call must have gotten someone's attention. The detective in charge of the case wasn't happy about giving it to me, but I got it."

"And?"

"They don't have much in the way of evidence. No fingerprints from the crime scene and no witnesses remembered seeing anyone near Weinberg's office the evening he was killed."

The mention of Saul Weinberg's name took my attention away from ruminations about the hearing, and I started paying more attention to the conversation between White and Horse.

"Anything on the ballistics?"

"Maybe. The report links the murder weapon to some other unsolved murders in other parts of the state. They've concluded that it was probably a professional hit, but they can't connect Weinberg and the other victims. All of them were two-bit criminals, and everything they have on Weinberg says he was an upstanding citizen."

"Do they have *any* leads?"

"They don't seem to. As far as they're concerned, it's a cold case. There aren't any entries in the file since a month after the murder."

"I'm not surprised. What about the other murders with the same gun? Did the police in those jurisdictions find anything useful?"

"Apparently not. The police in Shreveport managed to get a partial print from the crime scene, but not enough to prove anything. They had a guy they were looking at, but he had an alibi. It was a little shaky, but they couldn't break it."

"What do you have on their suspect?"

"Just a name. A guy named…" Horse rummaged through his files. I knew what he was going to say before he opened his mouth. "LaForrette, André LaForrette."

My whole body stiffened.

White must have seen my reaction. "What is it? Does that name mean something to you?"

"I…." I couldn't get the words out. I took a couple of deep breaths and tried to relax. "I almost represented him before I got disbarred. He works for Sonny Falco."

White didn't show any reaction to my announcement. It was as if he already knew there was a link between Falco and Weinberg's murder. I didn't know how it was possible for him to have made a connection, but he must have. Why else would he have had Horse investigating Saul's murder?

We drove on in silence. I knew that White and Horse

wanted me to tell them what I knew about LaForrette, but I wasn't ready to talk about it. I tried to remember if there was anything that I could tell them, but it was a long time ago, and my discussion with LaForrette had been exceedingly brief.

I also thought about whether I could even tell them what little I knew about him. I had never actually been LaForrette's attorney, but just having discussed the possibility of representing him may have made our conversation subject to the attorney-client privilege. I almost laughed when I realized what I was thinking. I'd spilled my guts about Falco, who had clearly been my client when I made my bargain with Blain, yet here I was thinking about my duty to withhold whatever I had learned from someone I never officially represented.

My thoughts moved on to the discussion about LaForrette that I had with LeBlanc after I'd first met with LaForrette. My memory of that talk was as vivid as if it had happened only a day ago. I distinctly remember what LeBlanc had said. "He does some work for us from time to time. He straightens out problems. Occasionally he finds missing people." I even remembered what I'd thought about LeBlanc's statements. My testimony could be damning if Falco was ever charged as an accomplice to Weinberg's murder. That was just another reason why Falco would want me dead.

My head was just beginning to clear when I realized we were nearing the exit for the causeway and White was shaking my arm.

"What do you know about the people Falco was in business with?"

"Like what?" I'm not so dense that I didn't know what White was talking about. I just hadn't decided what, and how much, I could tell him. I know it was a strange time for me to start thinking about my duty to keep client information secret, but Falco's business dealings weren't relevant to my present predicament.

"Do you know who he was in business with?"

"Not really. I know his records identify the other owners in the businesses he has an interest in. I don't remember any of their names, but they're all identified in the records at Saul's warehouse."

"Were his partners also clients of Saul Weinberg?"

"I think most of them were, but I'm not positive. I only remember Saul telling me that all his clients did business together."

"Tell us what you know about Weinberg's business."

"I don't know much. I only worked with him for a few days, and we only talked about things that were relevant to the reorganization we were planning for Falco."

"But didn't you say he kept all his client files at his storage facility?"

"That's what he told me. And he said the records for each client were kept in a separate unit."

"Did Falco's files fill his storage unit?"

"No. It wasn't more than half full. Probably not even that."

"Then there was plenty of space to store more files in Falco's unit?"

"I suppose."

"As far as you know, did Weinberg's clients ever go to the storage facility with him?"

"No. We've already talked about this. Saul said that none of his clients even knew where the facility was." I was beginning to see where White was going. "You're thinking that the files were kept separate so that a warrant order authorizing the search of any one client's unit wouldn't reveal anything about the others?"

"Exactly."

I don't remember anything else about the drive back to Mandeville. White and Horse were chatting about things that didn't concern me. I had a dozen questions about the hearing we had just left, but I couldn't bring myself to ask them. I don't think I wanted to know the answers.

Traffic was unusually heavy, and our driver was concentrating on the road. White and Horse were engrossed in their discussion, and I was thinking about Becky and looking forward to what I hoped would be a relaxing afternoon by the pool.

No one noticed the old beige sedan that stayed a half a mile behind us with André LaForrette at the wheel.

44.

When we reached the Mandeville house, I was still reeling from the realization that Falco could be responsible for Saul's murder and that Saul could have been involved in other criminal activities. The thought had crossed my mind when I first realized how few clients he had, but I'd dismissed it. As I've said, I liked Saul and was willing to give him the benefit of all doubts, but now I had to face reality.

I stayed outside, sitting on the front steps while White and Horse went inside. I was sick to my stomach and hung my head between my knees, ready to retch. A minute later, I felt the warmth of Becky's body by my side. I was so consumed with thoughts about my failure to see, or accept, facts that were right in front of me that I hadn't even heard her come out.

Becky didn't say anything as she sat beside me rubbing my back. Her presence and her touch were comforting, and the gnawing in my stomach began to subside, but I couldn't bring myself to face her.

I was still curled over when I said, "You were right all along." I don't know whether I said it for her benefit or my own.

She didn't say anything in response. Instead, she merely leaned on my back and wrapped her arms around me.

I don't know how long we remained like that. It could have been just minutes, or it could have been much longer.

Eventually, I felt well enough to sit up, and we put our arms around each other.

"How could I have been so blind? How could everything have been so obvious to you without me seeing any of it?"

"It happens," she murmured softly. She could have given me an "I told you so," but that wasn't the kind of person she is, and I was grateful for that.

Several seconds passed before I said, "But it shouldn't have happened to me." I paused, wallowing in self-pity, before continuing. "I'm better than that!"

She laid her head on my shoulder and whispered in my ear. "You are. You were just too close to see it."

The next thing I knew, she'd taken my hand and was leading me inside.

Everyone else was on the patio when Becky and I came through the living room. Leslie and Rodriguez were drinking Hurricanes, Horse was sucking on a bottle of Corona and White held a glass of Diet Pepsi. Our driver was at the patio bar shucking oysters.

Apparently, White had already told everyone about our day in court, because no one was talking about what had to have been the most important event of the day. I wished I could have been there to hear what he thought about the proceedings, and I secretly felt a little left out of whatever discussion had occurred. I knew Becky also wanted to hear all about it, but I could tell her later.

Becky and I joined the others and the driver asked what we wanted to drink. Becky and I looked at each other and simultaneously said, "Hurricanes." I don't know what was funny about that, but everyone laughed.

I had just finished my first Hurricane and asked for

another when White signaled for me to come with him. I kissed Becky and followed him to the study.

We were just taking our seats when Rodriguez joined us. That was when it occurred to me that he hadn't been a participant in any of our activities for the past several days.

Rodriguez tossed me the keys to my Porsche. "I hope you don't mind, but I've been using your car while I conducted a little business."

I'm sure I said something about that being okay, but I don't really remember because I was too consumed with thoughts about what he'd been doing. He'd never mentioned having any business of his own in New Orleans, so I assumed he'd been doing something that related to me. I didn't have to wait long to find out.

White got right to the point. "Manny has a few acquaintances here that he has been visiting with." White paused, took a deep breath, and exhaled slowly. "Maybe it would be better if you told him, Manny."

My anxiety level was rising rapidly. Who could he have been talking to?

Rodriguez leaned forward with his elbows on his thighs and his face close to mine. "Lucius asked me to do a little digging into the issues that the prosecutor was trying to prove at Sonny Falco's last trial. I know some people who have an interest in what Falco has been doing."

I knew from the way he spoke that I wasn't going to like where this conversation was going.

"What can you tell me about Louis LeBlanc?"

My heart beat faster. "What about him?"

"Just what I asked. I know you represented him on a cocaine possession case, and I know you've met with him and Falco on a number of occasions. I just want to know what you know about *him*."

"I… I don't know anything about him. I just know that he works for Falco."

"What *exactly* does he do for Falco?"

"I don't really know. I've heard that he's sort of Falco's…" I paused while I tried to find the right word to describe what I knew about LeBlanc. "I guess you could say he's Falco's man in Baton Rouge. He's sort of a lobbyist. He knows the political actors and the people in the agencies that regulate some of Falco's interests."

Rodriguez nodded in a way that said I had confirmed something he already knew.

"Why are you interested in LeBlanc?"

"It isn't so much that *I'm* interested in LeBlanc. What I'm getting at is that the people I have been talking to have a particular interest in him."

"Why? What's their interest in anything he's done?"

"You know what Falco was charged with, right?

"I've read the pleadings and the trial transcript. Bribery of public officials, aiding and abetting a scheme to influence public officials."

"And who are the defendants?"

"Falco and a bunch of politicians and agency people."

Rodriguez sat back and waited like he was expecting me to say more. I tried to visualize the charging documents and remember who all the named defendants were. Suddenly it dawned on me.

"LeBlanc wasn't a named defendant!"

"That's right. And the people I've been talking to want to know why."

45.

For the second day in a row I was up before dawn. The judge's ruling wouldn't be docketed for at least another four hours, but my future hung in the balance and I couldn't sleep.

I brewed some coffee and searched for something to snack on. Nothing looked especially tempting, so I took my coffee out to the patio and hoped the tranquility of the lake would help take the edge off my anxiety. The fresh air smelled great, and my mind drifted to the bungalow that I still considered my home, where, as everywhere in the French Quarter, the air always had a faint smell of discarded oyster shells waiting to be collected by the garbage trucks.

I had an intense craving for fresh beignets and chicory coffee at the Café du Monde. Thinking that this might be the last time I would be able to have such a morning treat I was about to wake Becky and head for the Quarter when White appeared at the door.

"Worried?" he said.

"Is it that obvious?"

"No. Just natural."

He sat down opposite me and took a sip of his coffee. "You make good coffee."

"Thanks. Maybe they'll put me to work in the kitchen when I'm in prison waiting to testify."

ALAN P. WOODRUFF

"I doubt it. I'm usually good at reading judges. I think we made a decent case yesterday."

"Maybe I'm just a pessimist."

"Possibly. Are you up for some breakfast? I thought I'd make some eggs Benedict."

"That sounds great," Leslie said from the doorway.

White tilted his head back as she leaned over and kissed him.

"I'd better go wake up Becky. Do I have time for a shower?"

"That depends," Leslie said. "Will you be alone or will Becky be joining you?"

"What's the difference?"

Leslie smiled. "About a half an hour if you do it right."

Coffee spurted from White's nose, and he choked and laughed at the same time.

White stood, announced that he was going to make breakfast and headed for the kitchen.

I decided that Becky and my shower could wait and lingered on the patio as White and Leslie went inside. I took another sip of coffee, yawned, and stretched my legs. Two bass boats drifted along the shore of the lake and a pair of pelicans glided low over the water. Half a dozen seagulls perched on the railing of the gazebo at the end of the pier. The scene was so peaceful that for a few minutes I put my problems out of my mind.

Breakfast was as good as I have ever had—even better than at Brennan's, which is famous for its eggs Benedict.

Becky and Leslie were chatting about whatever women chat about, and Horse and Rodriguez were just finishing their breakfasts when I excused myself and went to get my computer. It was probably too early for the judge to have filed his ruling, but I wanted to be ready as soon as it was released.

I took my computer into the study, logged onto the court's website and entered the password the clerk had given us. In a few seconds I was able to open the file containing the docket for the Falco case in which the pleadings relating to me had been filed. As I started scrolling down the pages, I was again reminded that Louis LeBlanc was not a named defendant in the case. I'd thought about this fact several times since discussing it with White and Rodriguez the previous evening and had still not come up with a reasonable explanation for his omission. I kept scrolling past all the pretrial motions and rulings and the trial transcript until I reached the last entry, a one-line entry stating that our hearing had taken place the previous day.

"Anything?" White called from the dining table.

"Not yet."

I checked my watch. It was only 8:32.

I switched from the docket page to the court calendar and saw that the judge's first hearing wasn't scheduled until eleven. I muttered a quiet curse. He could still be working on his opinion, and it might be hours before it was issued.

I returned to the dining room to join the others. The tension gnawed at me, but I tried to relax—as if that was going to happen. I tried to join in the conversation but couldn't concentrate. Becky reached under the table and squeezed my hand. When I tried to smile at her, I could see from the look in her eyes that she was feeling as anxious as I was.

I couldn't wait any longer and returned to my computer. It was only nine o'clock. Even if the judge had filed his ruling when he said he would, it would take some time for it to be entered into the electronic docket.

I returned to the docket file and found my case. Though

I didn't expect to find anything new yet, I had to do something to keep my mind occupied. I held my breath and slowly scrolled down the docket. At the end of the file, there was a new entry. I almost couldn't bring myself to read it.

"We have a ruling," I shouted to the others.

Everyone rushed to my side as I read it aloud: *MEMORANDUM OPINION: Movant's motions are GRANTED in part and DENIED in part.*

All I could think was, *Oh shit*!

I downloaded the file containing the opinion and did a quick Wi-Fi search for the wireless printer in the study. As soon as I was connected, I printed out a copy of the opinion, and we all gathered around the desk in the study to read it.

The judge had obviously had a busy night. The opinion was forty pages long and included a detailed recitation of the facts and analysis of the legal authorities on which he had relied. We only gave those pages a cursory look. They would have to be analyzed in detail later if an appeal was necessary. The only thing that mattered at the moment was the summary and the specific provisions of the ruling.

To make a long story short, the judge ruled that I didn't have to testify at Falco's next trial and didn't have to answer any further questions Blain might want to ask. He also quashed the material witness warrant. But he ruled that I still had to assist the government in identifying the source and, if I knew it, the location of all documents pertinent to the government's charges against Falco and the other defendants.

White was delighted by the ruling and proclaimed that a celebration was in order, and everyone started filing out. But I was still staring at the ruling when White closed the door and walked back to the desk. "Why the long face? You won."

I hesitated, looking for the right words to say what I was thinking. I had hoped it wouldn't come to this, but now it was unavoidable. Finally, I summoned enough courage to speak.

"We need to talk. There are a few other things you need to know."

46.

White took a seat in one of the chairs in front of the desk. He leaned back and stretched his legs as he waited for me to speak.

"It's about this part where I have to tell the prosecutor everything I know about the location of any documents."

"What's the problem? You'll just tell her where Falco's files are stored. She'll get a search warrant, and that will be the end of it."

"I'm afraid it's not that easy."

White sat up straight but didn't say anything.

"It's about the files."

White's breathing slowed, but he remained silent.

"Not all the documents Blain may want to see are at the storage facility."

"Where are they?" I'm sure he knew the answer to his question but wanted to hear it from me.

"I have them… on my computer."

White frowned and exhaled slowly, making a soft whistling sound.

"The documents she really needs…" I paused as I thought about how much I could say without compromising him or his continued representation of me. I wanted his advice—I *needed* his advice—but what was I willing to risk? Finally, I decided that he had a right to know everything.

"The documents Blain needs to really prove her case are

documents I created when I did some work for Falco. There won't be anything in his files at the warehouse, because he shredded his copy after I went over my report with him. I didn't realize how important my document was until I read the transcript of Falco's first trial and realized what she was trying to prove."

"Why didn't you tell her about what you had when she was first questioning you?"

"I didn't know how relevant my documents were. She never told me what her case was all about. I answered all of her questions, but she didn't ask anything suggesting that my documents would even be relevant."

"And you can't just tell her now—"

"I know… because my plea agreement only protects me from prosecution for anything I said in response to what she's *already* asked me about."

"And after what we've put her through, she won't be inclined to ignore your role in Falco's scheme."

White stood and began slowly pacing the length of the study and tapping his lips with his index finger as he went. I watched as he seemed to think about a solution to my dilemma. At least, I hoped that what's what he was thinking about. He might have just been pissed at me and deciding what to do about that. I'd terminated representations of clients who lied to me or withheld important information, and I hoped White would see that I hadn't intentionally misled him.

There was a knock at the door and Horse stuck his head into the study. "What are you guys talking about? There's a party going on out here."

White waived Horse in and told him to shut the door. Horse's smile faded as he took a seat beside White.

"We have a little problem with the judge's order," White said.

Horse listened quietly as White explained what I had done—or, rather, what I had not done—and how the judge's order affected my plea agreement. When White finished, Horse began chewing on the inside of his cheek and looked toward me. I couldn't tell if he was disappointed with me or merely trying to gauge my state of mind. Either way, I was unable to meet his eyes and lowered my head, pretending to reexamine the judge's order.

After what felt like an hour but was probably only a few minutes, White finally spoke. "There may be a way out of this mess."

I didn't see how, but I was ready to listen to anything.

"I'm sure Blain has read the ruling by now and knows you don't have to answer any more of her questions." White paused as if thinking through what he was about to say. "Since she has already tried Falco once, she now knows what the defense lawyers are going to do about her evidence and witness testimony and where the problems are with her case."

I was following him so far. Second trials are always more difficult for defense attorneys because the prosecution knows what questions are going to be asked of witnesses and are prepared to address anything the defense may say. But I still wasn't clear where White was going.

"Blain is going to want to ask you more questions about what you know, but the judge's order doesn't provide for that."

I nodded my concurrence with White's observation but remained uncertain about what White was thinking.

"What if we sweeten her up by offering to let her question you all over again. If she doesn't ask all the right questions, you can volunteer whatever she doesn't ask about."

I thought about the idea for a minute. It sounded like a logical solution, and I was sure Blain would love having a chance to reexamine me, but something still didn't feel right. I couldn't put my finger on it, but something in the back of my mind said it was important. I reached for a copy of my plea agreement and began rereading it. Nothing jumped out at me, but I knew there was something there that was the source of my concern. I read it again, line by line, while trying to recall what had transpired when Blain and I had first negotiated the agreement. In retrospect, I wished I'd retained a more experienced attorney to represent me in the original plea negotiations. Maybe someone else would have spotted the flaw I was looking for. I gave up my search and returned my attention to White, who was engrossed in reading the whole of the judge's opinion. I suspected he was looking for some flaw we could capitalize on. Several times he huddled with Horse and pointed to passages that held his interest. I waited nervously until he returned the ruling to the desk before I spoke.

"Isn't Blain going to be suspicious if we offer her something without asking for anything in return?'

"Probably," White said. "So I propose that we make our offer of further questioning contingent on a renegotiation of your plea agreement. She already knows she has problems with the plea. She won't want to go through another hearing like the one we had yesterday. She came off looking foolish, and I think she'll jump at the chance to amend the agreement."

I was confident that White could negotiate a better deal for me than I had done on my own, but I was still concerned about something. "What effect would a new agreement with Blain have on the agreement you negotiated with Graham Brochette?"

"That agreement still won't take effect until you have completely discharged your obligations to Blain. He won't be happy about a delay, but I can take care of him."

"What if Blain insists that any new agreement requires me to testify?"

"That won't make any difference. The whole point of your provisions in the agreement was to keep Falco from knowing that you were working with the government, but Blain's material witness warrant contains both your own name and your name as a protected witness. He now knows that you're working for the government, so appearing as a witness can't do you any more harm."

I hated to admit it, but White was right. If Falco hadn't been sure before, now he knew who he had to eliminate.

47.

White accompanied Horse and me out to the patio where the others were drinking mimosas in celebration of my apparent victory. Becky ran to me, hugged me and asked, "What were you guys talking about?"

I put on my best party face. "Nothing important." I hated to lie to her. She was truly happy for the first time since we had been reunited and I couldn't bring myself to tell her that everything might not be over after all. Horse returned to a chair in front of an unfinished mimosa. I dragged another chair to the table and sat down beside Becky, who reached over and held my hand.

White wiggled a finger toward Rodriguez indicating that he needed to talk to him in private. Rodriguez excused himself and followed White into the study. Leslie watched them go and the happy face she had shown when I arrived turned to a look of concern. She looked toward me. I understood what she was thinking and shook my head as I put a finger to my lips and pointed at Becky. Leslie gave me a faint nod of understanding and returned her attention to the rest of us.

I did my best to participate in the celebration, but I couldn't concentrate. Every few minutes I glanced toward the study in the hope that White and Rodriguez would return with some kind of good news. I didn't really expect that to happen, but I had to hold onto even the faintest of hopes. I couldn't imagine what they had to talk about without me, but I'd learned that there were times that White had to do things he didn't want me to know about. I don't know which was worse, knowing or not knowing.

About twenty minutes later, Rodriguez came out of the study and walked over to me. "I need to borrow your car again."

I told him my keys were on the dresser and watched as he went to my room. When he came out, he went to his own room, where he stayed for a few minutes before emerging and heading for the front door. He was wearing a sports jacket in spite of the fact that the temperature was already pushing ninety and the humidity was just as high. I didn't have to think about why he was wearing a jacket. I instinctively knew what he had under it.

White remained in the study for almost half an hour after Rodriguez had left. Whatever he was doing, I knew it was related to our earlier conversation, and the fact that I didn't know what was going on was killing me.

§

Rodriquez returned to the house around four in the afternoon and went straight to the study where White had been holed up most of the day making phone calls. I was lounging on the deck by the pool where Becky and Leslie were floating on inflatable rafts. I hadn't seen Horse since he'd been summoned to join White an hour earlier.

Being able to drink my Bloody Mary while watching two beautiful women in skimpy bikinis had helped take the edge off my anxiety, but I was never able to completely relax and join them. Things were happening that I didn't know about. I had to trust White, but putting my future in someone else's hands was foreign to me. Now I knew how my clients felt—not that it mattered anymore.

White finally came out of the study and, with a tilt of his head, beckoned me to join him. I felt a surge of acid in my stomach as I entered the room. White closed the door behind me and began talking before I had taken my seat. "I've made some progress on the problem presented by your plea agreement."

That part of the news was obviously good. However, the tone in White's voice suggested that there was a big "but" or "if" coming.

"I've been on the phone with Graham Brochette. I told him about the judge's order and our plan to offer more cooperation to Blain if she'll amend your plea agreement."

"Why did you do that? Won't it screw up the agreement you negotiated with him?"

"That's why I had to tell him. The good news is that the more we talked, the more I thought that you're in a strong negotiating position. He's anxious to get you with his team. But as we've discussed before, DOJ policy prevents him from doing anything as long as you have an agreement with Blain."

"Then my position hasn't changed."

"Maybe it has. After we first talked, he called Blain and told her he needed you as a witness in another case. I assume he didn't tell her about his task force, but I don't really know. He didn't volunteer anything, and I didn't ask. But the short version is that he proposed that she vacate her agreement with you so that his agreement can be put into effect. He apparently told her she could have everything that we were prepared to offer, but you would be subject to the terms and conditions of the agreement with him instead of the agreement she'd made."

I couldn't help thinking that this was where the "but" was coming. I was right.

"But she wanted the agreement to include your testimony at trial."

"I thought we agreed that testifying wouldn't put me in any more danger because Falco already knew I was cooperating with the government."

"That's right. And I still think it's the only conclusion that can be drawn under the circumstances."

"I still don't like it. But if you think it's necessary, I guess I can accept it."

"There's just one other thing."

Oh, shit. There's always just one more thing. "What's that?"

"She wants you to be somewhere that she can have access to you whenever she needs it."

"I don't know about that. I still think there's a leak in her office. If there is, Falco can still find me. That's why I thought I had to leave Tennessee."

"I know. But I proposed that her only contact with you has to come through me. I'm not going to let her interview you without me being present anyway."

"Did she agree to that?"

"Reluctantly. But Graham isn't sure he can accept that. He wants you to be protected by the Marshals Service just like anyone else in the Witness Protection Program."

"And what does that mean?"

"You have to go where they want you to go. You'll be given another new identity and be protected like anyone else in the Program. The only difference is that any contact with you by anyone except the Marshals will have to come through me."

"I don't know. How do I know that Falco can't still find out where I am?"

"I'm not thrilled about it either. If you're in the Program, even I can't contact you directly. But it may be our only option."

"I don't like it. And what about Becky? Can she come with me?"

"Graham agreed to that. But she'll have to agree to the terms of the Program."

"You mean she won't be able to contact anyone else—family, friends?"

"That's how the Program works. It's the only way it *can* work, and the Marshals have never lost a witness who has abided by all the requirements of the Program."

"I don't know," I said, which was perhaps the most honest thing I'd said in a long time. I knew that I could deal with the Program again. What other choice did I have? But Becky, well, *cautiously optimistic* was the phrase that came to mind. "I'll have to discuss it with her. It was hard enough for *me* to accept the terms of the Witness Protection Program. My parents are both dead, I don't have any brothers or sisters and I was only going to be in it for a little while. Becky's situation is different. She'd spent her whole life in New Orleans, and we're talking about being in the Program forever."

"I understand. But before you talk to Becky, you need to hear what Manny was doing today."

48.

Rodriguez pursed his lips and swallowed hard before beginning. "After we got the judge's order this, morning, Lucius asked me to get in touch with Falco and tell him what had happened. I was also told to offer him a deal."

I was furious, and it took all the willpower I could muster to not immediately ask White what he was doing offering Falco any kind of deal without my knowledge. I was sure as hell going to ask him that, but it was a question that should only be asked when we were alone.

Rodriquez must have seen my reaction because he paused and looked toward White.

White ignored me and waved a hand, signaling Rodriquez to continue.

"Like I was saying, I was told to tell Falco that we were ready to tell Blain where all his records were unless he was willing to guarantee your safety."

"That's it? What did he say?"

"At first he didn't say anything. He wanted to have someone else hear what I had to say." Rodriguez paused and studied me. I think he was considering whether to continue and what my reaction would be if he disclosed who else Falco wanted in the meeting.

I saved him from having to make a decision. "Who?" I thought I knew, but I hoped I was wrong.

Rodriguez hesitated before responding. "Louis LeB-lanc."

I swallowed hard. I would have given anything to have been wrong, but there it was.

As I considered the significance of Rodriguez's words, my mind flashed to the many meetings I'd attended with Falco and LeBlanc. There had always been a reason for LeBlanc's presence, and I desperately wanted to believe he was just one of Falco's associates. Now I couldn't continue to lie to myself. LeBlanc was, as I had tried so hard to avoid believing, more than a mere cog in the machinery of Falco's organization.

I was still engrossed in my thoughts when I heard White ask, "Are you okay?"

It took me several seconds to refocus my attention. "Yeah… I think so." I wasn't ready to hear whatever was coming next, but nothing I could do now would change what had happened. Ready or not, I had to know—my future depended on it.

Rodriguez gave a half shrug before continuing. "I repeated what I had told Falco about our offer. LeBlanc wanted to know where the documents were, how you knew about them and what documents you had seen personally. Of course, I didn't answer any of his questions. I just said we'd tell him whatever he wanted to know after we had an agreement."

I could feel the tension leaving my body. I was sur-prised to realize just how stressed I'd become since Rodri-guez explained the offer that had been made to Falco. But I still didn't know where I stood with him. "It sounds like you were negotiating a plea agreement." I'm not sure why I said that or how I intended the statement to be received. I only know that I had to say something, and that was the only thing that came to mind.

I glanced at White, but his stoic expression didn't give me any indication about what he was thinking.

Rodriguez pursed his lips and narrowed his eyes. I think he was trying to decide how to interpret what I had said. Finally, he spoke. "I suppose you could think of it that way." I expected him to say more, but he didn't.

For a time, silence blanketed the room. Finally, I couldn't stand it any longer.

"What did Falco say? Did he accept your offer or not?"

"Neither. He wanted time to think about it."

"What's there to think about? If he gets control of the documents, he's virtually guaranteed that he won't be convicted at his next trial. How could he possibly turn you down?"

Rodriguez turned to White, who leaned forward with his elbows on the desk and rubbed his hands together as he appeared to think about how to respond to my question.

I'm not sure what I was hoping to hear. Falco wanted me dead, and for that I feared and hated him. I also blamed him for my present predicament even though it was my own fault. Now I just wanted out.

When he eventually spoke, White's voice was hesitant and subdued. "Falco's situation isn't as simple as you think. He has co-defendants in his trial, and he has partners in his businesses. All of their interests would be affected if he were to agree to what we proposed."

"So, what's he going to do?"

"I don't know. I don't expect him to consult with anyone outside his organization, but he has to know that accepting our agreement could put his own life in danger."

"Where does that leave us?"

"We gave Falco until the end of the day tomorrow to give us his decision."

There was nothing more for me to do or say about the

deal they'd offered Falco. I'm sure we all continued to discuss the deal, and I must have participated in the discussion, but I don't remember what was said. I was already thinking about what I was going to say to White when we were alone. I didn't expect it to be pleasant, and I readied myself for the consequences of what I knew I had to say. I needed White and I knew it, but I couldn't let him believe he could make major decisions without first discussing them with me.

After Rodriguez left the room and closed the door, White settled back in his chair behind the desk and looked at me. His expression was professionally detached, much as it had been on the first day when he, Horse and I met to discuss my situation. He had to know I wasn't happy about the events of the day and had probably already determined how he was going to respond to what I had to say.

49.

As much as I'd thought about it while White and Rodriguez told me about the things they'd been doing on my behalf, I had no idea where to begin. My initial anger at having been kept in the dark about their respective activities had been moderated by the fact that the results they'd obtained were generally favorable, but now I was facing a whole new array of problems.

I suppose I could have remained seated and discussed my concerns rationally, but my inner child had a mind of its own.

I stood and leaned over the desk and glared at White. "Do you have any fucking idea what you were doing?" I said in a voice that was shy of a shout and its tone just short of blatant sarcasm.

White was evidently prepared for my outburst, and his face didn't show any response, which was all the more infuriating. "I think so. But why don't you tell me?"

I stepped back from the desk and began to pace around the limited space between the chairs and the bookcases that lined the walls. I rubbed the back of my head, still trying to absorb the reality of what I was ready to say. "Jesus Christ! You were telling Falco that I was willing to engage in the obstruction of justice. Blain would go ballistic if she found out. She'd have my ass."

White waited silently until it became clear that my initial tirade was complete. I expected his response to come with the same level of emotional verve as my challenge. Instead, he simply said, "Do you really think I'd let that happen?"

"You can't do anything about it."

"*I* can't, but Graham Brochette can."

His response was totally unexpected, and it took me a moment to register what he'd said. "What the hell does he have to do with it?"

"He approved the plan."

I stopped pacing and leaned against the bookcase with my arms crossed. "Plan. What plan? What the hell are you talking about?"

"We're setting up a trap." He spoke with such calm self-assurance that I was left nonplussed. "The storage facility will be under FBI surveillance, and they're ready to grab Falco with the documents when he picks up his files."

It sounded so simple and reasonable when he said it that I felt disarmed. My anger had temporarily fled, leaving me flushed and naked. Unsure of what to do, I emotionally doubled down. I couldn't—I *wouldn't*—let the issue go unchallenged. "What are you going to do if Falco doesn't get the files himself? What if he sends LeBlanc or someone else to get them?

"That's not likely to happen. Falco has gone to such great lengths to protect the files and keep anyone else from knowing where they've been stored that he isn't likely to want anyone else to know where Weinberg was keeping them."

"But that's just your assumption. What's your plan if he *does* send someone else?"

"Then the FBI would grab whoever picks up the files."

"And do what?"

"Find out where the files were going to be taken."

"You seem pretty confident that you can find out."

"The FBI is good at interrogating people."

"If it's only a matter of getting the files, we could just tell Blain where they are."

"But she'd have to get a search warrant before she could get them. We believe Falco has a source in the U.S. Attorney's office."

I stiffened. "Who told you that?"

"You did. You said you thought someone in the office had told Falco where you were when you told me about the break-in at your cabin in Tennessee. If you're right, which I think you are, Falco would know about the search warrant and could recover his files before the warrant was executed."

I relaxed and leaned back as I considered what White had said. "It sounds like you've thought of everything."

White smiled. "This isn't my first rodeo." There was a touch of smugness in his look and the tone of his voice. It killed me to admit it, but he'd earned it.

"That may be. Your plans may all work out well, but you had no business putting them into action without discussing them with me."

"I *am* sorry about that, but things were moving fast, and decisions had to be made on the fly. Besides, I didn't want you to have anything more to worry about than you already have."

I had difficulty responding to White's apology. It was logical, and I believed that he was genuinely sorry he hadn't kept me more involved. I wasn't completely ready to let bygones be bygones, but there was work to be done, and there wasn't any point in prolonging our discussion of what couldn't be changed.

I was only vaguely aware that White had already moved on and was asking me to review the plea agreement he'd negotiated with Brochette. He handed me the draft document, and I began to read it. It was as complete an agreement as I'd ever seen and covered every contingency I could imagine. It even provided me with some benefits I hadn't thought of.

When I finished reading and laid my copy of the agreement on the desk, White began to speak. "As you know, participation in the Witness Protection Program is voluntary. But if you sign the plea agreement, you're going to have to be enrolled in the Program for as long as Graham's task force wants access to you and until any cases they bring are concluded. After that, participation in the Program is voluntary on your part."

I said I understood all of that and reminded him that I'd been a temporary participant in the Program before.

"Now we're going to have to amend your plea agreement to incorporate the provisions needed to accommodate Barbara Blain and the Falco case. Do you think you're up to doing that now?"

I said I wanted to get the matter resolved as soon as possible so I could talk to Becky about our future. I still wasn't sure what I was going to say to her and was even less sure of how she would respond. When we had previously discussed relocating she was ready for that. But witness protection—that's something else entirely.

For the next few hours, we discussed the changes we wanted to make. White had to make several calls to Brochette to discuss our requests. My ability to concentrate was fading, and I was only vaguely aware of White's side of the conversations. All I remember was that the conversation was, at times, heated, but eventually we came to an agreement that I was willing to sign. I suppose I should have felt relieved, but I was thinking ahead to my impending discussion with Becky.

White was putting the files in his briefcase as I stood to leave. "There's just one more thing," he said.

"Isn't there always?"

"Graham needs your answer about the witness protection issue tomorrow."

"Why so soon?"

"Some things are happening that make it necessary. He wants to send some people from his task force to start interviewing you the day after tomorrow, and he needs to make arrangements for the Marshals to take over."

"But—"

"It can't be helped. The task force has gotten some information from a wiretap that makes it necessary."

I knew I wouldn't like the answer, but I had to ask the obvious question. "What kind of information?"

White hesitated and locked onto my eyes as he tapped a loosely closed hand against his chin.

"It's about me, isn't it?"

White considered my question for several seconds before responding. "Brochette isn't sure what it all means. The people whose phones are tapped are careful about what they say. All Brochette's people can do is try to read between the lines, but Falco's partners must be worried about the deal we offered. Brochette thinks your life is in danger."

50.

I hadn't realized how long we'd been meeting until I left the study and saw that everyone else was dressed for an evening out. My eyes settled on Becky, who was wearing a black silk jumpsuit I'd never seen before. She stood and started toward me then stopped and turned around slowly. "Like it?" she asked.

"What's not to like? You look fantastic."

"Leslie loaned it to me," she said as she came to me and kissed me. I put my arm around her and pulled her close. The sheer fabric was soft and smooth and clung to her in all the right places, and I could tell that she wasn't wearing anything underneath. I reached for her ass, but she spun away. "Later," she said. "Now hurry up and get dressed. We're all famished."

"Where are we going?"

"It's a surprise."

I thought I'd already had more than enough surprises for one day, and there were things we had to talk about, but she was so gorgeous and excited that I couldn't even consider disappointing her.

I quickly showered, shaved, and dressed, and as soon as I rejoined the others, we headed out the door to where a white stretch limousine was waiting.

"What the... Whose idea was this?" I said.

Becky, Leslie, and Horse all pointed to Rodriguez. Rodriguez smiled. "I thought we all needed a break. Tonight's on me."

Instead of turning onto the causeway and heading for New Orleans, we went north to I-12 and turned east. "Where are we going?" I said.

Rodriguez grinned. "Gulfport, Mississippi. We're going to do some gambling."

It occurred to me that we hadn't been doing anything but gamble since we'd arrived in New Orleans and gambled with my life. But this didn't seem to be the time to engage in gallows-humor. Instead of saying what I was thinking, I simply asked, "Why Gulfport?"

Rodriguez's grin morphed into a solemn look. "You'd probably be safe enough in New Orleans, but there's no point taking any chances. You're tense enough."

I couldn't have agreed more. Gulfport was a great choice, and I immediately felt myself relaxing. I hadn't had a fun night out with Becky for more than a year. I needed it, and she deserved it, so I vowed to enjoy the moment. The discussion we needed to have later would be difficult enough.

§

The evening in Gulfport was everything we needed. Good food, good fun, and good stories. We danced and drank and gambled way too much, but Becky, who had never been to a casino, had the time of her life. I couldn't take my eyes off her, and for a few hours I was able to put Falco and my other problems out of my mind.

Over White's objection, Rodriguez told story after story about things that had happened during the trials in which White had represented him. White was the central feature of most of the stories, and even he laughed at them. I think it was the first time I'd seen him laugh.

It was almost two in the morning when we arrived home from Gulfport. I knew it was too late to discuss plans for the future with Becky, or at least that's what I told myself. I had been dreading it and I think I was glad to have a reason to put off our discussion. I still didn't know exactly what I was going to say, and I was afraid of what her answer might be.

§

The sun was shining through our bedroom window when I woke the next morning. Becky was still asleep, lying naked against me with her arm over my chest. I slipped out of bed and headed for the bathroom.

A couple of aspirin and a long shower later, I was ready to face the day—and the moment of truth.

Becky was sitting up in bed, leaning against the pillow with her arms behind her head, when I came out of the bathroom. She pulled the blanket aside and patted the mattress beside her. She rolled to my side and gave me a concerned look but didn't say anything. I inhaled deeply and let my breath out slowly. What I had to say couldn't wait any longer.

I sat down on the edge of the bed. Becky sat up, pulled the sheet up around her chest, and moved to my side.

"There's something we need to talk about," I said. My mind was racing, but it was too late to stop now.

"I know. Leslie sort of told me last night."

I wasn't certain if Leslie knew what was happening. Because she was also an attorney, White could share everything with her without breaching any confidentiality requirements or violating the attorney-client privilege, but I was surprised that Leslie had said anything to Becky. Usually, whenever anything relating to me had come up in conversation, Leslie had found a reason to take Becky somewhere else so she wouldn't hear anything that might upset her. But none of that mattered now.

"What did Leslie tell you?" I was stalling, but I also hoped Becky already knew enough that what I had to say wouldn't come as a complete surprise.

"She told me that Lucius and Graham Brochette have worked out a new immunity agreement for you."

I hesitated before asking, "Did she tell you what's involved?"

Becky tensed, and there was a tone of concern in her voice when she responded. "Just that you have immunity for your part in anything illegal Sonny Falco might have done."

I think she already knew more than that but wanted to hear it from me. "It's a little more complicated than just that."

She didn't say anything.

"If I agree to everything Brochette wants, I'll have to go back into the Witness Protection Program for at least as long as he may need me."

"Like you did when you made your agreement with Barbara Blain?"

"For starters."

I felt her body grow tense. "For starters? What does that mean?"

This was harder than I'd thought it would be. "Falco was only one man. Brochette is going after dozens of people." I could feel my heart beating faster and wondered if Becky could feel it, too. "That means I could be in danger even after Brochette's cases are finished."

Becky looked at me with sad eyes. "You're still not telling me everything, are you?"

I rolled over and propped myself up on my elbow. "No. If I agree to what they're asking, they want me to go into the Witness Protection Program permanently. But I don't think I can do it if you don't come with me."

She wiped away the small tears that had formed in the corners of her eyes. "You know you have to do it."

I hesitated—struggling with my last vestiges of hope. I had come to New Orleans to get my life back. I had won the battles, but I had still failed. When I continued, my voice was hardly more than a whisper. "I know." I heard the sound of resignation in my voice.

"But I need to be with you, and Brochette has agreed to let you come with me."

She laid back down beside me and I felt her body quiver. "What will that mean?"

I explained how the Witness Protection Program worked: relocation, new identities and all.

She listened quietly as I spoke. She seemed to understand everything I was saying—at least she understood the words—but I couldn't tell if she fully comprehended what it would mean to be in the Program. I don't think anyone does until they're in it.

Becky pursed her lips and narrowed her eyes. I had seen the look before and knew she was thinking about what I had said. After a minute she asked, "When do you have to decide?"

"Brochette wants my answer about the plea agreement today."

Becky closed her eyes and buried her face against my shoulder. I felt her body shudder as she fought to hold back the tears.

51.

Becky and I joined the others on the patio around ten. They'd already finished breakfast, but White asked if he could make anything for us. Becky said she only wanted some orange juice, and I said the same.

Leslie must have sensed that Becky was feeling troubled and gave her a hug before taking her hand and leading her to the end of the pier. I watched as Leslie put her arm around Becky. Becky laid her head on Leslie's shoulder. I could tell from the way her body was shaking that Becky was crying. I wanted to do something to help, but there wasn't anything for me to do. As much as I wanted us to stay together, I knew what that would mean. Part of me wanted to convince her to join me, but another part told me that would be selfish. It was her decision to make. I had put in her in this position, but I couldn't do anything more now.

As I sat watching the women, a pair of pelicans sailed by just barely above the surface of the lake. I wondered if they were the same pelicans I'd seen on the previous mornings. Two bass boats drifted along the banks. I knew they were the same two boats I had seen before. The reeds along the shore must make for good fishing.

White reminded me that Brochette expected a decision today. He didn't say it like he was pressuring me, just stating a fact. I still didn't have any idea what Becky would do about the Witness Protection Program, but that decision, for both of us, was separate from my plea agreement with Brochette.

White and I went to the study to call him. White and Brochette made a few final revisions to the agreement, and five minutes later the fax machine began to purr. White glanced over the printout, making certain that all the agreed changes had been made, and handed it to me. I signed without reading the final document and White faxed it back to Brochette.

A minute later, we had a copy of the agreement signed by Brochette. The deal was done and my future was sealed. What kind of a future that would be was yet to be determined.

White and Brochette continued to talk for another ten minutes. I was thinking about Becky and I didn't pay much attention to what was said. After they hung up, White returned his attention to me.

"Three members of Graham's task force will be here tomorrow morning. They're probably going to be in town for a couple of days."

"What about Barbara Blain?"

"She gets you for two hours the day after tomorrow."

"Then what happens?"

"The Marshals Service is ready to take custody as soon as Graham's people are finished with you."

He didn't ask about Becky, and I didn't volunteer anything—mostly because I didn't know anything.

As soon as we left the study, I went to the patio and looked for Becky, but she wasn't there. Rodriguez looked up from his newspaper and said she and Leslie had gone shopping. I guess that's what women do when they're upset. Men shout and kick things; women shop.

The concern I felt when I heard what Rodriguez had said must have been obvious because he assured me that both Horse and our driver had gone with them and they would be safe.

§

By four o'clock we still hadn't heard from Falco about his response to the proposal Rodriguez had presented to him the previous day. Nobody else seemed concerned, but why should they? *Their* lives weren't at stake. I, on the other hand, was so filled with anxiety that I was ready to scream. I didn't know what I wanted to scream or who I would scream at—I just needed some relief from the pressure that was building. I excused myself and headed for the exercise room over the garage, where I spent the next hour running on the treadmill, punching the speed bag and throwing karate kicks at the heavy bag.

When we hadn't heard anything by seven o'clock, even White was showing signs of concern: taut muscles in his face and neck and a slightly clenched jaw. He glanced toward the door and tilted his head in a sort of jerking movement. I didn't understand the significance of whatever signal had been passed, but Rodriguez left the room and went out to the patio. He moved out of sight, and I couldn't see what he was doing, although I assumed that he was making a phone call. He returned a few minutes later and reclaimed his seat in the recliner facing the sofa where White and Horse were seated.

"I called Falco's number," Rodriguez said, "but I didn't get an answer, so I called LeBlanc. He said Falco was out at a meeting and he didn't know when to expect Falco back."

"Did he give you any indication of where Falco was?" I said.

"That isn't something we ask."

His use of the word "we" reminded me that Rodriguez lived in a world I wasn't familiar with.

At seven-thirty I heard a car pull into the driveway and rushed to the door. Horse and our driver got out and held the doors for Leslie and Becky, who were each carrying bags with the names and logos of stores that I'd seen but wasn't familiar with. Becky smiled when I went down the front steps and let me kiss her as I took her bags.

"Did you have a good day?" I said.

Becky gave me a smile that looked more forced than happy. "What do you think? We were shopping."

I followed her into our bedroom, where she immediately flopped onto the bed.

"I'm exhausted."

I didn't know what to say, so I went with something safe. "What did you buy?"

"Some girl things. I didn't have time to pack much when Leslie showed up and told me you were coming to New Orleans."

"I've been wondering about that. How did she connect with you?"

Becky didn't respond immediately. I couldn't tell whether she was thinking or just hadn't heard my question. I was about to ask her again when she sat up.

"Tell me. How much trouble are you in?" Her voice was firm, and she was no longer even trying to feign a smile.

"Honestly... I don't know."

I told her that I'd signed Brochette's plea agreement and that FBI agents were coming the next day to interview me. I also told her that the Marshals would be coming for me in two days. She listened without showing any reaction.

I desperately wanted to know what she was thinking

about joining me in the Witness Protection Program, but I knew she would tell me when she was ready.

Leslie knocked on the door and told us that dinner was ready and that she'd made it herself. Becky and I looked at each other, both wondering what Leslie could possibly have made.

Neither Becky nor I was particularly hungry. My stomach was still churning over the lack of response from Falco and the uncertainty about my future with Becky. I'm not sure why Becky wasn't hungry. I suspect it had something to do with her concerns about our future, but I was afraid to ask. Whatever decision she made, it had to be made by her alone. I was ready to talk more about it if she wanted, but she would have to initiate the conversation.

Notwithstanding our lack of hunger, we decided to join the others if only to see what Leslie had made. As we walked onto the patio and saw what was for dinner, we both laughed. We had to have been thinking the same thing. On the table were three pizzas.

Becky hugged Leslie and said, "When you said that you *made* dinner—"

"You thought I'd actually *made* dinner?" Leslie laughed. "Well, I sort of did. I *made* the call to the pizza joint."

White gave us all a "What can I say?" shrug, and Leslie punched him playfully on the shoulder.

§

By midnight we still hadn't heard from Falco. Becky and Leslie had long since gone to bed (I guess a day of shopping can be pretty tiring) and the rest of us were speculating about why we hadn't heard from Falco. It was a meaningless exercise, but it helped fill the time.

At one o'clock, White suggested that I turn in. The

interrogators from Brochette's task force were due early in the morning and I had to be ready for what was sure to be a grueling day. I had no idea just how grueling it was going to be.

52.

I didn't sleep the night before my visit from the FBI. I only had the vaguest idea what they might ask me and even less idea what I knew that would be of assistance to them. I hadn't done any work for Sonny Falco for more than a year, and any number of things could have occurred in the meantime. I took some solace in the fact that my plea agreement only required me to provide any information I had, and I knew I could do that. But witness protection is generally only made available to those who provide material evidence that the government deems to be valuable. I was beginning to wish I'd already signed on to the Witness Protection Program.

At eight o'clock, I was standing by the window at the front of the house when a black Chevy Suburban pulled into the driveway and three men got out. All of them wore FBI "uniforms"—dark suits, crisply starched white shirts, solid-color ties, and utilitarian but highly polished black shoes.

Two of the men waited by the car, briefcases in hand, while the third removed what I knew was a box of recording equipment. White joined me by the front door and opened it before any of the agents had a chance to knock. We exchanged introductions and handshakes, and White led the men into the library, where they began setting up their equipment.

Half an hour later I was summoned to the library and my interrogation began.

It didn't come as any surprise that their first questions concerned my knowledge about the location of any of Falco's documents. White gave them the address of Saul's facility and the unit number where Falco's files were stored.

The rest of the morning is something of a blur. The agents asked the same questions six different ways, and none of them struck me as being particularly pertinent to what I thought they were investigating. Or maybe I was just distracted by the untied threads in my life—Becky and the Witness Protection Program.

As their questioning continued, I added Falco—and the fact that we hadn't heard from him—to the list of things that were occupying what little remained of my capacity for cogent thought.

By noon I was exhausted. The lack of sleep and the many other things on my mind were taking their toll, and I asked if we could take a break while I took a short nap.

As I was leaving the library, one of the agents' cell phones rang and I stopped to listen just in case the call had something to do with me. The agent turned toward the corner so that I couldn't hear him or see his expression, but it was soon obvious that it was good news.

"That's great!" he shouted as he signaled for the other agents to come nearer. "Fantastic!... Yes, we'll be there ASAP." After hanging up, he turned to the other agents. "They've already executed the search warrant. We have all of Falco's files."

I suppose I should have been as pleased as the agents were, but all the news meant to me was that I could take a longer nap. I staggered toward our bedroom, where I found Becky curled on the bed with her arms around a pillow. I let myself fall face-forward onto the bed and almost immediately I fell asleep.

§

The next thing I remember was Becky shaking me awake. "You're wanted in the library. Everyone seems pretty tense, but no one's talking to the rest of us."

I rolled over and realized that the sun had already set. I must have been more drained than I'd thought. I looked for my watch and couldn't believe I'd been allowed to sleep until after seven.

When I walked into the library, White and two of the FBI agents were seated at the table in the middle of the room. The third agent was pacing in front of the window with his cell phone pressed to his ear. I could feel the tension in the air. "What's going on?"

White put a finger to his lips, and I slumped into a nearby chair and tried to listen to the third agent's conversation. "How sure are you?... When will you know?... Tell Quantico I want the results ASAP.... No! Tonight.... Same to you!" The agent turned away from the window. "It looks like it's him."

I had no idea what was happening. "Him? Who? What's going on?"

White turned to me. "They found a body in City Park this morning. It may be Falco."

"It *may* be Falco. Don't they know?"

"Shotgun blast to the face. Acid on the fingertips."

I shuddered at the picture that formed in my mind.

"They have Falco's DNA on file. The FBI is trying to get a match now."

"What makes them even think it's Falco?"

"Height. Weight. Hair and skin coloring and a tattoo on one arm."

"If Falco is dead, does that mean the FBI is through with me?"

"Hardly. The FBI has wiretaps on the cell phones of some other criminals and they're picking up rumors that someone is already trying to consolidate power in Falco's organization."

"Who?" I thought I knew the answer, but I didn't know if I wanted to be right or wrong.

"Your old friend… Louis LeBlanc."

"Do you think he had anything to do with Falco's murder?"

"What do you think? You knew him better than any of us."

I had a hard time seeing LeBlanc as a murderer, or even as someone who would order Falco killed. I knew that Falco was capable of ordering a murder, but LeBlanc… I didn't think so.

"No. I don't think LeBlanc is behind it."

"Do you have any other ideas?" the FBI agent said.

I looked toward White. He seemed to know what I was thinking and responded to the agent's question. "My guess is that one of his business partners is behind it."

"What makes you think that?"

"Why do you care? Falco's killing is a local matter. You don't have any jurisdiction."

White was right, and the agent should have been relieved.

"Maybe not now," the agent said. "But if his death has anything to do with our investigation I might be stuck with the case."

53.

When Barbara Blain arrived around nine the next morning, none of the FBI agents were there. I assumed they were all working together, but when I asked about it, her eyes narrowed and grew cold. I asked if she'd seen the evidence seized from Falco's storage unit. When she said the FBI hadn't given her access to it yet I understood her pique. I suppose I would have felt the same way if our roles were reversed, but I was secretly pleased that the FBI was treating her so unpleasantly. After what she'd put me through, I wasn't inclined to give her any sympathy. Petty? Perhaps, but I was the person who was going on a third identity. My largesse, evidently, has limits.

The body found in City Park had been confirmed as that of Sonny Falco, so there wasn't much I could tell her that would help what remained of her case.

She finished her questioning in a little over an hour and was leaving just as the FBI agents and two U.S. Marshals arrived. Blain glared at the agents but didn't say anything, and she completely ignored the Marshals. At least for today, the federal authorities weren't one big happy family.

White offered everyone coffee, but our visitors hesitated.

"Chicory?" one of the agents said. I wasn't sure whether he hoped it was or wasn't chicory, and I didn't care.

"Yes," White said.

The new arrivals took a pass, and they all went into the library as I went out to the patio to join Horse and Rodriguez. For the first time since we'd arrived in New Orleans, they were both wearing jackets. I yawned and stretched and looked toward the lake, hoping to see more pelicans. They're truly graceful birds, and after my year in Tennessee—where I guarantee you there are no pelicans—I'd come to look forward to seeing them every morning. But all I saw were the now-familiar bass boats.

I was just sitting down when the first shot ricocheted off the table and shattered a pane of glass in the French doors. The next thing I knew, Horse was pulling me down by the arm and Rodriguez was crouching by the table blasting away at the boats. Within seconds, the three FBI agents and two Marshals had joined the fray and were shelling the boats. I watched as three bodies fell into the water and a fourth slumped over the console of the boat.

That was it. No more than fifteen seconds from start to finish. Whoever had attacked us—me—had obviously not planned for the possibility that on that of all days there would be three FBI agents and two U.S. Marshals in the house.

White, Leslie and Becky came running out of the house.

"Oh my god! All you all right?" Becky said as she knelt beside me.

I was too stunned to answer. She pulled me to a seated position and ran her hands over me. I assume she was looking for blood because she already knew where all the important parts were.

It took me a minute to regain awareness of my surroundings. I didn't feel any pain, so I was reasonably certain I hadn't been hit.

The acrid smell of gun smoke still hung over the patio

as White pulled me to my feet. The leaders of both the FBI team and the Marshals were talking on their cell phones. I couldn't make out what they were saying, and I didn't care.

§

Becky sat quietly by my side as the Marshals reviewed the terms and conditions of the Witness Protection Program. All the documents had been completed, and the only thing left for me to do was sign my name. I still didn't know what Becky was going to do, and I didn't know if she did either, but all the logic in the world said I should sign. In fact, I didn't have a choice. My plea agreement required me to go into the Program for as at least as long as Brochette wanted me.

I signed and held my breath. I knew what was coming.

The Marshal gathered all the forms I'd signed, put them in a folder, and laid it in his briefcase. Then he took out a second folder and put it on the table. He looked at me, but I knew that what he was about to say was addressed to Becky. "What about her?" he said.

Becky put her arms around me and held me tight. I held my breath.

EPILOGUE

As long as Lucius White was my attorney of record, we were able to meet whenever I had a problem with the Marshals but always at places they chose, and I was prohibited from telling him where I was or what my new name was. That was okay with me. We didn't need to meet often, and there was no need for him to know my new name. He continued to refer to me as Masters and that was enough. I was sorry I couldn't invite him to be with Becky and me when we got married or tell him that Becky was pregnant— although the events did not occur in that order—but we'd known what participation in the Program meant when we signed on.

It had been almost a year since I'd last seen White or testified in any of Brochette's cases, but I'd followed the work of his task force on the Internet. They'd been particularly successful in Louisiana and along the Gulf Coast, so I guess some of my information had been helpful. It probably didn't hurt that Saul Weinberg's mini-storage facility had held a trove of financial records for fifteen of the biggest crime bosses in the region. I was disappointed to find that out about Saul, but it did explain a lot.

I'd thought I was through with the FBI and the rest of the criminal justice system when Becky and I came home from the beach one particularly lovely day in paradise only to find a Marshal waiting for us. I couldn't imagine why, but I was being summoned to a command appearance that would take me away for… I didn't know how long. I wasn't thrilled, but that's the way the Program works. They say jump and I say, "How high?"

The Marshals never tell you where you're going or where you are after you have arrived, but as we were on final approach to the airport, I recognized the landmarks of Fort Myers. I hadn't been given time to pack a bag, so I knew this would be a quick in-and-out visit.

§

White, Horse and an elderly man I didn't recognize were sitting in the living room of White's apartment when the Marshal and I arrived. Horse, White and I greeted each other like old friends and were given a few minutes to chat under the Marshal's watchful eye.

I was still wondering about the black Lincoln Navigator parked in front of the warehouse with two men standing rigidly beside it. I assumed its presence had something to do with the man who remained seated on the sofa. There was something about him—I can only describe it as an authoritative presence—that made me think he was important.

I crossed the room and introduced myself. The newcomer stood, smiled and extended his hand. "I'm Graham Brochette."

To say that I was stunned would be an understatement. My mind began to race. Graham Brochette! What could he possibly be doing here?

I took his hand and we shook. His grip was firm and seemed to reflect a genuine interest in meeting me. "We were just talking about you."

I let myself collapse into a chair beside Horse. "Why? Your people have already finished debriefing me."

"And we're very grateful for your cooperation." Brochette said as he returned to his seat, "I just wanted to tell you myself how much my whole team and I appreciate what you've done for us. I know it couldn't have been easy."

I mumbled some sort of thanks as I wondered why he was here.

"There are just a few details we need to go over again if you're up to it."

I was suddenly on high alert. "We? Who's 'we'?"

From behind me, I heard the running water in the bathroom sink being turned off. The door opened and another man entered the room.

I turned and gasped.

Brochette stood and said, "I think you know Special Agent Richard Gray."

I was still in shock. Brochette was right. I knew Richard Gray. But I knew him by another name. I knew him as Louis LeBlanc.

THANK YOU READERS

Thank you for buying and reading my book and I sincerely hope that you enjoyed it. As an independently published author, I rely on my readers to spread the word, so, if you like my book, please tell your family and friend. And if it's not too much trouble, mention me on your social media pages and **post a review on Amazon**. If you would like to tell me your opinion directly, please visit my website – **www.alanpwoodruff.com** – and send me a message. If you have a question, I will respond as soon as possible.

Turn the page for an excerpt from

THE INMATE

THE NEXT BOOK IN THE
LUCIUS WHITE NOVEL SERIES

1.

Lucius White and Buford "Horse" McGee, White's investigator of almost fifteen years, were seated in White's spacious office savoring their morning coffee while engaged in a heated, but collegially friendly, debate over the latest college football rankings.

Both of them had played football in college. White, whose six-foot-two-inch, one-hundred-ninety-pound frame had not changed since his college days, had been a reserve wide receiver and safety at the University of Michigan. Horse, at six foot five and a gym-rat solid three hundred ten pounds, had been a tackle and linebacker at the University of Florida. Both of their teams ranked in the just-released top ten, so today's debate was unusually lively.

"There's no way that a one-loss Michigan team should be ranked ahead of undefeated Florida," Horse said. "No fucking way!"

White shook his head slowly and emitted a chuckled in a way that suggested he a sadness at the weakness of Horse's argument. "But Florida has only beaten teams with losing records."

"Maybe, but they didn't just beat them. They humiliated them."

"Wait until Florida goes up against the big boys in the SEC. Michigan has already beaten two ranked teams, and its only loss was a three-pointer to a top-five team."

White, now satisfied that his argument had carried the day, leaned his desk chair as far back as it would go and propped his ever-present embroidered cowboy boots on the corner of his desk. His boots, and his black Stetson hat, were something of a fashion trademark for which he was well-known in legal circles, but White was the real thing. He had been reared on his family's ranch in northern Idaho and had been riding since he was old enough to grip a saddle horn. By the age of twelve, he was riding with the rest of the ranch hands in the annual roundup.

Horse was about to make another argument in support of his beloved Gators when Grace Matthews, White's longtime and indispensable administrative assistant, came into the office with the morning mail.

"Is there anything interesting, Grace?" White asked as he accepted the small stack of letters.

"Just one."

White's raised eyebrows asked his unspoken question.

"It's from an inmate at the Atlanta Federal Penitentiary."

White sat up abruptly. "Who? It can't be one of *my* clients."

"It isn't. It's from someone who wants you to represent him."

Creased lines formed on White's forehead. "Me? Why me?"

"You should read the letter," Grace said as she turned to leave the office. "It's on top."

"You know I don't represent inmates. I have enough work just keeping people *out* of prison."

Grace paused at the door and turned toward White. "I know," she said. "But I have a good feeling about this one."

White glanced toward Horse, who responded with an indifferent shrug.

White's eyes narrowed and his eyebrows drew close together as he reached for the letter, then read it aloud.

Dear Mr. White,

My name is José Lopez. I am an inmate at the Atlanta Federal Penitentiary. I have served twelve years of a life sentence for a murder I did not commit. I did not get a fair trial, and I believe the government used perjured testimony against me.

I read about you in a magazine in the prison library and know you are committed to seeing that justice is done. I believe you are the only person who can help me. I am sure you receive letters like this all the time, and I know that mine is not the kind of case you usually take. But please, Mr. White, I know that if you investigate my situation you will find me worthy of your consideration.

Yours in God,
José Lopez

"Well, he's articulate," Horse said. "You have to give him that."

White mumbled a noncommittal "Uh-huh" as he reread the short letter. Then he slid it onto his desk, scratched his chin and called out to Matthews, "Grace, would you please call Leslie and ask her to come down here?"

"Are you thinking about taking this case?" Horse asked.

"Probably not. Mr. Lopez doesn't have much to say other than claim he's innocent. I get this kind of letter all the time. Usually, Grace just sends a note saying I'm too busy."

"Why do you want Leslie to read the letter?"

"You know Leslie," White said as he stifled a yawn. "She always needs a cause."

Leslie Halloran, White's paramour, was a social activist lawyer. She, like White, fought for people who had been mistreated or ignored by the machinery of government.

"But," Horse said, "she's only practiced administrative law. Besides, she's always had enough work to keep her busy fighting with bureaucrats. Why would she be interested in this case?"

White leaned back and returned his boots to the edge of his desk. "She finished the last of her cases a year ago, and she's been filling in for the director of the legal aid office while he was on sabbatical. The work appeals to her do-gooder side, but it's all routine and a waste of her talents. Now the director is back, and Leslie needs something to keep her busy and challenged."

"She could get a job with any firm in town."

"She knows that, but they'd want her for her skills in administrative law, and she's burned out with that. She wants to do something new."

"But why would she want to work with us?"

"She already knows all of our associates, and she's helped most of them when they were writing appellate briefs. She especially enjoys the writing part of practicing law, and her appellate briefs are always great. I wish more of our trial lawyers had her creative mind."

"What about her painting? I'm no art critic, but I think she's very talented."

"She is that. In fact, pursuing a career in art was her original plan."

Horse's eyebrows rose. "You mean she hadn't always planned to be a lawyer?"

White took a sip of coffee before responding. "No. She

was an art major when she was at Wellesley. She was going to be an art restorer."

"I just assumed…"

"No. When it comes to career planning, she's like me. I was going to run the family ranch, until…"

It wasn't necessary for White to complete his thought; Horse already knew the story. White was only sixteen when the FBI arrested his father on dubious charges of criminal trespass on government property. Those were the days when patriotic militia units, of which his father was an active member, were flourishing throughout the northwest and the government was doing everything it could to crush the movement. The young White wasn't permitted to attend the trial, but he knew about the allegations of paid informers and the questionable authenticity of the evidence used by the government against his father. White worshiped his father and never doubted the rightness of his cause, but the prosecutors wanted his father in prison and weren't concerned with how they got him there.

His father's conviction, his death as a result of a stabbing by another inmate and the government's seizure of the family ranch were why he'd become an attorney. They were also the reasons he was obsessed with battling with the government in general and criminal prosecutors in particular.

White's ruminations about the events that had changed the course of his life were interrupted when Horse asked, "What made Leslie give up art and become a lawyer?"

White chuckled softly as he often did when he thought about Leslie's past and had an opportunity to talk about her. "She's always been active in social causes, and one of the organizations she was working with got involved in a dispute over how the government was regulating some of the clinics where she volunteered. Their dispute ended up in court, and the clinics won the case. That made Leslie realize how the law could be used for social good, and she decided to go to law school. It's the best thing that could have happened. I think she's a born lawyer, and now she says she wants to get involved in some of our cases."

Horse frowned. "Do you think it's a good idea? I mean, I know she's a good attorney and all. But working together…that can put a strain on a relationship."

White sighed, and his expression turned pensive. "I know. That's why I've resisted for so long. But she's been a big help when I need to talk through a case."

"That's not the same as working together. Besides, she's your girlfriend. What are the others going to think?"

"I've thought about that. But she's helped most of them in one way or another, and they love her. Some of them have even asked why I haven't hired her already. I'd love to work with her, but the criminal law work we do is very different from the administrative law she's accustomed to. I not sure she'd even like doing what we do."

"Isn't that something for her to decide?"

"Of course it is. But I don't want her to get into something she's not happy with … and I certainly don't want her to feel like she has to stay with it just because she's been asking for an opportunity to work on some of our cases."

"There's only one way to find out."

"I know. I'll let her take a look at the letter. She can decide if it's something she wants to follow up on."

Horse responded with narrowed eyes and a skeptical frown. White was the boss, but he and Horse had worked together for so long that Horse's opinion counted for something. "Why? It's not the kind of thing we usually do. We keep people from *going* to jail. We've never had to get someone *out*."

"You're right," White said as he took a sip from his University of Virginia law school coffee mug. "The letter isn't enough to get me interested, but it's the kind of thing she might be interested in."

"I suppose," Horse said. His guarded tone indicated that he wasn't convinced of White's assessment but didn't have sufficient interest in the subject to continue that part of the discussion. "But if the guy's been in prison for twelve years, you can be sure he won't be able to pay anything."

White snorted. "Since when have we worried about a client's ability to pay? We take pro bono cases all the time."

The ability of clients to pay for legal services was no longer of concern to White. He was already a wealthy man and he no longer needed to work—at least not for the money. Thanks to the multimillion-dollar fee he had earned in a patent infringement case and three decades of success in his criminal practice, he could afford to be, and was, selective in the cases he undertook. Now he was dedicated to pursuing his vendetta against the government—prosecutors and other people who abused their power, and he only accepted cases where the stakes were the highest and a win would be the most embarrassing to the prosecutors. He rarely had more than a few cases at any time, but those he undertook with an all-consuming vengeance. The long hours he put in rivaled those of any associate trying the make partner in a large firm

As they waited for Leslie, White and Horse resumed their debate over the football standings. Their discussion was interrupted when Leslie bounded down the stairs from White's apartment on the top floor of the converted warehouse that also contained his office. She strolled across the mezzanine. At five foot six, she was as lithe and graceful as the college tennis player she had once been. The brick-red hair that cascaded like a waterfall halfway down her back swung rhythmically from side to side as she cheerily bid Grace a good morning and entered White's office.

"You beckoned, Master?" she said in a playful manner that implied a relationship dynamic that everyone knew was just the opposite.

White and Horse both chuckled. White shook his head. "What am I going to do with you?"

"I have a few ideas," she said as she batted her eyelashes coyly. "But we'd have to go upstairs to do them."

Leslie could be, and was, a proper lady when the occasion required it. But otherwise she exhibited a careless lack of inhibition. Horse, who had grown accustomed to the suggestive banter she engaged in with White, stifled a chuckle.

"Later, Leslie," White said. "I have something else you might be interested in."

Leslie's hands shot upward, covering her mouth. "A case? A real case? You're going to let little ol' me look into a real case?"

White rolled his eyes, moved his head slowly from side to side and made a sound somewhere between a sigh and a subdued "harrumph." "Sarcasm isn't your strongest suit."

Leslie raised her eyebrows and gave him a wry smile—something she reserved for moments when she knew White was teasing her. "That's why I have to practice."

White looked at Horse. "See what I have to put up with?"

Horse held up his hands. "Leave me out of this."

Leslie cast an impish glance toward Horse. "Coward."

"Practical," Horse said as he rose and started for the door. "Let me know what you decide to do about…" Horse pointed to the letter lying on White's desk.

Leslie eyes followed Horse's gaze and landed on the letter. "Okay, Lucius. What's up?"

"I received this letter this morning," White said as he handed her the letter from José Lopez. "I thought it might interest you."

Leslie sat on the sofa in the place vacated by Horse. As she read, her smile gave way to a look of intense concentration. When she finished reading, she raised her head and looked at White. "Are you considering taking this case?"

"I don't know. Nothing Lopez said excites me, but Grace said she had a good feeling about the letter, and Grace usually has good instincts. I thought you might want to look into it."

Leslie reread the letter. "It's not the same as the others you've received from inmates. He sounds intelligent, and he's done some research on you. But he's a little cryptic."

"Maybe he thought putting a little mystery in his letter would get my attention."

"It seems to have worked. What do you want me to do?"

"See what you can find out about his case."

"What am I looking for?"

"Anything you can get. There may be some old newspaper stories about the case, and you should look at the case file. Get Horse to help you. He's familiar with searching for information on criminal cases.'

"Is it okay if I use Harry's old office?"

"Harry" was Harry Harris, White's former partner who had died after suffering a stroke more than a year before. At the mention of his name, White's mind returned to thoughts of what Harris had meant to the firm. He and White had practiced together for over a decade and were more than just partners. Harris had once been a peerless litigator, but the accident that killed his wife and daughter and shattered his legs had crippled more than his body. He'd tried to resume his trial practice, but his stock-in-trade was pure theater—gestures, postures, dramatic movements around the well of the courtroom. He was Hamlet with a briefcase. But after the accident, he couldn't do it anymore.

He had fallen into a deep depression and turned to alcohol. Most of his friends abandoned him, but not White. White got him into AA (with White as his sponsor) and brought him into the firm where Harris assumed the role of mentor to White's young associates. But more importantly, Harris had been a rock of stability when the demons that drove White threatened to overwhelm him. For reasons even White could not explain, he couldn't bring himself to let anyone else have Harris's office.

"Lucius?" Leslie said.

"What? Oh, I'm sorry. I was thinking about Harry."

"I could tell. Maybe it's time to—"

White knew what she was going to say and cut her off before she could complete her thought. "I'm not ready to replace Harry. Not yet. Soon. But not yet."

ABOUT THE AUTHOR

Alan Woodruff was born in Pittsburgh, Pennsylvania, raised in Cleveland, Ohio. He holds bachelors and masters degrees in chemical engineering (Virginia Tech), a doctorate in administration (Harvard), a law degree (Florida State) and a post-graduate degree in tax law (Univ. of Washington).

Before going to law school, Alan was a researcher and consultant to local, state, federal and international agencies and organizations and the founder and CEO of multiple companies.

As a lawyer, Alan has twenty years of experience as a trial attorney. He has more than fifty published articles and professional papers and is the author of one legal reference book.

Alan lives in North Carolina. He can be reached through the "Contact" page of his website at **www.alanpwoodruff. com** or at **alan.jd.llm@gmail.com**.

Made in United States
Orlando, FL
13 April 2023

32057888R00174